VOIDHAMMER

THE SOULFORGED ERA

VOIDHAMMER

VOLUME ONE – THE SHATTERED GATE

JOHN RAPOSIO

VOIDHAMMER

Copyright © 2026 John Raposio

All rights reserved. No part of this book may be reproduced, stored in a retrieval system, or transmitted in any form or by any means—electronic, mechanical, photocopying, recording, or otherwise—without prior written permission from the publisher, except in the case of brief quotations used in reviews or critical articles.

This is a work of fiction. Names, characters, places, and events are products of the author's imagination or are used fictitiously. Any resemblance to actual persons, living or dead, or actual events is purely coincidental.

Cover design by John Raposio

Interior design by John Raposio

Published by John Raposio

https://books.by/voidhammer-saga

ISBN: 978-1-7645314-0-5

First Edition

Printed in Australia

CHAPTER ONE — EMBERHOLD BREATHES

The Last Realm woke slowly. Dawn crept over Emberhold's walls in a wash of ember-gold, catching on soot-black stone and the iron braziers lining the battlements. The city always looked half-forged, half-ruined — as if someone had hammered it into shape in a hurry and never quite finished the job.
Smoke curled from the forges. Lanterns guttered in the morning wind. Somewhere in the distance, a bell tolled the changing of the watch.
Kaelren stood atop the eastern wall, hands resting lightly on the cold stone, watching the light spread across the valley like a promise the world no longer believed in. The wind tugged at his cloak. His breath misted in the air. He didn't move.
Bootsteps approached behind him.
"You're up early again," Lysa Emberbow said, leaning her elbows on the parapet beside him. Her bow hung across her back, a quiver of mismatched arrows rattling at her hip. "Either you're avoiding sleep, or sleep's avoiding you."
Kaelren's jaw shifted. "Dreams."
"Dreams," she echoed, huffing. "Right. The same ones?"
He didn't answer, but the way his fingers tightened on the stone told her enough.
Below them, the city stirred. Children darted between market stalls. Emberguard recruits jogged across the training yard while Captain Thalen barked orders behind them. Mareth Hollowhands swept the steps of her clinic with a broom that looked older than she was.
Near the central forge, Bren Ashforge —
broad-shouldered, soot-stained, and perpetually earnest — wrestled with a crate twice his size.
Kaelren watched him for a moment, head tilting slightly.
"He's going to drop that," Lysa said.

"He's going to try not to," Kaelren replied.

Sure enough, Bren's foot caught on a loose stone. The crate lurched. He flailed, recovered, and set it down with a triumphant gasp.

Lysa grinned. "See? Progress."

Kaelren didn't smile, but his shoulders eased a fraction, the breath he'd been holding slipping quietly out of him.

For a moment, Emberhold felt almost peaceful.

A low rumble rolled across the valley — distant, muted, wrong.

Lysa frowned. "Thunder?"

"There's no storm," Kaelren murmured.

The sky above them was clear, pale gold with dawn. No clouds. No shift in the wind. But the rumble came again, softer this time, as if swallowed before it reached them.

Kaelren's fingers tightened on the stone. Something in the air felt stretched thin, like a drumhead pulled too tight.

Then the Shattered Gate pulsed.

A ripple of ghostlight shivered across its cracked archway, bending the air around it. The braziers along the wall flickered. The wind shifted, carrying a faint whisper that raised the hairs on Kaelren's arms.

Lysa straightened. "That's new."

"No," Kaelren murmured. "It's getting worse."

He didn't look away from the Gate. His hand drifted unconsciously toward the hilt at his hip, fingers brushing the worn leather grip. The pressure he'd felt in his dreams — that weight behind the world — pressed against him again, subtle but insistent.

A memory stirred at the edge of his mind. Heat. Fire. A crown of flame. A voice he once swore to follow.

His breath caught. He forced it steady.

Not now.

A shout rose from the courtyard.

"Kaelren!" Bren waved up at him, face bright with soot and enthusiasm. "Captain Thalen wants you! Something about a patrol!"

Lysa groaned. "Of course he does. Can't let you brood in peace for five minutes."

Kaelren pushed away from the parapet. His hand lingered on the stone for a heartbeat longer than necessary before he turned. "Come on."

As they descended the steps, Emberhold came fully awake around them — the clang of hammers, the murmur of merchants, the distant hum of ghostlight drifting from the Gate. Kaelren adjusted the strap of his scabbard as they walked, the familiar motion grounding him even as his spine straightened under an old, unwelcome pressure.

Life. Fragile, stubborn life.

He didn't know why the dreams were returning. He didn't know why the Gate was weakening. He didn't know why the air felt wrong, as if the world were holding its breath. But he knew one thing with absolute certainty:

Something was coming.

And Emberhold was not ready.

CHAPTER TWO — THE GATE STIRS

The Shattered Gate had always been a wound in the world. But today, it felt like it was trying to breathe.

Kaelren felt it before he heard it — a pressure behind his ribs, a faint tightening in the air, like the moment before a forge hammer falls. He turned toward the Gate.

A low tremor rolled through the courtyard stones — not enough to shake dust loose, but enough to make his breath catch.

Lysa glanced upward. "Weather's turning strange."

The sky above Emberhold was clear, but a thin band of clouds on the horizon twisted in a slow, unnatural spiral, as if stirred by a wind that hadn't reached the ground.

"That's not weather," Kaelren said. His jaw tightened. The air felt stretched, brittle, as though the world were bracing for something it didn't want to name.

A thin line of ghostlight pulsed along the cracked archway — faint as a dying ember. The runes carved into its stone flickered weakly, as if remembering a language they no longer had the strength to speak.

Lysa stopped mid-stride. "Okay. That's new."

Bren swallowed. "It's… glowing."

"It shouldn't be," Kaelren said quietly.

Talla stepped behind Jorren, eyes wide. "I thought the Gate was dead."

"It is," Jorren murmured. "Or it was."

Kaelren stepped closer, shield slung over his back, hand resting on his sword. The air around the Gate felt wrong — colder, thinner, stretched too tight.

A faint whisper drifted from the archway.
Not words. Not sound. Something older.

Lysa shivered. "Tell me that was the wind."

"That wasn't the wind," Kaelren said.

Bren moved beside him. "Captain Thalen said the Gate used to connect to other Realms, right? Before they fell?"

Kaelren nodded. "Realm Bridges. Stable once. Anchored by the Codex's runes."

"And now?"

"Now it's a scar," Kaelren said. "A memory of something that doesn't exist anymore."

The Gate pulsed again — harder.

A ripple of ghostlight crawled across the courtyard stones. Mareth emerged from her clinic, wiping her hands. "What's happening?"

"It's waking up," Kaelren said, not taking his eyes off the archway.

"That's impossible," Mareth said. "There's nothing left on the other side."

Lysa drew an arrow. "Then what's pushing?"

No one answered.

The Gate pulsed a third time — a deep, resonant thrum that made the braziers flicker and the stones tremble.

Kaelren felt something stir in the back of his mind.

Heat. Light. A crown of fire. A familiar voice he had once sworn to follow.

He staggered, gripping the wall.

"Kaelren?" Bren asked. "You okay?"

"Just… a memory," Kaelren muttered.

But it didn't feel like a memory.

It felt like a warning.

The Gate pulsed again — violent, shuddering, alive. Cracks spiderwebbed across the archway. Ghostlight bled from the fractures, drifting upward like dying fireflies.

Lysa took a step back. "Nope. Nope. I don't like this."

Mareth's voice dropped to a whisper. "Something is coming."

Kaelren's hand tightened around his sword. "Not something," he said.

The Gate screamed.

A sound like a thousand memories tearing at once. The courtyard shook. The braziers went out. The sky dimmed. Ghostlight erupted from the archway in a blinding flash.

OFFICIAL

Talla screamed. Bren shielded her. Lysa fired an arrow into the ground just to steady her hands.

Kaelren stood his ground, teeth clenched, eyes locked on the Gate.

The light twisted.

Not outward — inward.

Like the Gate was folding in on itself, collapsing into a wound. Through the swirling ghostlight, fractured visions flickered:

A sky of molten gold. A forest of whispering shadows. A storm fortress chained to lightning. A river of magma beneath a burning city. Lanterns drifting through mist.

Dead Realms. Lost Realms. Remembered only by the Codex.

Then something fell through.

A body. A man. A streak of light and shadow, tumbling through the collapsing Gate like a star torn from its orbit. He hit the courtyard stone with a force that cracked the ground.

The shockwave knocked Kaelren to one knee.

Lysa scrambled backward. "What—what is that?!"

Bren stared, breathless. "Is he... alive?"

Ghostlight swirled around the fallen figure, flickering like dying fireflies. The runes that had flared on the Gate now crawled across his skin — glowing lines pulsing in unstable rhythm.

Kaelren approached slowly.

The man lay on his back, chest rising and falling in ragged breaths. His clothes were scorched, torn, half-burned by whatever force had hurled him through the Gate. His hair was matted with ash. His hands were scarred with symbols Kaelren didn't recognize.

But his face—

His face looked like someone who had lived a thousand lives and remembered none of them.

Mareth knelt beside him, hands trembling. "He's breathing. Barely."

The man's eyes snapped open.

They glowed.

Not with light. Not with magic.
With memory.
Kaelren froze.
The man stared upward, pupils dilated, chest heaving. His lips parted, and a single word escaped — a whisper in a language no one in Emberhold had ever heard.
But Kaelren felt it.
Like a spark in his bones. Like a name he should have known.
The man's gaze shifted — not to Kaelren, not to the sky, but to something only he could see.
A vision.
A woman. A lantern-lit figure drifting through mist.
Elyndra.
He reached upward, fingers trembling, as if trying to touch someone who wasn't there.
Then he collapsed.
The glow beneath his skin flickered once—
—and went dark.
Silence fell over the courtyard.
Lysa swallowed. "Kaelren… what just happened?"
Kaelren didn't answer.
Because he didn't know.
But he felt it — deep, instinctive, undeniable.
This man was not from Emberhold. Not from any surviving Realm. Not from anything that should still exist.
He was something else.
Something unwritten.
Kaelren exhaled slowly.
"Get Mareth," he said. "Get Thalen. Get everyone."
He looked down at the unconscious stranger.
"Because whatever he is… the world just changed."

CHAPTER THREE — ELYNDRA ARRIVES

The courtyard was still trembling when the Lantern Path opened.

Not with the violent crack of the Gate — but with a soft, resonant chime, like a memory being spoken aloud.

Ghostlight drifted into existence, swirling into a thin, shimmering trail that cut across the courtyard stones. The air grew colder. The noise of Emberhold dimmed, muffled as if wrapped in fog.

Above them, the sky flickered — a faint pulse of light behind thin clouds, too rhythmic to be lightning, too soft to be natural.

"That again…" Lysa muttered, glancing upward.

Kaelren felt the hairs on his arms rise. The storm on the horizon hadn't moved closer, but it had changed shape — spiraling inward, as if drawn toward the Gate's wound.

Elyndra stepped through the Path just as the pulse faded, her lanterns dimming in response. She paused, eyes lifting briefly to the sky, a crease forming between her brows.

"The air is wrong," she murmured. "Something is listening."

Kaelren turned toward the light.

Lysa raised her bow. Bren stepped protectively in front of Talla. Mareth froze mid-breath.

A figure stepped through the drifting ghostlight.

Tall. Cloaked. Lanterns orbiting her like small moons.

Elyndra Vaelis.

A Veilborn. A memory-walker. A woman who did not appear unless the world was about to change.

Her eyes swept the courtyard — and then landed on the man lying unconscious in the cracked stone.

The Unwritten.

The stranger who had fallen through a dead Gate. The man she had seen only in visions.

Her breath caught.

"No," she whispered. "Not yet. Not now."
Kaelren stepped forward. "You know him?"
Elyndra didn't answer.
She moved toward the fallen man slowly, lanterns dimming as she approached. Ghostlight curled around her feet, drawn to him like iron to a magnet.
She knelt beside him.
His skin still glowed faintly with dying runes. His breath was shallow, uneven. His hands twitched as if reaching for something he couldn't grasp.
Elyndra reached out — then stopped, fingers trembling inches above his chest.
Lysa lowered her bow. "Who is he?"
Elyndra swallowed hard.
"I don't know," she said. "But I've seen him."
Kaelren frowned. "In Spiritveil?"
"In visions," Elyndra whispered. "Fragments. Echoes. A man falling through memory. A spark that refused to die."
She looked at Kaelren, eyes wide with something close to fear.
"But he saw me."
Bren blinked. "What does that mean?"
"It means," Elyndra said softly, "that he is not bound by the Codex. That he is not written. That he is something the Realms were never meant to contain."
She looked down at the Unwritten again.
"And that terrifies me."
The man stirred.
His eyes snapped open — glowing faintly, unfocused, searching.
He looked at Elyndra.
Not with confusion. Not with fear.
With recognition.
"You..." he whispered, voice raw. "From the light..."
Elyndra recoiled as if struck.
Kaelren stepped forward. "He knows you?"
"No one sees a Veilborn through visions," Elyndra said, voice shaking. "No one."

9

OFFICIAL

The Unwritten reached toward her — fingers trembling, glowing faintly with dying runes.

Then he collapsed again, breath hitching, spark flickering.

Mareth rushed to him. "He's fading!"

Elyndra pressed her lantern to his chest. Ghostlight flowed into him, stabilizing his breath, slowing the flicker beneath his skin.

But her hands were shaking.

Kaelren saw it. "What is he?" he asked quietly.

Elyndra didn't look up.

She stared at the man who had fallen through a dead Gate, who had seen her in visions, who had spoken to her as if remembering a dream.

Her voice was barely a whisper.

"Something unwritten."

She rose abruptly.

"I need to return to Spiritveil."

Lysa blinked. "Now? You just got here!"

Elyndra shook her head. "I need answers. And the Lantern Council must hear of this."

Bren stepped forward. "We'll come with you."

Elyndra raised a hand sharply.

"No. You cannot."

Talla frowned. "Why not?"

"Because only Veilborn can walk the Lantern Paths," Elyndra said. "Anyone else would be unmade. Lost. Turned into an echo."

Silence fell.

Kaelren looked down at the Unwritten. "Will he survive?"

Elyndra hesitated.

"I don't know."

She stepped back into the Lantern Path.

Ghostlight swirled around her.

Her final words echoed through the courtyard as she vanished.

"Do not let him die. If he does… the Last Realm falls with him."

The Path sealed shut.

And Emberhold was left with a stranger who had fallen through a dead Gate — and a prophecy none of them understood.

"I need to return to Spiritveil."

Lysa blinked. "Now? You just got here!"

Elyndra shook her head. "I need answers. And the Lantern Council must hear of this."

Bren stepped forward. "We'll come with you."

Elyndra raised a hand sharply.

"No. You cannot."

Talla frowned. "Why not?"

"Because only Veilborn can walk the Lantern Paths," Elyndra said. "Anyone else would be unmade. Lost. Turned into an echo."

Silence fell.

Kaelren looked down at the Unwritten.

"Will he survive?"

Elyndra hesitated.

"I don't know."

She stepped back into the Lantern Path.

Ghostlight swirled around her.

Her final words echoed through the courtyard as she vanished.

"Do not let him die. If he does... the Last Realm falls with him."

The Path sealed shut.

And Emberhold was left with a stranger who had fallen through a dead Gate — and a prophecy none of them understood.

CHAPTER FOUR — THE LANTERN COUNCIL

The Lantern Path carried Elyndra in a rush of cold air and drifting ghostlight. For a heartbeat she was nowhere — weightless, suspended between echoes, drifting through the memory-roads only the Veilborn could walk. Lanterns flickered in the distance like drowned stars. Voices whispered fragments of forgotten lives.

But today, the Paths trembled beneath her feet.

Spiritveil was afraid.

She stepped out of the Path and into the mist-shrouded clearing where the Lantern Council convened. Ancient stones ringed the space, each carved with runes older than the Realms themselves. Lanterns floated above them, dim and unsteady.

Four figures waited.

Not leaders. Pillars.

High Seer Vaelith stood at the centre, tall and still, her eyes reflecting centuries of memory. Her presence always felt like standing in the shadow of something ancient and unbroken.

Her voice was calm but strained. "Elyndra. You felt it."

Before Elyndra could answer, Sythra stepped forward, lantern clutched to her chest. "The Paths screamed," she whispered. "They haven't done that since—"

"Do not say it," Oryn snapped, hand tightening on the hilt of his ghost-iron blade.

Sythra flinched. The lanterns dimmed.

Archivist Lume hovered near the Lantern Codex, runes drifting around him like dust motes. His eyes flickered with agitation. "We all know what it means," he muttered. "Pretending otherwise is pointless."

Oryn turned sharply. "You speak too freely, fragment."

"And you too slowly," Lume shot back. "The Paths are collapsing. The echoes are screaming. Something tore through the Shattered Gate. We cannot afford your pride."

Oryn's jaw clenched, but Vaelith lifted a hand. "Enough."
The word carried the weight of centuries. Even the lanterns steadied.
Vaelith turned to Elyndra. "Tell us what you saw."
Elyndra stepped into the circle, breath unsteady. "The Gate ruptured. Something fell through."
The mist tightened. The lanterns dimmed.
Vaelith's voice sharpened. "What came through?"
"A man."
Sythra gasped. Oryn's blade half-drew. Lume's runes flared in alarm.
Elyndra continued. "He fell like a star torn from the sky. His body was covered in dying runes. His spark was fractured — flickering like a memory trying to remember itself."
Lume's expression twisted. "Impossible. A mortal spark cannot survive a dead Gate."
"He is not mortal," Oryn growled.
Sythra shook her head. "Then what is he?"
Elyndra swallowed. "He spoke. A word I didn't recognize. And then… he looked at me."
Lume froze. "Through the Gate?"
"No," Elyndra whispered. "Before that."
The Council stiffened.
"In visions," she said. "He saw me in visions."
Sythra's lantern flickered violently. "No one sees a Veilborn through visions. Not unless—"
"Unless the prophecy is waking," Lume finished.
Oryn stepped forward, voice low. "We do not speak of the prophecy lightly."
"We don't have the luxury of silence," Lume snapped. "Not anymore."
He opened the Lantern Codex. The book shuddered, pages turning in a frantic blur until it stopped on a single glowing symbol.
Vaelith's breath caught.
"The Eternal Voyager," she whispered.

OFFICIAL

The lanterns flared. The echoes screamed. The Paths trembled.

Sythra pressed a hand to her mouth. "He has returned... after all this time."

Oryn's voice was a blade. "Then the cycle is restarting."

Elyndra's pulse quickened. "So it's true. He is the Eternal Voyager."

Vaelith nodded slowly. "The title is his. The prophecy is his. The cycle recognizes him."

"But the name," Lume said sharply, "is another matter."

Elyndra frowned. "The... name?"

Oryn exhaled through his teeth. "Must we do this now?"

"Yes," Lume hissed. "Because she has already seen him. And he has already seen her."

Vaelith stepped closer to Elyndra, her expression grave. "The Eternal Voyager is a mantle. A myth. A warning. But beneath the title lies a name older than the Realms."

Sythra's lantern dimmed. "Older than the Codex."

"Older than the Hammer," Lume whispered.

Oryn's voice dropped to a growl. "And dangerous."

Elyndra's breath caught. "Dangerous?"

Vaelith nodded. "His spark is fractured. His memory shattered. His identity unstable. If you speak his true name before he remembers it himself..."

Lume finished the sentence.

"...it will tear him apart."

Silence fell.

The lanterns flickered like dying stars.

Vaelith placed a hand on Elyndra's shoulder. "You may call him the Eternal Voyager. But you must never speak the name beneath the title."

Elyndra nodded slowly, though her pulse thundered in her ears. "I understand."

Vaelith's eyes softened with sorrow. "No, child. You do not. Not yet."

The Lantern Path opened behind Elyndra, ghostlight swirling like a storm.

As she stepped into it, Vaelith's final words followed her like a prophecy.

"Protect him. Anchor him. Guide him. If he fails to awaken… the Realms will never rise again."
The Path sealed shut.
And Spiritveil trembled.

CHAPTER FIVE — THE UNWRITTEN AWAKENS

The world returned to him in fragments.
Light. Cold stone. Voices muffled by distance. A weight in his chest like something trying to break free.
He inhaled sharply.
The breath burned.
Mareth jerked back from his bedside, hand flying to her mouth. "He's waking!"
Kaelren was already moving — a single step forward, hand resting on the hilt at his hip, eyes narrowing with focus.
Lysa hovered near the doorway, bow half-drawn. Bren stood behind her, wide-eyed, shifting his weight like he wasn't sure whether to run or help.
The man on the cot — the stranger who had fallen through a dead Gate — opened his eyes.
Ghostlight flickered beneath his skin, pulsing in uneven rhythms. His gaze darted around the room, unfocused, searching for something he couldn't name. His fingers curled against the blanket as if bracing for impact.
"Easy," Mareth murmured, her voice soft but steady. "You're safe."
He flinched at the word.
Safe. As if it were foreign.
Kaelren stepped closer, posture controlled, every movement deliberate. "Do you understand me?"
The man blinked slowly, as though dragging himself back from somewhere far away.
"I…" His voice cracked, raw and unused. "I don't…"
He stopped.
His breath hitched.
His hand rose to his chest, fingers trembling as they brushed the faint, dying runes etched into his skin. The marks pulsed once beneath his touch, then dimmed.
"What… happened to me?"

Lysa shifted her stance, bowstring creaking softly. "You fell out of the sky," she muttered.
Bren elbowed her. "Lysa—"
"What? He did."
Kaelren ignored them. His attention stayed fixed on the stranger. "You came through the Shattered Gate."
The man frowned, as if the words were familiar but wrong. "The Gate…" he whispered. "It shouldn't… it shouldn't be open."
Mareth's breath caught. She exchanged a quick look with Kaelren. "You know the Gate?"
He shook his head.
"No. Yes. I—"
His fingers dug into his temples. His breath quickened.
Images flickered behind his eyes:
A Realm collapsing into liquid light. A crown of fire shattering. A woman of lanterns reaching for him. A voice calling a name he couldn't grasp.
He gasped.
Kaelren steadied him with a hand on his shoulder — firm, grounding. "Easy. Don't force it."
The man looked up at him, eyes glowing faintly with ghostlight.
"What… am I?"
Silence filled the room.
Lysa lowered her bow slightly. Bren swallowed hard.
Mareth's hands hovered near the man's shoulders, unsure whether to comfort or brace him.
Kaelren answered first.
"We don't know."
The man exhaled shakily.
Of course they didn't.
He didn't know either.
He closed his eyes, trying to grasp the fragments slipping through his mind like sand.
A Realm of molten rivers. A sky of golden pillars. A storm fortress chained to lightning. A woman in ghostlight whispering—
You must remember.

His eyes snapped open.

"Where is she?"

Kaelren frowned. "Who?"

"The woman," he said, breath quickening. "Lanterns... light... she—she was here."

Mareth shook her head. "No one's been here except us."

"No," he insisted, voice rising. "I saw her. Before I fell. Before the Gate. She—"

He stopped.

Because the memory was already fading.

Lysa stepped forward, bow lowered but ready. "Do you remember your name?"

He opened his mouth.

Nothing came out.

He tried again.

Still nothing.

His chest tightened. His pulse hammered. His hands curled into fists against the blanket.

"I... I don't know," he whispered. "I don't know who I am."

Mareth placed a gentle hand on his arm. "It's alright. Memory loss after something like that—"

"This wasn't a fall," he snapped, voice cracking. "This was—this was—"

He couldn't finish.

Because he didn't know.

Kaelren crouched beside him, voice steady, grounding. "Listen. You're alive. That's what matters right now. We'll figure out the rest."

The man stared at him, searching for something solid to hold onto.

Kaelren offered his hand.

After a long moment, the man took it.

His grip was weak. Uncertain. But beneath it — a spark trying to remember itself.

"What do we call you?" Lysa asked quietly.

The man hesitated.

He didn't know his name. He didn't know his past. He didn't know why he had fallen through a dead Gate.

But he knew one thing:
He was not meant to be here.
"I…" He swallowed. "I don't know."
Kaelren nodded once. "Then we'll call you something until you remember."
The man looked down at his trembling hands.
"Unwritten," he whispered.
Kaelren's expression shifted — not confusion, not judgment, but recognition of something heavy beneath the word.
Lysa's fingers tightened on her bow. "Names matter here," she said quietly. "Blank ones… usually mean trouble."
Bren shot her a look, but she didn't take it back.
The man didn't hear them.
Because in the corner of the room — just for a heartbeat — a lantern flickered with ghostlight.
And he saw her again.
The woman of Spiritveil. Elyndra. Her outline soft, luminous, impossible.
She whispered something he couldn't hear.
Then she vanished.
A shiver ran through him.
Kaelren noticed. "What is it?"
The man shook his head.
"Nothing," he lied.
Because he didn't have words for the truth.

CHAPTER SIX — EMBERHOLD REACTS TO THE UNWRITTEN

The first whisper rose before dawn.
Two sentries huddled beneath a frost-bitten archway, their torches guttering in the wind.
"I saw him," one breathed. "Runes under the skin. Fading like embers."
"Stop. If Thalen hears—"
"He fell through the Gate, Ryn. Through a dead Gate."
A long, brittle silence.
"Then the Last Realm is finished."
The wind carried their fear across Emberhold like drifting ash.
By morning, the fortress-city was alive with murmurs. Not gossip — aftershocks. The kind that ripple through stone and bone alike.
Kaelren heard them as he crossed the courtyard with Lysa and Bren.
"Did you see him?" "They say he's Voidborn." "No — a ghost. A memory given flesh." "Captain Thalen wants him watched." "What if he's a sign the Gate is failing?" "What if he's a sign the Void is coming?"
Lysa snorted. "One unconscious man and suddenly everyone's a prophet."
Bren didn't laugh. "They're scared, Lys."
"Everyone's always scared," she muttered. "Fear's the only thing Emberhold has left."
Kaelren didn't respond.
Because the whispers weren't wrong.
He felt it too — a pressure in the air, a tension humming beneath the stone, as if the Last Realm itself were bracing for something it couldn't name.
They reached the courtyard's edge.

The Shattered Gate loomed before them, cracked and trembling, ghostlight leaking from its fractures like dying embers. The glow pulsed unevenly, as if struggling to remember how to shine.
Bren swallowed. "It looks worse."
"It is worse," Kaelren said quietly.
Lysa nudged him. "You think it's connected to him?"
Kaelren didn't answer.
Because something in his bones — something old, something he didn't have a name for — whispered the truth:
When the Unwritten fell through the Gate, the world shifted.
Something fundamental changed.
Something familiar.
Something he had felt once before, long ago, in a burning city beneath a dying sky.

Inside the Infirmary
The Unwritten sat on the edge of the cot, staring at his hands.
The runes beneath his skin had faded to pale scars, but he could still feel them — like echoes of a language he once knew, a script carved into his bones.
Mareth checked his pulse. "You're stabilizing. That's good."
He didn't respond.
She tried again. "Do you remember anything new?"
He shook his head.
But that wasn't entirely true.
Flashes haunted him.
A Realm of molten rivers. A sky of golden pillars. A woman illuminated by drifting lanterns, whispering a name that wasn't his — but felt older, deeper, truer.
He winced.
Mareth noticed. "Pain?"
"No," he lied. "Just… noise."
It wasn't noise.

It was pressure. A presence. Something brushing against his thoughts like a hand against glass.
Calling to him. Or hunting him.
Something that felt like recognition.
The door slammed open.
Captain Thalen strode in — broad-shouldered, scarred, eyes sharp as a drawn blade.
He looked the Unwritten up and down.
"So. You're the one who fell out of the sky."
The Unwritten didn't look away. "So, they tell me."
Thalen crossed his arms. "What are you?"
"I don't know."
"Where did you come from?"
"I don't know."
"What do you remember?"
The Unwritten hesitated.
Mareth stepped between them. "Captain, he's still recovering—"
Thalen ignored her. "Answer the question."
The Unwritten met his gaze.
"I remember falling."
Thalen's jaw tightened. "Through a dead Gate."
"Yes."
"That Gate hasn't opened in years."
"I know."
"How?"
The Unwritten blinked. "I don't know."
Thalen exhaled sharply. "You're either lying or you're dangerous."
"Maybe both," the Unwritten said softly.
Mareth glared at Thalen. "Enough. He needs rest."
Thalen turned to leave — then paused at the door.
"If anything else comes through that Gate," he said without looking back, "we won't survive it."
A chill crawled up the Unwritten's spine.
Because Thalen was right.
And because something else was true:
Something was coming. Something that felt like it knew him.

Outside — The Storm Learns
Kaelren, Lysa, and Bren stood atop the battlements as the sky darkened. Clouds twisted unnaturally. Wind reversed direction. Ghostlight flickered along the horizon like dying stars.
Lysa whispered, "Kaelren… the storm's moving wrong."
Kaelren nodded slowly. "It's reacting."
Bren swallowed. "Reacting to what?"
Kaelren didn't answer.
Because he didn't want to say it. Because the truth pressed against his mind like a weight he couldn't name.
It wasn't watching Emberhold. It wasn't following the Gate.
It was circling the spark that had fallen through it. The stranger in Mareth's infirmary. The man with runes under his skin and a memory that wasn't a memory.
The Unwritten.
Kaelren exhaled, breath tight. "Something out there knows he's here."

Back in the Infirmary
The Unwritten stood at the window, staring at the sky. The storm pulsed — once, twice — in perfect rhythm with his heartbeat.
He whispered, "What are you?"
The storm answered.
Not in sound. Not in words.
In memory.
A crown of fire. A Realm collapsing. A voice calling his true name.
He staggered, gripping the windowsill.
Mareth rushed to him. "What's wrong?"
He shook his head.
"I think…" He swallowed hard. "I think something out there remembers me."
Mareth froze. "Is that possible?"
He didn't answer.
Because he didn't know. But he felt it.

Something in the storm was calling to him. Something in the storm was searching for him. Something in the storm recognized the spark inside him — the one he couldn't remember.

Across the battlements, Kaelren felt the pressure too — a distant echo, a shift in the air — but nothing more. He felt the storm react, not to him, but to the stranger in Mareth's care.

It was remembering him — the one who had fallen through the Gate, the one whose spark refused to die, the one the storm had known long before the Realms fell.

CHAPTER SEVEN — THE LOST SCOUT

The call came at dawn.
A fist hammered on Kaelren's door, followed by Thalen's voice — clipped, urgent.
"Scout missing. Ashfall District. Move."
Kaelren was already pulling on his gear.
"Lysa, Bren, Jorren, Talla — with me."
Lysa groaned as she slung her bow over her shoulder. "Of course. The one morning I thought we might not almost die."
Bren tightened his gauntlets. "Someone's missing. We can't leave them."
Talla swallowed hard. "Do we… know what took him?"
Kaelren shook his head. "No. That's why we're going."
Jorren simply nodded, already checking the edge of his knives.

The Ashfall District
The district lived up to its name.
Ash drifted through the air like slow, grey snow. Buildings leaned at odd angles, half-collapsed from old battles. The forges here had gone cold years ago, their chimneys cracked and silent.
Lysa wrinkled her nose. "Smells like burnt socks and regret."
Bren laughed. "You say that about everywhere."
"Because everywhere smells like that," she shot back.
Kaelren allowed himself a small smile.
This was why he brought them.
They made the darkness feel less heavy.

Tracking the Scout
Jorren crouched beside a set of footprints in the ash.
"He was running," he murmured. "Fast."
Talla knelt beside him. "From what?"

Jorren pointed to a second set of tracks — deeper, heavier, wrong.

"Something big."

Lysa drew her bow. "Fantastic."

Kaelren scanned the rooftops. "Stay close. Eyes up."

They moved deeper into the district.

The ash grew thicker. The silence heavier. The air colder.

Bren whispered, "Kaelren... do you feel that?"

Kaelren nodded.

Ghostlight.

Faint. Drifting. Wrong.

Something was waiting for them.

The First Sign

They found the scout's cloak snagged on a broken beam.

Talla rushed forward. "He was here!"

"Careful," Kaelren warned.

She froze — just as the ash beside her shifted.

A ripple. A distortion. A shape rising from the ground like a memory trying to take form.

Not a Voidborn. Not an echo. Something in between.

A mutation — twisted by the Gate's instability, half-formed, half-remembered, its body flickering like a broken lantern.

Lysa reacted first.

An arrow snapped through the air — passed through the creature — and came out burning.

"Okay," she breathed. "That's new."

The creature lunged.

Not at one of them — at all of them. A blur of limbs and ghostlight, its form stuttering like a corrupted memory.

Kaelren moved.

Shield up. Feet braced. Impact like a hammer to the ribs. The blow rattled him, driving him back a step.

"Jorren!" he barked.

Jorren was already moving — a shadow peeling off the wall, blades flashing in a tight arc. The creature twisted unnaturally, its torso bending in ways no living thing should.

Bren roared and charged, hammer swinging in a wide, brutal arc.
The creature slipped aside — too fast, too fluid, too wrong.
Talla froze.
Her breath hitched. Her spear trembled. Her eyes locked on the thing as it turned toward her.
"Talla!" Lysa shouted. "Move!"
Too late.
The creature lunged.
Kaelren's heart lurched—
—but Bren slammed into it like a falling boulder, knocking it off its path.
"Talla!" he yelled. "Eyes up! Breathe!"
She gasped, nodding shakily, tears pricking her eyes.
The creature reformed — its body flickering, glitching, ghostlight leaking from its seams.
Kaelren didn't hesitate.
He stepped in, shield high, and drove his blade down through the creature's core.
A burst of ash. A hiss of ghostlight. A sound like a memory tearing.
Then silence.
The creature dissolved into drifting embers.
Talla trembled. "I'm sorry. I—I froze."
Lysa placed a hand on her shoulder. "Freezing is fine. Staying frozen isn't."
Bren smiled gently. "You did good. You warned us."
Talla blinked. "I… did?"
"Yeah," Bren said. "You saw the cloak first. That matters."
Kaelren watched them — the way Bren steadied her, the way Lysa softened, the way Jorren kept silent but close.
This was a team. A family.
And he felt a sudden, sharp fear.
He couldn't lose them.
Not again.

Finding the Scout
They found him in the ruins of an old forge.
Alive. Barely.

He was curled against the wall, clutching his side, breath shallow.

Kaelren knelt. "Easy. We've got you."

The scout's eyes fluttered open. "Captain… the Gate… it's changing…"

Kaelren stiffened. "What do you mean?"

"It's… leaking," the scout whispered. "Ghostlight… everywhere… and something… something is calling…"

His voice broke.

"Calling him."

Kaelren's blood ran cold.

"Who?"

The scout's eyes widened in terror.

"The man who fell."

Return to Emberhold

They carried the scout back through the Ashfall District. Lysa kept watch. Jorren scouted ahead. Bren supported the scout's weight. Talla stayed close to Kaelren, silent but steady.

As they neared Emberhold's gates, Kaelren looked back at the ruined district.

The ash was shifting again. The storm was gathering. And the Gate was waking.

CHAPTER EIGHT — THE STORM LEARNS HIS NAME

They brought the scout straight to the infirmary.
Mareth worked quickly, hands steady even as her eyes flicked to the door every few breaths. Lysa paced in tight circles. Bren hovered protectively. Talla wrung her hands. Jorren stood silent as stone, watching everything.
Kaelren remained at the foot of the cot, jaw set, shoulders tense.
The scout stirred.
His eyes fluttered open, unfocused at first — then sharpening when they found Kaelren.
"You... pulled me out," he rasped.
Kaelren nodded. "What's your name, soldier?"
The scout swallowed, voice rough but steady. "Rynn," he said. "Rynn Halveth. Third-watch scout."
Lysa crossed her arms. "Well, Rynn Halveth, you gave us a nice jog through the Ashfall District."
Rynn managed a weak smile. "Glad I could... keep you fit."
Bren chuckled. "He's got spirit."
Talla stepped closer, hesitant. "Are you... going to be alright?"
Rynn nodded. "Thanks to all of you."
Kaelren studied him — the alert eyes, the stubborn will, the way he tried to sit up even though he clearly shouldn't.
This was no ordinary scout.
"Rest," Kaelren said. "We'll talk when you're stronger."
Rynn shook his head. "Captain... I meant what I said out there. The Gate is changing. And whatever's calling... it's not done."
Kaelren's jaw tightened. "We know."
Rynn hesitated — then spoke the words that would change his future.

"If you need another blade... another pair of eyes... I want to help. I don't want to sit on the sidelines while Emberhold burns."
Lysa raised a brow. "You want to join us?"
Rynn nodded. "If you'll have me."
Kaelren didn't answer immediately.
Because the door opened.
And Thalen stepped inside.

Thalen Arrives
Thalen entered like a storm contained in armour — sharp-eyed, controlled, dangerous.
His gaze swept the room, landing on Rynn, then Kaelren.
"Your squad stirred up half the city," Thalen said. "Ashfall lit up like a forge fire."
Kaelren didn't flinch. "We found the scout. He's alive."
Thalen folded his arms. "And you walked straight into a ghostlight surge without backup."
Kaelren's jaw tightened. "My call. My responsibility."
Thalen stepped closer, voice low. "Your calls affect the entire Realm."
Kaelren didn't back down. "So do yours."
The air between them tightened — not superior and subordinate, but two commanders with different philosophies.
Thalen turned to Rynn.
"You said something was calling the man who fell."
Rynn nodded. "Yes, sir."
Thalen studied him with cold precision. "You want to join Kaelren's unit?"
Rynn hesitated. "If he'll have me."
Kaelren nodded once. "I will."
Thalen's eyes narrowed.
"Then he proves he won't get you all killed."
Kaelren stepped forward. "Thalen—"
"No," Thalen said, not as an order, but as a challenge. "You trust too easily. I don't. Let's see which of us is right."

Kaelren exhaled slowly. "Fine. But the test happens on my terms."
Thalen nodded once.
"Then let's see what your new recruit is made of."

EMBERHOLD — Rynn's Trial
The training yard was silent when they arrived — the kind of silence that gathers before a storm.
Ash drifted on the wind. Lanterns flickered. Recruits paused their drills to watch.
Rynn stepped into the sand, rolling his shoulders, trying to hide the tremor in his hands.
Thalen stood opposite him, spear in hand, posture relaxed in a way that was somehow more threatening than any battle stance.
Kaelren watched from the edge of the yard, arms folded, expression unreadable.
Lysa leaned close to Bren. "He's dead."
Bren whispered back, "He's not dead. Just... mostly dead."
Talla wrung her hands. "He'll be fine. He must be."
Jorren said nothing — but his eyes never left Rynn.
Thalen planted the spear in the sand.
"This isn't a duel," he said. "It's a measure."
Rynn nodded, breath steadying.
Thalen moved.
Not fast — correct. Every strike was a lesson. Every step a test.
Rynn blocked the first blow. Barely dodged the second. Took the third across the ribs.
He staggered, breath knocked out of him.
Thalen didn't pause.
"Your stance is weak."
Rynn reset.
Thalen swept his legs.
Rynn hit the sand hard.
"Your guard is sloppy."
Rynn pushed up.
Thalen struck again.

Rynn blocked — barely — but the force sent him skidding backward.

"Your fear is louder than your focus."

Rynn's jaw clenched. "I'm not afraid."

Thalen's spear slammed into the sand beside his head.

"Then stop fighting like you are."

Rynn rolled away, breath ragged, sweat stinging his eyes. He forced himself to his feet.

Kaelren watched, unmoving.

Lysa whispered, "He's going to step in."

Bren shook his head. "Not yet."

Thalen advanced again.

Rynn braced.

This time, he didn't dodge. He didn't retreat. He stepped into the strike, deflecting the spear with his forearm and driving his shoulder into Thalen's chest.

Thalen slid back a step.

Just one.

But it was enough.

The recruits watching murmured. Lysa's eyebrows shot up. Bren grinned. Talla gasped softly.

Thalen's expression didn't change — but something in his stance sharpened.

"Better," he said. "Again."

Rynn charged.

They clashed — sand spraying, ash swirling, the spear ringing against Rynn's bracers. Rynn fought like a man who refused to break, even as his legs trembled and his breath tore from his lungs.

Thalen swept him down one final time.

Rynn hit the sand and didn't rise.

For a moment, no one moved.

Then Rynn pushed himself up — shaking, bleeding, barely standing.

"I can keep going," he rasped.

Kaelren stepped forward.

"That's enough."

Thalen didn't move. "He's not ready."

"He's standing," Kaelren said. "That's enough for today."

Rynn swayed but stayed upright.
Thalen studied him for a long, cold moment.
Then he stepped back.
Rynn blinked. "So… I'm in?"
Kaelren extended a hand.
"You're in."
Relief flickered across Rynn's face as he took it.
Lysa smirked. "Congratulations. You survived Thalen's warm welcome."
Bren clapped him on the back. "Told you you had it."
Talla smiled shyly. "I'm glad you're with us."
Jorren gave a single approving nod.
Thalen crossed his arms.
"Don't thank me. I still don't trust him. Or the thing that fell through the Gate."
Kaelren's voice hardened. "You don't have to trust him. You trust me."
Thalen held his gaze for a long, tense moment.
Then he turned away.
"We'll see if that's enough."
A cold wind swept across the yard, carrying the faint scent of ozone.
Kaelren frowned.
The storm was shifting.

EMBERHOLD — The Wind Changes
As the squad left the yard, the wind tugged at their cloaks, sharp and unnatural. The sky above Emberhold had darkened — not with clouds, but with something heavier, a pressure that made the air feel too tight.
Rynn glanced upward. "Is it always like this?"
"No," Lysa said quietly. "This is new."
Kaelren felt it too — a pulse in the air, faint but insistent, like a heartbeat echoing through stone.
Bren noticed him tense. "Captain?"
Kaelren didn't answer.
Because the pulse came again.
And this time, he felt it in his bones.

SPIRITVEIL — Elyndra Feels the Same Pulse
Far away, ghostlight rippled across the Lantern Paths.
Elyndra stumbled mid-stride as the same pulse struck her — a thrum of power, distant but unmistakable.
Her lanterns flared.
"He's waking," she whispered.
The Paths trembled beneath her feet.
She ran faster.

EMBERHOLD — The Unwritten Reacts
The Unwritten sat on the edge of the infirmary cot, staring at his hands.
The pulse hit him like a blow.
He gasped, clutching his chest as ghostlight flickered beneath his skin.
Mareth rushed to him. "What's wrong?"
He shook his head, breath ragged.
"It's... learning me."
Outside, thunder rolled — but not from the sky.
From the Gate.

THE VOID — The Harrowed King Hears It Too
In the endless dark, the Harrowed King lifted his head.
The pulse reached him like a whisper through eternity.
He smiled — a slow, broken thing.
"So," he murmured. "The spark stirs."
Voidborn shadows writhed in anticipation.

EMBERHOLD — The Pulse Becomes a Tremor
Kaelren and the squad reached the courtyard just as the ground shuddered beneath their feet.
Rynn stumbled. "What was that?"
Jorren's voice was low. "The Gate."
Kaelren's heart dropped.
"Positions!"
The squad snapped into formation.
Thalen appeared on the battlements, barking orders to the Emberguard.
"Shields up! Eyes on the Gate!"

The storm above them twisted, spiralling inward like a great eye opening.
Ghostlight bled through the cracks in the Shattered Gate.
Talla whispered, "It's waking…"
Kaelren raised his shield.
"Steady."
The Gate pulsed again — harder.
The air rippled. The stone screamed. The world held its breath.
Rynn swallowed hard. "Captain… what do we do?"
Kaelren glanced at him — bruised, exhausted, but standing with the squad.
"Welcome to the team," Kaelren said.
The Gate split open.
"Time for the real test."

CHAPTER NINE — THE FIRST BREACH

The courtyard stones still held the warmth of the day when the first tremor rolled through Emberhold.
It was subtle at first — a faint vibration beneath Kaelren's boots, the kind that made a soldier pause and listen without knowing why. He felt it again a heartbeat later. A pulse. Deep. Resonant. Like something enormous stirring beneath the world.
Rynn felt it too. He steadied himself beside Kaelren, still bruised from the trial, still breathing hard, but refusing to show weakness. Talla hovered just behind him, spear clutched tight, trying to hide the tremor in her hands. Lysa scanned the rooftops, bow half-drawn, while Bren rolled his shoulders, hammer ready. Jorren was already gone — melted into the shadows like he'd never been there at all.
The pulse came again.
This time, the Shattered Gate answered.
A thin crack of ghostlight split across its surface, bright enough to paint the courtyard in pale fire. The air warped. The wind twisted. The storm above Emberhold tightened into a spiral, as if the sky itself were holding its breath.
Kaelren lifted his shield.
"Steady."
The Gate screamed.
Not metal. Not stone. Something older. Something alive.
A shape pushed through — flickering, half-formed, like a memory trying to become real. It lunged the moment it found shape, claws of ghostlight slashing toward the squad. Lysa's arrow flew past Kaelren's shoulder, pinning the creature to the ground for a heartbeat before the ghostlight burned the shaft away. Bren was already moving, hammer crashing into the creature's side, sending it skidding across the courtyard. Jorren appeared behind it, blades flashing, cutting through its unstable form.
Talla saw an opening and stepped forward.

"I can do this," she whispered.
Kaelren turned sharply. "Talla—"
But she was already moving.
The creature twisted faster than she expected. It slammed into her, knocking her flat, breath ripped from her lungs. She gasped, scrambling backward as it reared up—
Rynn threw himself between them, shield raised. The impact drove him back several steps, boots carving lines in the stone, but he held. Barely. His teeth clenched. His arms shook. But he held.
Kaelren was there a heartbeat later — shield bash, sword strike, clean and controlled. The creature dissolved into ash and ghostlight.
Talla coughed, pushing herself upright. "I'm sorry. I—"
"You were brave," Kaelren said, helping her to her feet. "Next time, be smart too."
She nodded, cheeks burning, determination hardening behind her eyes.
But the Gate wasn't done.
The crack widened. Ghostlight poured out in a wave that made the courtyard tiles shudder. More shapes pushed through — three, then five, then more, flickering like broken lanterns.
Thalen's voice rang from the battlements, sharp and commanding. "Emberguard — brace! They're coming through in waves!"
Kaelren raised his sword. "Squad — on me!"
They formed up without hesitation. Lysa took the high angle, arrows ready. Bren anchored the front with Kaelren. Rynn guarded the flank. Talla steadied herself, spear trembling but held firm. Jorren slipped between shadows, waiting for the perfect moment.
The creatures surged.
And the squad met them head-on.
Far above, the storm twisted tighter, spiralling like a great eye opening. Ghostlight flickered across the clouds, pulsing in rhythm with something — or someone.

In the Infirmary

The Unwritten staggered to the window as the pulse hit him again. His breath caught. Ghostlight flickered beneath his skin. He felt every creature that crossed the Gate. Felt their hunger. Felt their recognition.
They knew him.
"They're here for me," he whispered.
Mareth grabbed his arm. "You can't go out there!"
He didn't answer.
Because he wasn't sure she was wrong.

On the Lantern Path
Far away, Elyndra stumbled as the same pulse struck her. Her lanterns flared violently, ghostlight swirling around her like a storm of memories.
"He's waking," she whispered.
She ran faster.

Back in Emberhold
The courtyard was chaos.
Bren shattered one creature with a hammer swing that cracked the stone beneath it. Lysa's arrows pinned another long enough for Jorren to finish it. Rynn blocked a strike meant for Talla, grunting as the impact rattled his ribs.
Talla steadied herself and drove her spear through a creature's flickering chest, ghostlight bursting around her.
Kaelren moved like a force of nature — shield and blade in perfect rhythm, anchoring the squad with every step.
But the Gate pulsed again.
Harder.
The courtyard shook.
A massive shape pressed against the Gate from the other side — not flickering like the others, but solid, heavy, wrong. The stone arch groaned under the pressure. Dust drifted from the cracks. The air thickened, pulling inward as if the world were inhaling.
Rynn swallowed hard. "Captain… something else is coming."
Kaelren didn't answer. He could feel it too.

The Gate didn't crack this time. It bulged — as if something enormous pressed against it from the other side.
A deep, resonant thud echoed from within — not a scream, not a tear, but a knock.
Once. Twice. A third time.
Each strike heavier than the last.
Lysa's voice was barely a breath. "By the Titans…"
The Gate inhaled — a long, slow pull of air that dragged cloaks and hair toward it.
Kaelren planted his feet.
He looked at Rynn — bruised, exhausted, terrified, but refusing to step back.
A fierce, proud smile touched Kaelren's face.
"Welcome to the team," he said quietly.
The Gate exhaled.
Not a crack. Not a scream. A detonation of ghostlight that blew the courtyard open in a shockwave of violet fire.
Kaelren lifted his shield.
"Stay with me," he said. "All of you."
The shape that stepped through was massive — too solid to be a memory, too wrong to be flesh, its form shifting between shadow and bone.
Kaelren lowered his stance.
And the courtyard erupted into chaos.

CHAPTER TEN — THE BEAST OF THE BREACH

The creature stepped through the Gate like a nightmare forcing itself into flesh. Its body flickered between shadow and bone, its limbs too long, its movements too smooth — as if it remembered being something else before this.
The courtyard fell silent.
Even the storm paused.
Kaelren felt the pressure hit him first — a weight behind his eyes, a pull in his chest, like a hand reaching through time and memory to grab him by the spine.
He staggered.
Just for a heartbeat.
A flash — a hammer of burning metal, a battlefield of molten stone, a voice shouting his name across a collapsing sky—
Then it was gone.
Rynn didn't notice. Lysa didn't notice.
But Thalen did.
"Kaelren!" he barked from the battlements. "Stay with us!"
Kaelren blinked hard, forcing the world back into focus.
"I'm here."
But the echo of that other place clung to him like smoke.
The beast moved.
Not fast — inevitable. Each step cracked the stone beneath it, ghostlight bleeding from its joints like molten memory.
Bren tightened his grip on the hammer. "Captain… what is that thing?"
Kaelren didn't answer.
Because he didn't know.
But something inside him did.
A whisper. A warning. A memory that wasn't his.
It knows you.
The beast's head snapped toward him, as if hearing the thought.
Kaelren raised his shield.

"Form up!"
The squad closed in around him.
Rynn on the flank, shield up. Talla steadying her breath, spear trembling but ready. Lysa drawing an arrow. Jorren slipping behind the creature like a shadow. Bren bracing for impact.
The beast lunged.
Kaelren met it head-on.
The impact was like being hit by a falling tower. His shield buckled, metal screaming, and he slid backward across the courtyard, boots carving deep grooves in the stone.
Another flash — a battlefield of fire, a giant in obsidian armour, Kaelren raising a burning blade against it—
He gasped.
The beast's claws raked across his shield, ghostlight searing the metal.
"Kaelren!" Lysa shouted. "Move!"
He snapped back into the moment just in time to duck as the creature's arm scythed overhead, slicing a chunk of stone from the wall behind him.
Rynn charged in, shield-bash to the creature's knee. It staggered — not much, but enough.
Bren followed with a hammer strike that cracked the courtyard tiles.
Talla thrust her spear into the creature's side. Ghostlight burst from the wound, burning her hands, but she held on.
Jorren's blades flashed, carving lines of shadow from the creature's back.
The beast roared — a sound like a collapsing world.
Kaelren felt the roar inside his skull.
Another flash — a woman of lanterns screaming his name, a crown of fire shattering, a king kneeling before the Void—
He stumbled.
Rynn caught his arm. "Captain! What's happening?"
Kaelren shook his head, breath ragged.
"I… I don't know."
But the beast did.

It turned toward him, ignoring the others, ghostlight burning brighter in its eyes.

It remembered him.

Or the man he used to be.

Or the man he would become.

Kaelren raised his sword.

"Stay behind me."

Rynn stepped forward instead.

"No. We stand with you."

Kaelren looked at him — bruised, exhausted, terrified, but unbroken.

A fierce pride surged through him.

"Then let's finish this."

The beast lunged.

The squad moved as one.

And the storm above Emberhold finally broke.

The beast hit harder the second time.

Kaelren barely got his shield up before the creature's weight slammed into him, driving him backward across the courtyard. Stone shattered under his boots. His arm screamed. His vision blurred.

He dug in, teeth clenched, trying to hold the line—

—but the beast wasn't aiming to break his shield.

It was aiming to throw him.

The creature twisted, using its own momentum, and Kaelren felt the ground vanish beneath him. For a heartbeat he was weightless, suspended in ghostlight and storm wind.

Then he fell.

He hit the lower courtyard wall with a crack that echoed through Emberhold. His shield flew from his hand. His breath left his lungs in a violent rush. He slid down the stone, vision swimming, the world tilting sideways.

"KAELREN!" Lysa's scream cut through the chaos.

Bren roared and charged the beast. Rynn sprinted toward the fallen commander. Talla froze, terror locking her limbs. Jorren vanished into shadow, reappearing behind the creature with blades drawn.

But Kaelren didn't hear any of it.

Because the moment he hit the ground, the world went white.
Not from pain.
From memory.
A hammer of burning metal. A sky split open. A woman of lanterns reaching for him. A king of shadows kneeling before the Void. A voice — his voice? someone else's? — shouting across a collapsing realm.
Hold the line.
Kaelren gasped, dragging air into his lungs as the vision snapped away.
He tried to push himself up.
His arm buckled.
The courtyard spun.
The beast turned toward him, sensing weakness, ghostlight dripping from its claws like molten memory.
Rynn planted himself between Kaelren and the creature, shield raised, voice shaking.
"You want him," Rynn said, "you go through me."
The beast tilted its head, as if amused.
Then it lunged.

SPIRITVEIL — Elyndra Runs the Paths
Elyndra stumbled as the Lantern Path bucked beneath her feet, ghostlight flaring in violent bursts. She caught herself on a drifting lantern, breath ragged, heart pounding.
The pulse hit her again — stronger this time.
Not a call.
A scream.
She felt Kaelren fall. Felt the shock of impact. Felt the beast's hunger closing in.
"No," she whispered. "No, no, no—"
She pushed forward, lanterns swirling around her like frantic fireflies. The Path twisted, fracturing into three possible routes, each flickering with unstable light.
She didn't hesitate.
She took the one that hurt.

The one that burned her feet. The one that felt like running through broken glass. The one that led straight toward the breach.
"Hold on," she whispered. "Please hold on."
The Path screamed as she ran.

EMBERHOLD — The Voyager Stirs
In the infirmary, the Unwritten collapsed to his knees.
His breath fogged the air. Ghostlight crawled beneath his skin. His eyes unfocused, staring at something far beyond the walls.
He whispered a name he didn't remember learning.
"Kaelren…"
Mareth grabbed him. "You need to lie down!"
He didn't hear her.
Because the breach was calling him. Because the beast was hunting him. Because Kaelren was falling.
And because something inside him — something ancient, something broken, something vast — was waking.
A voice echoed in his skull.
You cannot run from what you were.
He clutched his head, gasping.
"No… no, I'm not— I'm not him—"
But the storm outside pulsed in perfect rhythm with his heartbeat.
The Voyager's shadow stretched across the Realms.

EMBERHOLD — Kaelren's Last Stand
Kaelren forced himself upright, vision swimming, ribs screaming with every breath.
Rynn braced for impact as the beast lunged.
Kaelren didn't think.
He moved.
He threw himself forward, grabbing Rynn's collar and yanking him aside just as the beast's claws tore through the space where the young scout had been standing.
The impact caught Kaelren instead.

Claws raked across his armour, tearing through metal, dragging him across the stone. He hit the ground hard, blood blooming beneath him.
The world dimmed.
Voices blurred.
The storm roared.
And Kaelren felt himself slipping.
Not dying.
Falling.
Falling through memory. Through ghostlight. Through a sky he didn't recognize. Through a realm that wasn't his. A woman of lanterns reached for him. A hammer burned in his hands. A king of shadows whispered:
You fall again.
Kaelren's eyes fluttered.
He exhaled.
And the world went dark.
Rynn screamed Kaelren's name as the commander hit the ground, blood blooming beneath him. The beast's claws had torn through armour and flesh, leaving deep, burning wounds that pulsed with ghostlight.
Kaelren didn't move.
For a heartbeat, the entire squad froze.
Not from fear.
From rage.
Bren was the first to break.
He roared and charged, hammer raised high, slamming it into the beast's flank with enough force to crack the courtyard tiles. The creature staggered, ghostlight spraying from the wound like molten sparks.
Lysa loosed arrow after arrow, each one striking true, each one burning away in the creature's shifting form.
Jorren appeared behind it, blades carving deep lines of shadow from its back.
Talla screamed and thrust her spear into its side, tears streaking her face.
But the beast didn't fall.
It turned.
And it chose its next target.

Talla.

She froze for a heartbeat — just one — but it was enough.

The beast lunged.

Rynn shoved her aside, shield raised, but the creature's claws caught the soldier behind her — a young Emberguard who had rushed down from the battlements to help.

His name was Dalen.

Barely twenty.

He didn't even have time to scream.

The beast's claws tore through him, lifting him off his feet and hurling him across the courtyard. He hit the wall with a sickening crack and slid down, leaving a smear of blood behind him.

Talla's voice broke.

"Dalen— Dalen— no—"

Bren roared in fury. Lysa's hands shook as she drew another arrow. Rynn's shield trembled. Jorren's blades dripped ghostlight.

Thalen's voice cracked from the battlements.

"Hold the line! HOLD—"

But even he faltered.

Because Kaelren wasn't moving. And Dalen was gone. And the beast was still coming.

SPIRITVEIL — Elyndra Sees It Happen

Elyndra burst out of the Lantern Path just beyond Emberhold's outer ridge — and collapsed to her knees.

She saw it.

Not with her eyes.

With her lanterns.

Kaelren falling. Dalen dying. The squad breaking. The beast towering over them. The storm twisting tighter. The breach widening.

She felt the moment Dalen's life slipped away — a lantern going dark.

"No— no, please—"

She pushed herself up, legs shaking, sprinting toward Emberhold with everything she had left.

But she was too far.
Too slow.
Too late.
She stumbled again, lanterns flickering violently, tears blurring her vision.
"I'm coming— I'm coming— please— hold on—"
But the Paths had taken too long.
And she knew it.

EMBERHOLD — The Voyager Breaks
The Unwritten felt Dalen die.
He felt Kaelren fall.
He felt Elyndra's despair.
He felt the beast's hunger.
And something inside him — something ancient, something buried, something that had been sleeping since the moment he fell through the Gate — snapped.
He staggered out of the infirmary, ignoring Mareth's screams, ghostlight pouring from his skin in violent pulses.
He stepped into the courtyard just as the beast raised its claws over Rynn and Talla.
He didn't think.
He didn't choose.
He reacted.
A scream tore from his throat — raw, terrified, furious, grieving — and the ghostlight exploded outward in a shockwave that shattered the air.
The pulse hit the beast first.
It didn't throw it. It didn't wound it.
It erased it.
One moment it was there — towering, snarling, victorious.
The next it was gone.
Ash. Memory. Nothing.
The courtyard fell silent.
The storm froze mid-swirl. Lanterns stopped flickering.
Even the wind held its breath.
Every eye turned toward the Unwritten.
His chest heaved. Ghostlight crawled across his skin. His eyes glowed with a light that wasn't human.

Then the glow flickered.

And he collapsed.

Rynn caught him before he hit the ground, dropping to his knees with the weight of him.

"Hey— hey— stay with me—"

But the Unwritten was unconscious, ghostlight fading from his skin like dying embers.

Lysa lowered her bow, hands shaking.

Bren stared at the empty space where the beast had been.

Talla sobbed over Dalen's body.

Jorren wiped ghostlight from his blades, eyes fixed on the Unwritten with something like fear.

Thalen descended the battlements slowly, expression unreadable.

And Kaelren lay bleeding on the stones, barely breathing.

Elyndra reached the courtyard entrance just in time to see the Unwritten collapse.

She fell to her knees.

Too late.

Too late.

Too late.

CHAPTER ELEVEN — THE KING OF FLAMEBORN

Darkness held him gently.
Not the cold void that had swallowed him in the courtyard — this was warm, like banked coals beneath a hearthstone.
He floated in it, weightless, until a voice reached him.
A laugh.
Deep. Warm. Alive.
"Again, little ember."
Kaelren blinked.
The darkness peeled away.
He stood in Flameborn.
The air shimmered with heat, carrying the scent of scorched basalt and iron. Ember lanterns hung from obsidian pillars, their flames steady and bright. Beyond the courtyard walls, molten rivers glowed like veins of gold, and the distant rumble of magma echoed through the realm.
This was home.
And the King stood before him.
Tall. Broad-shouldered. Laugh lines around his eyes. A beard streaked with early silver. A training sword of tempered embersteel in one hand, a battered shield in the other.
He looked like he belonged to the realm itself — forged from the same heat and stone.
Kaelren looked down.
He was small again — eight years old, maybe — holding a wooden sword too big for his hands, feet planted too wide, shield crooked.
The King crouched to meet his eyes.
"You're gripping it like it owes you a debt," he said gently. "Relax your hand."
Kaelren tried. The sword wobbled.
The King chuckled. "Better. Now — show me your stance."

Kaelren lifted the shield, trying to imitate the King's posture.

The King tilted his head. "That's a stance for someone bracing against a firestorm. You're not bracing. You're standing."

He stepped behind Kaelren, adjusting his shoulders, his feet, the angle of his shield.

"There," he said softly. "Now you look like a Flameborn."

Kaelren's chest swelled with pride.

A voice called from the archway.

"Is he giving you trouble yet?"

Kaelren turned.

His father stood there — General Aric Flameborn, commander of the King's armies, armour unbuckled at the collar, hair tied back, a grin tugging at his mouth. He carried the weight of a thousand battles, but his eyes softened the moment they fell on his son.

"Not trouble," the King said. "Determination."

Aric laughed. "He gets that from his mother."

Kaelren flushed. "I can hear you."

The King winked. "Good. Then hear this too — you're doing well."

Aric stepped into the courtyard, arms crossed, watching with a pride that made Kaelren stand a little taller.

"Show me what you've learned," Aric said.

Kaelren swallowed, lifted his shield, and nodded.

The King raised his practice sword.

"Ready?"

Kaelren nodded fiercely.

They moved.

The King's strikes were slow, deliberate, guiding Kaelren without overwhelming him. Kaelren blocked, stepped, adjusted — each movement smoother than the last. When he stumbled, the King steadied him. When he hesitated, Aric's voice cut through the heat.

"Trust your feet, boy!"

Kaelren did.

He blocked a strike cleanly — the first clean block of the day.

Aric let out a sharp, proud whistle. "That's my boy!"
Kaelren's grin nearly split his face.
The King lowered his sword. "Again."
They trained until Kaelren's arms trembled and sweat dripped onto the warm basalt. The ember lanterns brightened with dusk, their flames shifting from orange to deep red.
Kaelren finally collapsed onto the stone, chest heaving.
Aric knelt beside him, ruffling his hair.
"You did well."
Kaelren beamed. "I didn't fall as much."
"You fell plenty," Aric said, laughing. "But you got up every time. That's what matters."
The King sat beside them, lowering himself with a soft grunt.
"He has your heart," the King said quietly.
Aric's smile faded into something softer. "He has yours too."
Kaelren leaned against his father, small and tired and proud.
"Will I be strong enough?" he whispered.
Aric placed a hand on his son's back.
"You already are."
The King placed a hand over Kaelren's heart.
"This is your strength. Not the sword. Not the shield. This."
Kaelren covered the King's hand with his own.
"I won't let you down."
The King's smile faltered — just for a moment.
"You never could."
A gust of ember ash swept across the courtyard, glowing like fireflies in the dusk.
The memory wavered.
The heat dimmed. The basalt faded. The King's face dissolved into ember light. His father's voice echoed like a fading heartbeat.
Stand tall, Kaelren.
Kaelren reached for them.
"Wait—!"

But the world slipped away.

KAELREN WAKES
He gasped.
Pain lanced through his ribs. The warmth of Flameborn vanished, replaced by the cold stone and herbal scent of Emberhold's infirmary.
He blinked hard, vision swimming.
A lantern flickered overhead.
A soft groan sounded beside him.
Kaelren turned his head — slowly, painfully — and saw the Unwritten lying on the next cot. Pale. Still. Ghostlight flickering faintly beneath his skin like dying embers.
Kaelren stared at him.
The stranger who had obliterated a monster with a scream. The stranger who had collapsed the storm. The stranger who had saved them all. The stranger who had nearly died beside him.
Kaelren swallowed, throat tight.
"You... saved us," he whispered.
The Unwritten didn't stir.
Kaelren reached out, resting a trembling hand on the edge of the stranger's cot.
"You're not alone," he murmured. "Not anymore."
Outside, a mourning bell tolled — slow, heavy, grieving.
For Dalen. For the breach. For the Realms.
Kaelren closed his eyes.
And his father's voice echoed softly in his mind.
Stand tall, Kaelren.

CHAPTER TWELVE — EMBERHOLD IN MOURNING

The bell tolled through Emberhold like a wound that refused to close.
Slow. Heavy. Final.
Kaelren heard it even through the haze of pain and herbs, each strike vibrating through his ribs like a hammer on cracked stone. He forced his eyes open, the infirmary ceiling swimming above him.
The world felt muted. Dim. As if the courtyard's ghostlight pulse had drained the colour from everything.
A soft rustle drew his attention.
Talla sat on the edge of a cot across the room, her hands clasped so tightly her knuckles were white. Her spear lay beside her, snapped in half. She stared at it as if it were a body.
Lysa stood behind her, one hand on her shoulder, eyes red but dry. She had always been the one who cried last.
Bren sat on the floor with his back against the wall, hammer resting across his knees. His head hung low, shoulders shaking silently. Quiet grief didn't fit him — but it had found him anyway.
Rynn paced like a caged animal, stopping every few steps to glance at Kaelren and the Unwritten, then at the door, then back again. He looked like he wanted to scream but didn't know where to aim it.
Jorren was nowhere to be seen. He always vanished when the world hurt too much.
Kaelren swallowed, throat raw.
"Dalen…"
The name tasted like ash.
Lysa looked up sharply. "Don't speak. You're not healed."
Kaelren ignored her. "Is he…?"
Talla broke.

A sob tore from her chest, sudden and violent, and she folded forward, burying her face in her hands. Lysa pulled her close, holding her as she shook.
Bren's fist tightened around his hammer until the metal groaned.
Rynn stopped pacing, jaw clenched so hard it trembled.
Kaelren closed his eyes.
Dalen had been young. Eager. Brave. Too brave.
And Kaelren hadn't saved him.
A soft groan beside him made him turn his head.
The Unwritten shifted in his cot, ghostlight flickering faintly beneath his skin. His breathing was shallow, uneven, as if each inhale was a battle.
Kaelren stared at him.
The stranger who had obliterated a monster with a scream. The stranger who had collapsed the storm. The stranger who had saved them all. The stranger who had nearly died beside him.
The stranger who had killed Dalen's killer — but not in time.
The infirmary door slammed open.
Elyndra stumbled inside.
Her lanterns were dim, barely glowing. Her hair clung to her face, soaked with sweat and tears. She looked like she had run through fire.
Her eyes found Kaelren first.
She froze.
Then she saw the Unwritten.
Her knees buckled.
She caught herself on the doorframe, breath hitching, lanterns flickering violently around her.
"I was too late," she whispered. "I saw it. I saw him fall. I saw—"
Her voice broke.
Kaelren tried to sit up. Pain lanced through him, but he forced himself upright.
"Elyndra—"
She shook her head, tears spilling freely now.
"I should have been here. I should have—"

"You couldn't have stopped it," Kaelren said softly.
She looked at him with a grief so sharp it felt like a blade.
"I'm a Lanternkeeper. I'm supposed to guide. To protect. To see the paths before they break."
Her gaze drifted to the empty cot where Dalen's body had been laid before being taken for rites.
"I didn't see this."
The room fell silent.
Even the lanterns seemed to dim.
The door opened again — slower this time.
Thalen stepped inside.
His armour was still scorched from the battle. His face was drawn, older than it had looked yesterday. He scanned the room, taking in the wounded, the grieving, the unconscious stranger.
His eyes lingered on the Unwritten.
Then on Kaelren.
Then back to the Unwritten.
Something cold settled behind his gaze.
"Everyone out," Thalen said quietly. "Except Kaelren."
Lysa bristled. "Captain, with respect—"
"Out."
His voice left no room for argument.
One by one, the squad filed out — Bren supporting Talla, Lysa guiding Elyndra, Rynn lingering at the door until Kaelren gave him a small nod.
When the door closed, Thalen stepped closer to Kaelren's cot.
He didn't speak at first.
He just stared at the Unwritten.
Finally, he said:
"That wasn't human."
Kaelren's breath caught. "Thalen—"
"Don't lie to me." His voice was low, controlled, but shaking with something beneath it. "I've fought horrors. I've seen breaches. I've seen what ghostlight can do. But I've never seen anything like that."
Kaelren swallowed hard. "He saved us."

Thalen's jaw tightened. "He also destroyed a creature with a single scream. He froze a storm. He nearly tore the courtyard apart."

"He didn't mean to."

"That doesn't matter."

Thalen turned to Kaelren fully.

"What is he?"

Kaelren looked at the Unwritten — pale, still, fragile in a way that didn't match the power inside him.

"I don't know," Kaelren whispered. "But he's not our enemy."

Thalen's eyes hardened.

"Not yet."

A chill crawled down Kaelren's spine.

Thalen stepped back, voice quiet but heavy.

"The Council will want answers. And if they decide he's a threat…"

He didn't finish the sentence.

He didn't need to.

Kaelren's hand tightened around the edge of the Unwritten's cot.

Thalen turned toward the door.

"Rest while you can. Things are about to change."

He left without another word.

Kaelren stared at the Unwritten, heart pounding.

Outside, the mourning bell tolled again.

Slow. Heavy. Final.

Kaelren closed his eyes.

And Flameborn's heat felt very far away.

CHAPTER THIRTEEN — THE COUNCIL SUMMONS

The Council chamber of Emberhold was carved from black stone and lit by a ring of cold lanterns that cast long, sharp shadows across the floor. It always felt too large, too empty, as if built for giants rather than people.
Today, it felt like a tomb.
Kaelren stood near the back, leaning heavily on a crutch, ribs still bound beneath his tunic. Every breath hurt. Every heartbeat reminded him of the beast's claws. But he refused to sit. He refused to look weak.
The Unwritten sat beside him — pale, silent, wrapped in a cloak too large for him. His eyes were downcast, unfocused, as if listening to something no one else could hear. Ghostlight flickered faintly beneath his skin, dimming and brightening like a dying ember.
Thalen stood at the centre of the chamber, armour polished, expression carved from stone.
The Councillors watched from their raised seats — five of them, each older than the last, each wearing the same expression:
Fear.
The doors opened.
Elyndra entered.
Her lanterns were dim, their light trembling like her hands. She walked with purpose, but Kaelren saw the exhaustion in her steps, the grief in her eyes, the weight of the Paths clinging to her like frost.
She stopped beside Kaelren, not looking at him, not looking at the Unwritten — staring straight ahead.
The High Councillor rose.
"Lanternkeeper Elyndra," he said, voice echoing through the chamber. "You were summoned to speak on the matter of the stranger."
The Unwritten flinched at the word.
Elyndra's jaw tightened. "His name is—"

"He has no name," another Councillor snapped. "He has no history. No origin. No allegiance. And yet he wields power capable of annihilating a breach beast in a single breath."

A murmur rippled through the chamber.

Kaelren felt the Unwritten shrink beside him.

Thalen stepped forward. "With respect, Councillors, we all saw what he did. We all felt it. That was not controlled power. That was not training. That was instinct. And instinct that strong is dangerous."

Elyndra's voice cut through the room like a blade. "He saved us."

Thalen didn't look at her. "He also nearly killed half the courtyard."

"He didn't mean to."

"That doesn't matter."

Elyndra took a step forward, lanterns flaring. "It matters to me."

The High Councillor's gaze sharpened. "Lanternkeeper, you were seen running from the Paths moments before the pulse. You arrived breathless, distraught. You knew something was coming."

Elyndra froze.

Kaelren felt the tension coil in her like a drawn bowstring.

"I..." She swallowed. "I saw... possibilities."

"Possibilities," the Councillor repeated. "Or truths?"

Elyndra's hands trembled.

Kaelren stepped forward. "She can't tell you."

The Councillor turned on him. "And why not?"

Kaelren met his gaze without flinching. "Because Lanternkeepers are bound by oath. They cannot reveal what the Paths show them."

"That is convenient," another Councillor muttered.

Elyndra's voice cracked. "It is not convenience. It is law. It is survival. If I speak what I saw, I risk breaking the Paths themselves."

The High Councillor leaned forward. "Then tell us this: Is the stranger a threat?"

Elyndra's breath hitched.

Her lanterns flickered violently.
She looked at the Unwritten — really looked at him — and Kaelren saw the fear in her eyes, not of him, but for him.
"I cannot answer that," she whispered.
The chamber erupted.
Voices rose. Accusations flew. Fear thickened the air like smoke.
Thalen raised his voice above the chaos. "Councillors — we must act. If he is a danger, we cannot wait for another breach. We cannot risk another pulse."
Kaelren stepped between Thalen and the Unwritten, pain lancing through his ribs.
"You will not touch him."
Thalen's eyes hardened. "Kaelren—"
"No."
The word echoed through the chamber.
Silence fell.
Kaelren's voice was low, steady, unyielding.
"He saved my life. He saved all of us. And until we know what he is — until we understand him — he stays under my protection."
The High Councillor's expression darkened.
"You do not have the authority to make that decision."
Kaelren didn't blink. "Then strip me of it."
A ripple of shock moved through the chamber.
Elyndra's breath caught.
The Unwritten looked up for the first time, eyes wide, ghostlight flickering.
Thalen stared at Kaelren as if seeing him for the first time.
The High Councillor exhaled slowly.
"Very well," he said. "The Council will deliberate."
He raised a hand.
"Until then, the stranger is confined to Emberhold. He is not to leave the fortress. He is not to approach the Gate. And he is not to be left unguarded."
Kaelren's jaw tightened. "I'll guard him."
"No," the Councillor said. "You are injured. You are compromised."
He turned to Elyndra.

"Lanternkeeper. You will watch him."
Elyndra's breath stopped.
Kaelren's heart dropped.
The Unwritten stared at her, ghostlight trembling beneath his skin.
Elyndra bowed her head.
"I will."
The Councillor nodded.
"Then we are adjourned."
The lanterns dimmed.
The chamber emptied.
Kaelren stood frozen, breath shallow, ribs aching.
Elyndra didn't move.
The Unwritten whispered, voice barely audible.
"...why me?"
Elyndra closed her eyes.
"Because," she said softly, "I'm the only one who knows what you might become."
And she couldn't tell him why.

CHAPTER FOURTEEN — THE ANCHOR

The infirmary was quiet after the Council's storm. Too quiet. The kind of quiet that made every breath feel loud. Lanterns burned low, their light soft and trembling. Outside, the mourning bell had finally fallen silent, leaving only the distant hum of Emberhold's walls settling after the breach.

Elyndra stood in the doorway for a long time before she moved.

Kaelren was asleep — or unconscious — his breathing shallow but steady. The healers had forced him to drink something that smelled like crushed mint and bitter roots. He hadn't fought them. That alone told Elyndra how much pain he was in.

But her eyes weren't on Kaelren.

They were on the stranger.

The Unwritten.

He lay on the cot beside Kaelren, wrapped in a blanket too large for him, ghostlight flickering faintly beneath his skin. His face was peaceful in a way that felt wrong — like a storm pretending to be a pond.

Elyndra approached slowly, her lanterns dimming to a soft glow.

She sat beside him.

For a moment, she didn't speak. Didn't breathe. Didn't move.

She just watched him.

The man who had screamed a monster out of existence. The man who had collapsed a storm. The man who had nearly died doing it. The man the Council feared. The man she had seen in the Paths — not fully, not clearly, but enough to know he was a fracture in the Realms.

A fracture she was now responsible for.

She reached out, hesitated, then placed her hand gently on his forearm.

His skin was warm. Too warm. Like a lantern left burning too long.

"Can you hear me?" she whispered.

His eyelids fluttered.

Not open. Not awake. But aware.

Elyndra exhaled shakily.

"I know you're not ready," she murmured. "I know you're not supposed to wake yet. The Paths… they're not aligned. The Realms aren't ready. You're not ready."

Her voice cracked.

"But I need you to stay. Just stay. Don't slip."

The ghostlight beneath his skin pulsed once — faint, but unmistakable.

Elyndra's breath caught.

She tightened her grip on his arm.

"You're not alone," she whispered. "Not anymore. Kaelren is here. I'm here. You're safe."

The ghostlight flickered again — brighter this time, then dimmed.

His lips parted.

A sound escaped him.

Not a word. Not a breath.

A plea.

Elyndra leaned closer, lanterns trembling.

"I'm here," she said softly. "I'm your anchor. Just hold on to me."

His brow furrowed, as if he were fighting something deep inside — a memory, a voice, a darkness.

Elyndra felt it too.

A pressure. A pull. A whisper from the Paths.

She steadied herself, grounding her breath, letting her lanterns settle into a slow, rhythmic glow.

"Follow the light," she murmured. "Not the dark. Not the storm. Me."

The Unwritten's breathing eased.

The ghostlight steadied.

His hand twitched — reaching, searching — and Elyndra caught it gently, guiding it to rest against her lantern.

The lantern brightened.

Just a little.
Just enough.
Elyndra's eyes stung.
"You're not waking," she whispered. "Not yet. But you're here. And that's enough."
She stayed like that for a long time — holding his hand, guiding his breath, keeping the ghostlight from flaring too bright or fading too dim.
Kaelren stirred once, half awake, saw them, and relaxed again.
Outside, Emberhold slept uneasily.
Inside, Elyndra kept vigil.
The Unwritten did not wake.
But he did not slip away either.
And for now — for this fragile, trembling moment — that was victory.

THE PATH WITHIN
The Unwritten's breathing steadied under Elyndra's hand, but the ghostlight beneath his skin still pulsed too fast, too bright — like a lantern about to shatter.
She closed her eyes.
Lanternkeepers were forbidden from entering another's mind without consent. But this wasn't intrusion.
This was survival.
She let her lanterns dim until only one remained lit — the smallest, the softest, the one meant for guiding lost souls.
She placed it gently against his chest.
The world tilted.
Heat washed over her. Light bent. Sound folded inward.
And then—
She was standing in a place that wasn't a place.
A vast, empty expanse of shifting light and shadow. A horizon that curved like a broken mirror. A sky that flickered between storm and void.
The Unwritten stood in the centre of it.
Not awake. Not aware. Just... present.
His back was to her, shoulders tense, head bowed as if listening to something far away.

Elyndra approached slowly.

"Can you hear me?"

He didn't turn.

But the world around him rippled — a tremor of recognition.

She stepped closer, lantern held out before her. Its glow pushed back the darkness, revealing fragments floating in the air around him:

A shattered crown. A burning hammer. A woman made of lantern light. A king kneeling in shadow. A Gate splitting open. A scream that wasn't human.

Elyndra's breath caught.

These weren't memories. They were fractures.

Pieces of a life he didn't remember. Pieces of a life he wasn't ready to face.

She reached out, touching his shoulder.

The world snapped.

Suddenly they were standing in a training courtyard — not Emberhold, not Flameborn, but something older, something impossible. The ground was smooth obsidian. The sky a swirling storm of ghostlight. Lanterns hung from nothing, suspended in midair.

The Unwritten turned.

His eyes glowed faintly, unfocused but aware of her presence.

"Where... am I?" he whispered.

Elyndra steadied her breath. "Inside your mind. Inside the space between what you were and what you are."

He frowned, confused. "I don't... remember."

"You're not meant to," she said gently. "Not yet."

He looked around, fear flickering across his face. "It's broken."

"It's unfinished," she corrected. "And that's why I'm here."

He swallowed. "To fix me?"

"No." She stepped closer, lantern glowing brighter. "To teach you how not to break."

The ground trembled beneath them.

A shadow rose at the edge of the courtyard — tall, formless, reaching. The same presence she had felt during the breach. The same hunger.

The Unwritten staggered back, panic rising. "It's coming—"

Elyndra grabbed his hand.

"Look at me."

He did.

"Breathe," she said. "Match the lantern."

Her lantern pulsed slowly.

His chest rose and fell, shaky at first, then steadier.

The shadow hesitated.

Elyndra lifted the lantern higher.

"This place listens to you," she said. "It bends to you. But only if you're calm."

He stared at her, trembling. "I don't know how."

"That's why I'm here."

She guided his hand to the lantern.

"Focus on the light. Not the dark. Not the storm. Me."

The lantern brightened.

The shadow recoiled.

The world steadied.

The Unwritten's breathing slowed, his shoulders lowering, the panic fading from his eyes.

Elyndra exhaled.

"You're not ready to wake," she said softly. "But you're not lost."

He looked at her with something like trust — fragile, uncertain, but real.

"Will you stay?" he whispered.

Elyndra's throat tightened.

"Yes," she said. "Until you can stand on your own."

The lantern flared.

The world dissolved.

And Elyndra opened her eyes in the infirmary, still holding his hand, her lantern dim but steady.

The Unwritten slept peacefully.

For the first time since the breach.

CHAPTER FIFTEEN — THE WEIGHT OF FLAMEBORN

The corridor outside the Council chamber felt colder than it should have. Emberhold's stone always held a faint warmth, but now it felt as though the heat had been drained from the walls, leaving only the echo of the Council's verdict behind.

Kaelren walked slowly, each step sending a dull ache through his ribs. The healers had warned him not to move too much. He ignored them. Pain was easier than stillness. Stillness meant thinking. Thinking meant remembering.

He reached the end of the corridor and braced a hand against the wall, breath catching. The world tilted for a moment — not from injury, but from the weight of everything pressing down on him.

Dalen's face. Elyndra's trembling voice. The Unwritten's confusion. Thalen's suspicion. The Council's fear.

He closed his eyes.

A memory rose — unbidden, sharp, and brief.

Memory — The King's Warning

He was younger then — not a boy, but not yet the commander he would become. His armour was new, his shoulders unburdened, his future still unwritten.

He stood with the King on a balcony overlooking Flameborn's molten rivers. The heat shimmered in the air, turning the horizon into a wavering line of gold.

The King rested his hands on the railing, gaze distant.

"Power frightens people," he said quietly.

Kaelren frowned. "Yours doesn't."

The King smiled — a tired, knowing smile.

"That's because they trust me. But trust is fragile. It can shatter faster than steel."

Kaelren stepped closer. "Then I'll protect it."

The King shook his head.

"No, Kaelren. You protect people. Not their fear."

He turned, placing a hand on Kaelren's shoulder.
"One day, you'll stand beside someone the Realms don't understand. Someone they fear. And you'll have to choose whether to stand with them... or with the people who fear them."
Kaelren swallowed. "What should I choose?"
The King's eyes softened.
"Choose the one who needs you most."
The memory faded.
Kaelren opened his eyes, breath unsteady.
The corridor felt colder now.
He pushed himself upright, ignoring the pain, and made his way toward the infirmary. His steps were slow but determined, each one echoing the King's words.
Choose the one who needs you most.
He reached the doorway.
Elyndra sat beside the Unwritten, lantern dim but steady, her hand resting lightly on his. She looked exhausted — drained in a way that went deeper than physical fatigue.
Kaelren leaned against the doorframe.
"How is he?"
Elyndra didn't look up. "Holding. Barely."
Kaelren exhaled. "The Council wants him contained."
"I know."
"They want him watched."
"I know."
"They want him controlled."
Elyndra's jaw tightened. "They can't control him."
Kaelren stepped inside, lowering himself onto the cot beside hers.
"No," he said softly. "But we can help him."
Elyndra finally looked at him.
Her eyes were tired. Haunted. But resolute.
"We have to," she whispered. "Because if he slips... if he breaks... the Realms won't survive what wakes up inside him."
Kaelren nodded.
He looked at the Unwritten — pale, still, ghostlight flickering faintly beneath his skin.

The stranger who had saved them. The stranger the Council feared. The stranger who needed them most.
Kaelren rested a hand on the edge of the cot.
"I'm not leaving him," he said quietly.
Elyndra's lantern brightened.
"Neither am I."
Outside, Emberhold's bells were silent.
Inside, three lives hung in fragile balance.
And the Realms shifted — quietly, imperceptibly — toward the storm that was coming.

CHAPTER SIXTEEN — THALEN'S LINE

Thalen didn't go far after leaving the Council chamber. He walked until the noise of Emberhold faded behind him, until the torches thinned and the stone corridors narrowed into the older parts of the fortress — the places built before records, before the Realms were mapped, before Emberhold had a name.
He stopped in a small alcove carved into the wall, a place he had come to many times over the years. A place where no one followed him. A place where he could breathe.
He braced both hands against the cold stone and bowed his head.
For a long time, he said nothing.
Then, quietly:
"Dalen."
The name cracked in his throat.
He squeezed his eyes shut, jaw tightening until it hurt.
He had trained Dalen. He had vouched for him. He had promised his parents he would keep him safe.
And now the boy was dead.
Killed by a creature that should never have reached the courtyard. Killed while Thalen watched.
He slammed his fist into the wall.
The stone didn't move.
His knuckles split.
He didn't care.
Another strike. Another. Another.
Blood smeared across the basalt.
He pressed his forehead to the wall, breath shaking.
"I failed you," he whispered. "I failed all of you."
Footsteps echoed behind him.
He didn't turn.
Kaelren's voice was quiet, strained. "You didn't fail anyone."
Thalen let out a humourless breath. "Don't lie to me."

Kaelren stepped into the alcove, leaning heavily on his crutch. His ribs were bound tight beneath his tunic, but he stood tall anyway.

"You did everything you could," Kaelren said.

Thalen finally turned.

His eyes were red. Not from tears — Thalen didn't cry — but from holding them back.

"Everything I could wasn't enough."

Kaelren didn't argue.

Thalen looked at him for a long moment, then at the blood on his own knuckles.

"You should be resting."

Kaelren shrugged. "Couldn't sleep."

Thalen's gaze hardened. "Because of him."

Kaelren didn't flinch. "Because of everything."

Thalen stepped closer, lowering his voice.

"You're too close to him."

Kaelren's jaw tightened. "He saved us."

"He destroyed a breach beast with a scream," Thalen snapped. "He froze a storm. He nearly tore the courtyard apart. And you want me to pretend that doesn't terrify me?"

Kaelren held his gaze. "He didn't choose any of that."

Thalen's voice dropped to a whisper.

"That's what scares me."

Silence settled between them — heavy, suffocating.

Thalen looked away first.

"I've seen power like that before," he said quietly. "Not the same. But close. A man who couldn't control what he was. A man who thought he could handle it."

Kaelren frowned. "Who?"

Thalen's expression darkened.

"My brother."

Kaelren froze.

Thalen rarely spoke of his family. Almost never.

"He was gifted," Thalen said. "Touched by the Lanterns. Everyone thought he'd be a great Keeper one day. But the Paths… they twisted him. He saw too much. Felt too much. And one day he broke."

Kaelren swallowed. "I'm sorry."
Thalen shook his head. "I'm not telling you for sympathy. I'm telling you because I know what it looks like when someone is on the edge of losing themselves."
He stepped closer, voice low and fierce.
"And that stranger is standing on that edge."
Kaelren didn't back down. "Then we pull him back."
Thalen's eyes flashed. "Or we let him fall before he takes the rest of us with him."
Kaelren's hand tightened on his crutch. "I won't let you hurt him."
Thalen stared at him — long, hard, searching.
Then he said something Kaelren didn't expect.
"I don't want to hurt him."
Kaelren blinked.
Thalen's voice softened — barely.
"I want to protect Emberhold. I want to protect all of you. And I don't know how to do that if he's here."
Kaelren exhaled slowly. "Then trust me."
Thalen's jaw clenched. "I trust you. I don't trust him."
Kaelren stepped forward, pain forgotten.
"Then trust that I'll keep him in check."
Thalen looked at him for a long time.
Finally, he nodded — once, sharp, reluctant.
"I'll give you time," he said. "But not much."
Kaelren nodded back. "That's all I ask."
Thalen turned to leave, but paused at the edge of the alcove.
"Kaelren."
Kaelren looked up.
Thalen's voice was quiet. "If he slips... if he becomes what the Council fears..."
He didn't finish the sentence.
He didn't need to.
Kaelren's voice was steady.
"Then I'll stop him."
Thalen nodded.
And for the first time since the breach, Kaelren saw something in Thalen's eyes that wasn't fear.

OFFICIAL

It was trust.
Fragile. Wounded. But real.
Thalen left without another word.
Kaelren stood alone in the alcove, the King's memory echoing in his mind.
Choose the one who needs you most.
He turned toward the infirmary.
And he walked.

CHAPTER SEVENTEEN — THE WARNING BREACH

It began with a sound.
Not a roar. Not a scream. A hum.
Soft. Low. Wrong.
Kaelren felt it first — a vibration in the stone beneath his feet, a tremor that crawled up his spine. He froze, hand braced against the wall.
Not again.
He turned and tried to run. Pain detonated through his ribs — sharp, blinding — and his knee buckled. He caught himself on the wall with a gasp, breath punched out of him.
"Not now," he hissed through his teeth.
He forced himself forward anyway, half-running, half-stumbling, every step a jolt of fire beneath his ribs.
He burst into the infirmary just as Elyndra jerked upright, lanterns flaring violently around her.
"You felt it too," she whispered.
Kaelren nodded. "Where?"
Before she could answer, the Unwritten convulsed.
His back arched, ghostlight surging beneath his skin.
Elyndra grabbed his hand, lanterns trembling.
"Something's calling him."
Kaelren didn't hesitate.
"We take him with us."
Elyndra stared at him. "He can't walk."
"I'll carry him."
Elyndra grabbed his arm. "Kaelren — your ribs—"
"There's no time."
He hooked his arms under the Unwritten's shoulders and tried to lift — and nearly collapsed. Pain ripped through his side, white-hot, stealing his breath.
Bren surged forward instinctively. "Kaelren—"
"Help me," Kaelren rasped.
Bren and Rynn moved in without hesitation, each taking part of the Unwritten's weight. Kaelren kept one arm

around him, guiding, anchoring, but no longer bearing the full load.

And the hum deepened, as if the breach felt him move. They moved as fast as they could — Bren and Rynn carrying most of the Unwritten's weight, Kaelren limping beside them, one hand gripping the railing, the other keeping the stranger steady.

Every step up the stairs was agony. Twice Kaelren stumbled; twice Bren caught him without comment. They drove themselves toward the north wall. The hum grew louder with every step.

When they reached the rampart, the squad was already braced for a fight.

Bren and Rynn lowered the Unwritten to the stone, then instinctively moved into position — Bren stepping to the front, hammer raised, jaw clenched hard enough to crack stone. Lysa slid in beside him, bow drawn, three arrows fanned between her fingers. Rynn shifted behind them, shield trembling in his grip. Talla held her spear rigidly, eyes wide, haunted by the memory of Dalen's death. Jorren lingered near the wall, blades drawn, shadows curling around him like smoke.

Thalen turned at the sound of their approach — and his eyes widened when he saw Kaelren limping behind them, the Unwritten's weight still half supported by Elyndra's steadying hand.

"What are you doing? Get him away from here!"

Kaelren shook his head. "He's connected to it."

Thalen swore. "That's exactly why—"

A crack split the air.

Everyone froze.

A thin line of ghostlight tore open in the stone wall — no bigger than a handspan, but pulsing violently, like a wound trying to rip itself wider.

A micro breach.

Unstable. Hungry. Growing.

Bren stepped forward, hammer raised. "I'll smash it—"

"NO!" Elyndra snapped. "You'll make it worse!"

The breach pulsed.

Rynn stumbled back. "It's... it's looking at us."
Lysa's voice was tight. "It's not looking at us."
Her eyes flicked to the Unwritten.
"It's looking at him."
The Unwritten convulsed in Kaelren's arms, ghostlight flaring so bright it illuminated the entire rampart.
Elyndra grabbed his face, forcing his gaze to hers.
"Anchor to me. Not to it. To me."
The breach screamed.
A skeletal hand pushed through the crack — fingers made of ghostlight and shadow.
Talla gasped, stumbling back, spear shaking violently.
Bren roared and stepped forward, hammer raised.
"Bren, WAIT—!" Kaelren shouted.
Too late.
The breach reacted to Bren's aggression — the crack widening, the hand stretching toward him.
Jorren appeared behind Bren, grabbing his shoulder.
"Don't give it a target!"
Bren froze, chest heaving.
The breach pulsed again.
The Unwritten whispered:
"...stop..."
And the breach froze.
Just for a heartbeat.
Just long enough.
Elyndra thrust her lantern forward, its light exploding into a beam that struck the breach dead center.
The crack sealed.
The hand vanished.
The hum died.
Silence fell.
Bren lowered his hammer, breath shaking. Lysa exhaled slowly, bow trembling in her grip. Rynn collapsed to one knee, shield slipping from his hand. Talla covered her mouth, tears streaming silently. Jorren sheathed his blades, eyes fixed on the sealed wall.

Kaelren sagged with relief, legs shaking, ribs screaming. Bren and Rynn lowered the Unwritten the rest of the way as Kaelren braced himself on the wall, breath ragged. Thalen stared at them — at the sealed wall, at Elyndra's trembling lantern, at the unconscious stranger glowing faintly on the stone between them.
Then he said, voice low and shaken:
"That wasn't a breach."
Kaelren frowned. "What do you mean?"
Thalen pointed at the wall.
"That was a call."
Elyndra's breath caught.
Kaelren's blood ran cold.
Thalen stepped closer, eyes locked on the Unwritten.
"Something on the other side wasn't trying to get through."
He swallowed.
"It was trying to pull him back."

CHAPTER EIGHTEEN — THE SQUAD BREAKS

The rampart was still humming with the aftershock of the sealed breach when Bren and Rynn lowered the Unwritten to the stone. Kaelren sagged against the wall beside them, ribs screaming, while Elyndra dropped to her knees at the stranger's side, lanterns dimming to a soft, steady glow as she checked his pulse.

The squad gathered in a loose semicircle — not close, not far, caught between fear, awe, and the kind of silence that follows something no one has words for.

Bren was the first to speak.

"What in the burning hells were you thinking?"

Kaelren didn't look up. "I did what I had to."

"What you had to?" Bren's voice cracked. "You carried him toward the breach, Kaelren. Toward it."

Kaelren met his eyes. "He was connected. If we left him—"

"We don't know that!" Bren roared. "We don't know anything about him!"

Lysa stepped forward, bow still in her hand, knuckles white. "Bren's right. We're fighting blind. And you're making decisions for all of us."

Kaelren's jaw tightened. "Someone had to."

Rynn shifted nervously, glancing between them.

"Kaelren... we trust you. We do. But this — this is different."

Talla stood beside him, spear still trembling in her grip. She swallowed hard.

"He scares me," she whispered.

Kaelren's chest tightened. "Talla—"

"No." She shook her head, eyes shining. "I'm not saying he's evil. I'm not saying he meant to hurt anyone. But I watched Dalen die. I watched that thing tear him apart. And then I watched the stranger destroy it like it was nothing."

Her voice cracked.

"And now the breach is calling him."

Rynn placed a hand on her shoulder — gently, awkwardly, but with real warmth.

"You're allowed to be scared," he murmured.

Talla blinked at him, surprised by the softness in his voice. "Are you?"

Rynn hesitated, then gave a small, crooked smile. "Terrified."

Talla let out a shaky laugh — the first sound of anything close to joy since the courtyard — and Rynn's smile widened just a little.

Kaelren watched them, a flicker of relief threading through his worry.

But Bren wasn't done.

He stepped forward, hammer resting on his shoulder, eyes burning.

"You're protecting him," Bren said. "More than you're protecting us."

Kaelren stiffened. "That's not true."

"Isn't it?" Lysa asked quietly. "Because it feels like it."

Kaelren looked at each of them — Bren's anger, Lysa's fear, Rynn's uncertainty, Talla's trembling grief, Jorren's unreadable stare from the shadows.

He felt the weight of their trust. And the weight of their doubt.

"I'm protecting all of you," Kaelren said. "Including him."

Bren scoffed. "He's not one of us."

Kaelren's voice hardened. "He saved us."

"He almost killed us!" Bren snapped.

"He didn't choose that!"

"And what happens when he chooses something else?" Lysa whispered.

Silence.

Cold. Heavy. Suffocating.

Kaelren swallowed.

"I don't know," he admitted. "But I know this: if we turn on him now, we lose him. And if we lose him… we lose whatever chance we have of stopping what's coming."

Jorren finally spoke, voice low and quiet.
"He's right."
Everyone turned.
Jorren stepped out of the shadows, blades sheathed, eyes fixed on the Unwritten.
"I've seen things in the dark," he said. "Things that don't belong in this world. Things that are coming whether we want them to or not."
He looked at Kaelren.
"And I've seen the way he reacts to the stranger. He's not afraid of him. He's afraid for him."
Kaelren blinked.
Jorren shrugged. "That matters."
Bren looked away, jaw clenched.
Lysa exhaled slowly.
Rynn squeezed Talla's shoulder again, and she didn't pull away.
Elyndra stood, lanterns dim but steady.
"We don't have to trust him," she said softly. "Not yet. But we do have to keep him alive."
Kaelren nodded.
"And together," he said, "we can."
The squad exchanged glances — uncertain, shaken, but united by something deeper than fear.
Not trust. Not yet.
But loyalty.
To each other. To Kaelren. To the Realms.
Bren grunted. "Fine. But if he so much as twitches wrong—"
Kaelren smirked. "You'll be the first to hit him. I know."
Bren snorted. "Damn right."
Talla nudged Rynn with her elbow. "You jumped when the breach screamed."
Rynn flushed. "I— I didn't jump. I— repositioned."
Talla smiled — small, but real.
Kaelren felt something in his chest loosen.
The squad wasn't whole.
But they weren't broken.
Not yet.

CHAPTER NINETEEN — THE VEIL THINS

The Council chamber was louder than Kaelren had ever heard it.

Voices clashed like steel on steel, echoing off the stone walls, overlapping in panic and accusation. Lanterns flickered violently overhead, their light stuttering as if afraid.

Kaelren stood near the back, leaning on his crutch, ribs aching with every breath. Elyndra stood beside him, lanterns dim and trembling. The Unwritten lay unconscious on a stretcher between two healers, ghostlight pulsing faintly beneath his skin.

The High Councillor slammed his staff against the floor. "Silence!"

The chamber quieted — but the fear didn't.

Thalen stepped forward, jaw tight. "The breach wasn't an attack. It was a call."

A ripple of dread moved through the Council.

One of the elders leaned forward. "A call to what?"

Thalen's eyes flicked to the Unwritten.

"Not what," he said. "Who."

Elyndra's lanterns flared. "You don't know that."

Thalen didn't look at her. "I know enough."

The High Councillor pointed at the Unwritten. "That thing—"

Kaelren stepped forward, voice sharp. "He's not a thing."

The Councillor didn't blink. "—is a danger to Emberhold. And now the breaches are reaching for him."

Kaelren's pulse hammered. "He didn't cause it."

"But it reacted to him," another Councillor snapped. "It grew when he approached. It froze when he spoke. It sealed when he—"

"He didn't seal it," Elyndra cut in. "I did."

The Councillor's gaze sharpened. "And how did you do that, Lanternkeeper?"

Elyndra hesitated.
Kaelren saw it — the flicker of fear, the weight of the Paths pressing against her throat.
"I…" She swallowed. "I anchored him."
"Anchored him?" the High Councillor repeated. "To what?"
Elyndra's lanterns dimmed.
"I cannot say."
"You will say."
"I cannot," she whispered. "The Paths forbid it."
The chamber erupted again.
Kaelren felt the walls closing in — the fear, the suspicion, the weight of a hundred eyes turning toward the Unwritten like he was a loaded weapon.
His breath hitched.
And suddenly—
A memory rose.

Memory — The King's Burden
He was older now — a commander, not a boy. Flameborn burned bright around him, molten rivers glowing beneath the balcony where he stood with the King.
The King's armour was dented, soot-stained, his beard streaked with ash. He looked tired in a way Kaelren had never seen.
"Do you know what leadership is?" the King asked.
Kaelren frowned. "Responsibility?"
The King shook his head.
"Loneliness."
Kaelren blinked. "You're not alone."
The King smiled — sad, soft, knowing.
"Every leader stands alone, Kaelren. Not because people abandon them. But because they carry what no one else can."
He placed a hand on Kaelren's shoulder.
"One day, you will carry something no one else understands. And you will feel alone. But you must stand anyway."
The memory faded.

Kaelren opened his eyes.
The Council chamber felt colder.
Elyndra stood alone in the centre of the storm — lanterns dim, shoulders trembling, eyes hollow with exhaustion.
She was carrying everything.
The Unwritten. The squad. The Council's fear. The Realms' future.
And she was breaking.
The High Councillor slammed his staff again.
"Lanternkeeper Elyndra, you will answer this: Is the stranger a threat to Emberhold?"
Elyndra's breath caught.
Her lanterns flickered violently.
"I… I cannot answer."
"You refuse to answer."
"I am forbidden to answer."
The Councillor's voice rose. "Then you are unfit to serve."
Kaelren stepped forward. "Enough—"
But Elyndra spoke first.
"No."
Her voice was quiet. Steady. Breaking.
"I will not be stripped of my oath. I will not betray the Paths. And I will not abandon him."
The chamber fell silent.
The High Councillor's eyes narrowed. "Then you leave us no choice."
Elyndra stiffened.
Kaelren's heart dropped.
"Lanternkeeper Elyndra," the Councillor said, "you are hereby ordered to return to the Spirit Veil and seek guidance. You will not return until you bring us answers."
Elyndra's lanterns dimmed to embers.
Kaelren stepped toward her. "Elyndra—"
She shook her head.
"It's all right," she whispered. "I knew this was coming."
She turned to the Unwritten — pale, still, ghostlight flickering faintly.
"I'll be back," she murmured. "Hold on."
Then she turned and walked out of the chamber.

OFFICIAL

Her lanterns flickered behind her like dying stars.

CHAPTER TWENTY - THE SPIRIT VEIL

The Spirit Veil was silent. Too silent.

Not the soft, reverent quiet Elyndra had known all her life — the kind that hummed with memory and light — but a hollow, breathless stillness. A silence that felt wrong.

Mist curled around her ankles as she stepped forward, lanterns dimming to a faint, trembling glow. The air was cold in a way that wasn't temperature — a cold that lived in the bones, in the spark, in the spaces between thoughts.

The Paths shimmered faintly around her. Threads of light twisting through the fog. Whispering. Shifting. Refusing to settle.

Elyndra reached for the nearest thread.

It recoiled.

Not gently. Not shyly. Like a frightened animal snapping away from a hand it once trusted.

Her breath hitched.

She reached for another.

It flickered — once, twice — then went dark, dissolving into the mist like a dying ember.

Her lanterns dimmed in sympathy.

"Please," she whispered, voice trembling. "I need guidance. I need something. Anything."

The Paths twisted away from her.

All of them.

Like a tide pulling back from the shore. Like a thousand doors slamming shut at once.

The rejection cut deeper than any blade.

"I'm trying," she choked. "I'm trying to hold Emberhold together. I'm trying to anchor him. I'm trying to keep the Realms from tearing open. I'm trying to—"

Her voice broke.

"I can't do this alone."

The Veil did not answer.

The mist swirled around her, thickening, darkening. Her lanterns guttered. The Paths flickered like dying stars.
A faint sound drifted through the fog — not a whisper, not a voice, but something like a memory trying to speak and failing. A half-formed echo. A breath that wasn't hers.
Elyndra fell to her knees.
The cold seeped into her bones. Into her spark. Into the place where the Paths had always lived.
For the first time since she became a Lanternkeeper, she felt truly, utterly lost.
"Please," she whispered. "Tell me what to do."
The Veil remained silent.
The mist thickened around her, swallowing her lanternlight, swallowing her breath, swallowing her hope. It felt like kneeling inside a dying world.
Then—
Somewhere deep within the fog, faint and distant and trembling, a single thread of light pulsed.
Weak. Unstable. Calling.
Not to her.
To him.
Elyndra's breath caught.
"Oh no…"
The thread pulsed again — faint, frantic, desperate — and the mist shuddered around it, as if the Veil itself feared what it pointed toward.
She stood, lanterns flaring with sudden, terrified urgency.
She ran.
Through the mist. Through the silence. Through the dying light of the Paths.
Back toward Emberhold. Back toward the Unwritten. Back toward the storm that was coming.

CHAPTER TWENTY-ONE — ELYNDRA RETURNS

The Spirit Veil spat her out.
Not gently. Not gracefully. It threw her back into Emberhold like a wave rejecting a stone.
Elyndra stumbled into the lantern hall, catching herself on the cold stone floor. Her lanterns flickered violently around her, their light unstable, trembling like frightened birds.
She pushed herself upright, breath ragged.
The Paths had given her nothing. Not a whisper. Not a warning. Not a single thread to follow.
She had never felt so blind.
The hall was empty — too empty — the silence pressing against her ears. Emberhold always hummed with life, with footsteps, with distant voices. Now it felt like the fortress was holding its breath.
She moved quickly, lanterns dimming to a soft glow as she crossed the hall and pushed through the doors into the main corridor.
The moment she stepped inside, she felt it.
Fear.
Thick. Heavy. Clinging to the walls like smoke.
Soldiers whispered in corners. Lanterns burned lower than usual. Every face she passed turned away, as if afraid her eyes might reveal something they didn't want to know.
She walked faster.
Her heart hammered.
She reached the infirmary door and pushed it open.
Kaelren was there.
Sitting beside the Unwritten's cot, elbows on his knees, head bowed. His crutch leaned against the wall. His ribs were still bound, his breathing shallow, but he didn't look away from the Unwritten.
He looked like a man guarding a dying flame.
He looked up when he heard her.
"Elyndra."

Her breath caught.
He stood — too fast, pain flashing across his face — but he didn't stop.
"What happened?" he asked. "What did the Veil show you?"
She shook her head.
"It didn't."
Kaelren froze.
"What do you mean it didn't?"
Elyndra's voice cracked.
"It refused me."
Kaelren stared at her, disbelief and fear mixing in his eyes.
"The Veil refused you?"
She nodded, lanterns trembling.
"I reached for the Paths. They pulled away. I begged. They stayed silent. I asked for guidance. They gave me nothing."
Her voice broke.
"I've never been shut out before."
Kaelren stepped closer, lowering his voice.
"Elyndra… what does that mean?"
She swallowed hard.
"It means something is coming that the Paths cannot show. Something they cannot touch. Something they cannot predict."
Her gaze drifted to the Unwritten — pale, still, ghostlight flickering faintly beneath his skin.
"And it's tied to him."
Kaelren's jaw tightened. "Then we protect him."
Elyndra shook her head, tears burning behind her eyes.
"You don't understand. The Council is terrified. The breaches are calling him. The Veil is silent. And I—"
Her voice cracked.
"I'm trying to hold Emberhold together. I'm trying to anchor him. I'm trying to keep the Realms from tearing open. And I don't know how much longer I can do this."
Kaelren reached out, placing a hand on her shoulder.
"You're not alone."
Elyndra let out a shaky breath.
"Yes," she whispered. "I am."

Before Kaelren could respond, the door burst open.

The squad rushed in — Bren first, hammer in hand, Lysa close behind, Rynn and Talla shoulder to shoulder, Jorren slipping in silently like a shadow.

Bren's eyes widened when he saw Elyndra.

"You're back."

Lysa stepped forward. "What did the Veil say?"

Elyndra looked at them — at their fear, their hope, their exhaustion — and felt something inside her twist.

"It said nothing."

Silence.

Cold. Sharp. Cutting.

Rynn swallowed. "Nothing? As in… nothing nothing?"

Elyndra nodded.

Talla's hand found Rynn's without thinking. He squeezed it gently.

Bren swore under his breath. "We're blind."

Jorren's voice was quiet. "No. We're hunted."

Kaelren stepped between Elyndra and the squad.

"We don't panic," he said. "We don't break. We stay together."

Elyndra looked at him — at all of them — and felt the weight of the Realms pressing down on her shoulders.

She whispered:

"I don't know how to save us."

Kaelren met her gaze.

"You don't have to," he said softly. "We save each other."

Her lanterns flickered.

For the first time since the Veil, they didn't dim.

They steadied.

Just a little.

Just enough.

CHAPTER TWENTY-TWO — THE SECOND DREAM

The room was too quiet.
The squad stood in a loose circle around the Unwritten's cot — Bren tense, Lysa pale, Rynn and Talla shoulder to shoulder, Jorren unreadable in the corner. Kaelren sat beside the Unwritten, one hand gripping the edge of the mattress, the other pressed to his ribs.
Elyndra stood at the foot of the bed, lanterns trembling around her like frightened birds.
"He's slipping again," she whispered.
Kaelren leaned forward. "Can you anchor him?"
"I'm trying."
Her lanterns flickered.
The Unwritten's breath hitched — once, twice — then his back arched, ghostlight flaring beneath his skin.
Talla gasped. Rynn stepped in front of her without thinking. Bren raised his hammer. Lysa grabbed his arm.
Jorren didn't move.
Elyndra stepped closer.
"Stay with me," she murmured, placing her hand on the Unwritten's chest.
The lantern in her palm flared.
And then—
Her eyes unfocused.
Her breath caught.
Her lanterns froze mid-air.
Kaelren stood instantly. "Elyndra?"
She didn't answer.
Her body remained upright, steady, breathing — but her mind was gone.
Not unconscious. Not collapsed. Just… elsewhere.
Her voice came out soft, distant, layered with an echo that didn't belong in the room.
"I see it…"
Kaelren's heart dropped. "She's in his mind."

Bren swore. "She can't do that while awake."
"She's not doing it," Jorren said quietly. "He's pulling her in."
The Unwritten's eyes fluttered beneath closed lids, ghostlight pulsing in time with Elyndra's lantern.
Her voice trembled.
"It's calling him…"

Inside His Mind
Darkness stretched in every direction — cold, endless, shifting like smoke.
The Unwritten stood in the centre of it, trembling, breath shallow.
A thin crack of ghostlight tore across the void.
A breach.
A silhouette stood on the other side — tall, indistinct, reaching.
"…come back…"
The Unwritten staggered backward.
"No— no, I don't know you—"
Elyndra appeared beside him, lantern blazing.
"Don't look at it," she said, voice steady in the dream though her real body stood frozen in the infirmary. "Look at me."
He turned toward her.
The breach pulsed harder.
The silhouette leaned forward.
"…ours…"
Elyndra stepped between them.
"Not today."

In the Infirmary
Elyndra's lantern flared so bright the squad shielded their eyes.
Kaelren didn't move.
He grabbed her arm, grounding her.
"Elyndra, come back."
Her lips moved — but the words weren't for him.
"Anchor to me," she whispered. "Not to them."

The Unwritten gasped.
His hand shot up, grabbing hers.
Ghostlight surged between them — a bridge, a tether, a pulse of shared fear.
Talla clutched Rynn's sleeve. Rynn held her steady. Bren stepped back, hammer lowered. Lysa's breath shook. Jorren watched with a hunter's stillness.
Kaelren leaned closer.
"Elyndra. You're here. Come back."
Her eyes snapped into focus.
Just for a moment.
Then she whispered:
"They tried to take him."
The Unwritten whispered at the same time:
"...they know where I am..."
The lantern dimmed.
Elyndra sagged.
Kaelren caught her before she fell.
She clung to his arm, breath trembling, eyes wide with terror.
"I was in his mind," she whispered. "And he was in mine."
The squad stared at her — at the Unwritten — at the ghostlight still flickering faintly between their hands.
Kaelren swallowed hard.
"What did you see?"
Elyndra looked at the Unwritten, voice barely audible.
"Something on the other side is calling him."
Her lantern flickered.

CHAPTER TWENTY-THREE — THE BREAKING POINT

The Council summoned them before dawn.
No bell. No messenger. Just guards pounding on the infirmary door until Kaelren jolted awake, ribs screaming, hand flying to his sword before he remembered where he was.
Elyndra was still slumped in the chair beside the Unwritten, lanterns dim, face pale with exhaustion. She wasn't supposed to be back from the Veil yet — the Council had ordered her to remain until she returned with answers.
But she had come back anyway.
And now they knew.
Kaelren helped her stand, steadying her with one arm while the other clutched his ribs. The squad gathered quickly — Bren rubbing sleep from his eyes, Lysa already armed, Rynn and Talla half-armoured, Jorren silent as a shadow.
The guards didn't speak.
They didn't need to.
The Council chamber was colder than usual. The lanterns burned low. The air felt heavy, as if the fortress itself was bracing for something.
The High Councillor didn't wait for them to settle.
"You disobeyed a direct order," he said to Elyndra. "You were commanded to remain in the Veil."
Elyndra's voice was hoarse. "The Paths refused me. I returned because—"
"You returned because you are compromised."
Kaelren stepped forward — or tried to. Pain lanced through his ribs, forcing him to brace on his crutch.
"She saved his life."
"She endangered the realm," the Councillor snapped. "And so did you."
Kaelren's jaw tightened. "If we hadn't acted, the breach would have—"
"ENOUGH."

The word cracked through the chamber like a whip.
The Councillor pointed at the Unwritten, lying unconscious on a stretcher between two healers.
"That creature is a threat to Emberhold. The breaches are calling him. Lanternkeepers are being pulled into his mind. The Veil itself rejects guidance."
He turned to the guards.
"Take him to the Deep Cells."
The room erupted.
Bren: "Absolutely not." Lysa: "You'll kill him." Rynn: "He didn't do anything wrong." Talla: "He needs help, not chains." Jorren: "You're making a mistake."
Kaelren didn't shout.
He stepped between the guards and the Unwritten — slowly, painfully — sword drawn, voice low and steady.
"You're not taking him."
The Councillor's eyes narrowed. "You would defy us?"
Kaelren didn't blink. "I would protect him."
The Councillor raised his staff.
"Then you are relieved of command."
The words hit like a physical blow. Kaelren staggered, breath catching — but he didn't lower his sword.
Elyndra stepped beside him, lanterns flaring weakly.
"You cannot imprison him," she said. "If you do, the breaches will tear this fortress apart trying to reach him."
The Councillor's voice was ice. "Then we will deal with that when it comes."
Kaelren's heart dropped.
They weren't listening. They weren't thinking. They were afraid.
And fear made people dangerous.
The guards stepped forward.
Bren moved first, stepping in front of Kaelren, hammer raised. Lysa nocked an arrow. Rynn lifted his shield. Talla planted her spear. Jorren vanished into the shadows.
The Councillor stared at them — at the squad he had trained, trusted, relied on — and saw rebellion.
"So be it," he said. "You are all dismissed from service. Effective immediately."

Kaelren exhaled slowly.
Then he said the words that changed everything:
"Then we're not bound by your orders."
The squad moved as one.
Bren shoved the nearest guard aside. Lysa shot an arrow into the floor between two others, forcing them back. Rynn blocked a strike meant for Kaelren. Talla swept a spear across the guards' legs. Jorren appeared behind the healers, cutting the stretcher free.
Bren and Rynn lifted the Unwritten between them. Kaelren limped beside them, one hand on the stretcher, guiding but unable to carry.
Elyndra's lanterns flared, casting a blinding burst of light that filled the chamber.
"RUN!" she shouted.
They did.
Down the corridor. Through the hall. Past the stunned guards. Into the lower levels of Emberhold.
The fortress shook with alarm bells.
Kaelren's ribs burned. Elyndra stumbled beside him, lanterns flickering. The Unwritten trembled on the stretcher, ghostlight pulsing weakly.
Bren slammed a door behind them. Lysa shot out a lantern to plunge the hall into darkness. Rynn and Talla held the rear. Jorren led them through a hidden passage only he knew.
They didn't stop until they reached the old catacombs beneath Emberhold — a place so ancient even the Council had forgotten it existed.
Bren and Rynn lowered the Unwritten onto a stone slab. Kaelren sagged against the wall, breath ragged. Elyndra collapsed beside the slab, lanterns dimming to embers.
The squad gathered around them, breathless, shaken, terrified.
Bren broke the silence.
"So," he said, "we're fugitives now."
Kaelren looked at the Unwritten — pale, trembling, ghostlight flickering faintly.
"No," he said quietly. "We're protectors."

Elyndra lifted her head, eyes hollow but determined.
"And we're not letting them take him."
The squad nodded.
One by one.
A vow. A rebellion. A family.

Above Them — The Council's Decision
Far above them, in the Council chamber they had fled, silence hung like smoke.
The High Councillor stood alone, staring at the shattered lantern Elyndra's light had ruptured. Cracks spiderwebbed across the floor. The air still hummed with ghostlight.
One by one, the remaining Councillors stepped from the shadows.
"They've gone to ground," one whispered.
"They won't get far," muttered another.
"They have the Lanternkeeper," a third said. "And the stranger. The breaches will follow them."
The High Councillor closed his eyes.
"No," he said. "Something else will."
He lifted his staff.
A deep, resonant thrum rolled through the chamber — not ghostlight, not lanternlight, but something older.
Something forbidden.
The Councillors stiffened.
"You cannot mean—"
"We have no choice," the High Councillor said. "The Lanternkeeper has defied us. Kaelren has turned traitor. The squad is lost. And the Unwritten…" His voice tightened. "The Unwritten cannot be allowed to awaken."
A single rune ignited beneath his feet — black, sharp, cold.
A summoning sigil.
The others recoiled.
"High Councillor, the Hunters are not loyal to us—"
"They are loyal to the Codex," he snapped. "And the Codex is silent. Silence means danger."
The sigil pulsed.
Once. Twice. A third time.
The temperature dropped.

Shadows lengthened.
A whisper crawled across the stone.
The High Councillor exhaled.
"Send word to the Deep Vaults," he said. "Tell them the order is given."
His eyes hardened.
"Release the Hunters."
The lanterns guttered.
The sigil flared.
And somewhere in the depths of Emberhold, something ancient and merciless woke.

CHAPTER TWENTY-FOUR — THE FIRE THAT NEVER DIED

The catacombs were cold.
Kaelren sat with his back against an ancient pillar, the Unwritten unconscious beside him, Elyndra barely awake, lanterns flickering like dying stars.
The squad gathered close, shaken and silent.
Kaelren exhaled.
"My Realm died believing in someone like him."
The others looked up.
Kaelren stared into the lantern flame.
"Flameborne wasn't just fire. It was prophecy. It was rebellion built on a warning older than the Realms."
He swallowed.
"My father used to tell me the old stories — stories passed down through the Emberclad. Stories the King himself believed."
Lysa leaned forward. "What stories?"
Kaelren's voice softened.
"Of the Unwritten One."
The squad froze.
Kaelren nodded.
"A being the Codex could not record. A wanderer born from a Realm that never survived. A soul the Void feared more than any army."
He looked at the Unwritten — pale, trembling, ghostlight flickering beneath his skin.
"Flameborne believed he would return one day. Not as a child. Not as a king. But as a fracture in fate."
Bren swallowed. "And your Realm... fought for that?"
Kaelren nodded.
"We fought because the Void was terrified of him. We fought because the Codex was silent about him. We fought because the King believed that if the Unwritten ever

returned, he would be the spark that could break the Void's hold."
He looked at the squad — at his family.
"And now he's here."
Silence.
Heavy. Electric. Transformative.
Talla whispered, "Kaelren... are you saying Flameborne died waiting for him?"
Kaelren nodded.
"Yes."
Rynn's voice trembled. "Then we're not just protecting a stranger."
Lysa's eyes widened. "We're protecting the prophecy Flameborne died for."
Bren exhaled. "We're protecting the one the Void fears."
Jorren stepped forward, voice low.
"Then we protect him with our lives."
Elyndra lifted her head, lanterns glowing faintly.
"And we don't let the Council take him."
Kaelren placed a hand on the Unwritten's shoulder.
"No," he said softly. "We don't."
The lantern flame steadied.
The catacombs felt less cold.
And the squad — for the first time — understood the truth:
They weren't fugitives.
They were the first defenders of the Soulforged Era.

The Council's Fear
Silence settled again — heavy, electric, charged with something none of them could name.
Elyndra sat with her back against the stone, eyes half-closed, breath slow and uneven. Her lanterns drifted lazily around her, dim but no longer trembling.
For the first time since the breach, she looked... calm.
Kaelren noticed it first.
"You're breathing easier," he said softly.

Elyndra opened her eyes. "Because I'm not alone."
The squad exchanged glances — surprised, touched, unsure how to respond.
Elyndra gave a faint smile.
"You've all earned something," she said. "A truth I've carried alone for too long."
Bren leaned forward. "About him?"
Elyndra nodded.
"About what he is. And what he must become."
The lanterns brightened slightly, casting ghostlight across the stone walls.
She looked at the Unwritten — pale, still, ghostlight flickering beneath his skin like a heartbeat trying to remember its rhythm.
"There is an artifact," she said quietly. "Older than Emberhold. Older than the Realms. Older than the Codex itself."
Jorren's eyes narrowed. "A weapon?"
"No," Elyndra said. "A tool. A truth. A memory forged into metal."
Kaelren's breath caught.
"The Hammer."
Elyndra didn't deny it.
But she didn't confirm it either.
She simply continued.
"It responds only to one thing: identity. Not strength. Not training. Not will."
She placed her hand gently on the Unwritten's arm.
"Identity."
Lysa frowned. "But he doesn't remember anything."
"Exactly," Elyndra whispered. "He cannot wield what he cannot remember."
Talla's voice was soft. "So he needs to regain his strength?"
Elyndra shook her head.
"Strength won't help him. Memory will."
Rynn swallowed. "But he doesn't have any."
Elyndra's lanterns dimmed.

"He has fragments. Echoes. Instincts. But until he remembers who he is — truly is — the Hammer will remain silent."

Kaelren leaned forward. "And if he does remember?"

Elyndra hesitated.

The lanterns flickered.

Her voice dropped to a whisper.

"Then the Realms will change."

Silence.

Heavy. Electric. Terrifying.

Bren exhaled. "So, the Council… they're afraid he'll awaken it."

Elyndra nodded. "Yes."

"And you?" Lysa asked softly. "Are you afraid?"

Elyndra looked at the Unwritten — at the man who didn't know his own name, who trembled in his sleep, who the breaches called to like a lost child.

"No," she said. "I'm not afraid of him."

She closed her eyes.

"I'm afraid of what will happen if he never remembers."

Kaelren placed a hand on her shoulder.

"We'll help him."

The squad nodded — one by one.

Elyndra let out a long, slow breath.

For the first time since the Veil rejected her, she looked like she believed it.

CHAPTER TWENTY-FIVE — THE HUNTERS IN THE DARK

The catacombs breathed around them — slow, cold, ancient. The squad had fallen quiet, the weight of Kaelren's story settling like ash.
Elyndra leaned back against the stone, eyes half-closed, lanterns drifting lazily around her. For the first time since the breach, she looked almost peaceful.
Almost.
Kaelren watched her, relieved to see the tension easing from her shoulders. He opened his mouth to speak—
And froze.
A sound drifted through the tunnels.
Soft. Sharp. Wrong.
A metallic click.
Not loud. Not echoing.
A deliberate sound.
A signal.
Jorren's head snapped up instantly. His hand went to his blade.
"Everyone up," he whispered. "Now."
Bren frowned. "What? Why—"
"Up," Jorren hissed. "We're not alone."
The squad moved.
Slow. Silent. Instinctive.
Kaelren reached for his sword, ribs screaming. Lysa nocked an arrow. Rynn pulled Talla behind him. Elyndra's lanterns flickered, reacting to something she hadn't yet consciously sensed.
Then—
A second sound.
A soft scrape of metal on stone.
Kaelren's blood ran cold.
"Hunters."

The word was barely a breath.
But it hit the squad like a hammer.
Bren swore under his breath. "They found us."
Lysa's voice trembled. "How? These tunnels aren't mapped."
"They don't need maps," Jorren said. "They follow heat. Breath. Fear."
Elyndra pushed herself upright, lanterns flaring weakly. "We have to move."
Kaelren shook his head. "We can't outrun them."
Rynn swallowed. "Then what do we do?"
Kaelren looked at the Unwritten — still unconscious, ghostlight flickering faintly beneath his skin.
"We protect him."
The lanterns dimmed.
The tunnel ahead went silent.
Too silent.
Then—
A whisper.
Not a voice. A breath.
A Hunter stepped into view.
Clad in obsidian armour that drank the light. Mask smooth and featureless. Blades curved like broken runes.
Ghostlight sigils etched into their gauntlets.
A second appeared behind it. Then a third. Then more — shadows peeling from the walls.
Talla's breath hitched. "There's too many."
Kaelren stepped forward, sword raised.
"You're not taking him."
The lead Hunter tilted its head — a gesture almost curious.
Then it spoke.
Not with a voice.
With a rune.
A glowing sigil flared across its mask, pulsing once.
Surrender.
Elyndra's lanterns flared violently.
"No."
The rune flickered.
The Hunter stepped forward.

Kaelren braced himself.
Bren roared and lifted his hammer. Lysa drew the string to her cheek. Rynn raised his shield. Talla planted her spear. Jorren vanished into the shadows.
The Hunters moved.
Fast.
Too fast.
The first one lunged for the Unwritten.
Kaelren blocked the strike, steel ringing through the catacombs. Pain tore through his ribs, but he didn't fall.
Bren slammed his hammer into another Hunter's chest — the blow barely staggered it.
Lysa loosed an arrow — it shattered against a Hunter's mask.
Rynn took a hit to the shield that sent him skidding back into Talla.
Jorren reappeared behind a Hunter, blade slicing across its armour — sparks flew, but the Hunter didn't bleed.
Elyndra staggered forward, lanterns blazing.
"Stay away from him!"
Her lantern burst into ghostlight, flooding the tunnel with pale fire.
The Hunters recoiled — not in fear, but in calculation.
They adjusted. Shifted. Adapted.
Kaelren's heart dropped.
"They're learning her light."
Elyndra's breath trembled. "Then I'll burn brighter."
She raised her lantern—
And the Unwritten gasped.
Everyone froze.
His eyes snapped open — glowing faintly, unfocused, terrified.
"...they're here..."
Elyndra grabbed his hand.
"We know."
The Hunters surged forward.
Kaelren shouted.
"FORM UP!"
The squad closed ranks around the Unwritten.

Elyndra's lantern flared.
The Hunters descended.
And the catacombs erupted into chaos.

CHAPTER TWENTY-SIX — THE MEMORY THAT MOVES

The catacombs erupted into violence.
Steel rang. Ghostlight flared. Lanterns screamed.
Kaelren blocked a Hunter's blade, ribs tearing with pain.
Bren swung his hammer in a wide arc, sparks exploding as it struck obsidian armour. Lysa loosed arrows that shattered on impact. Rynn held the line with his shield while Talla thrust her spear between gaps in the Hunters' formation.
Elyndra stood over the Unwritten, lantern blazing, breath ragged.
"Stay with me," she whispered. "Please— stay—"
But he wasn't here.
Not fully.
Not anymore.
He drifted.
Through darkness. Through memory. Through echoes of things he did not understand.
A sky of molten gold. A city of floating stone. A crown made of broken light. A woman's voice whispering his name — a name he couldn't hear. A hammer glowing like a dying star. A king kneeling in shadow. A scream that split a Realm in half.
He reached for one memory— It dissolved.
He reached for another— It burned.
He reached for a third—
And something reached back.
A voice.
Not the silhouette. Not the breach. Not the thing calling him.
A different voice.
Soft. Warm. Familiar.
"Come back."

Elyndra.
Her voice cut through the drifting fog of memory like a lantern through mist.
"Come back to us."
He turned toward the sound.
The darkness trembled.
The memories shattered.
And the world snapped into place—
He opened his eyes.
Just for a moment.
Just long enough.
The Hunters were closing in — blades raised, masks glowing with runes of capture and silence.
Kaelren was bleeding. Bren was staggering. Lysa was out of arrows. Rynn's shield was cracked. Talla was shaking. Jorren was cornered. Elyndra was burning herself out.
And the Unwritten saw it.
All of it.
His breath hitched.
Ghostlight surged beneath his skin.
Elyndra gasped. "No— don't— you're not ready—"
But instinct moved before thought. Before fear. Before memory.
A Hunter lunged for Elyndra.
The Unwritten sat up.
His hand rose.
Ghostlight erupted.
Not a blast. Not a scream. Not the catastrophic force from the courtyard.
Just a pulse — sharp, precise, instinctive.
A shockwave of pale fire rippled outward, slamming into the nearest Hunters and hurling them back into the stone walls.
The squad froze.
The Hunters staggered.
Elyndra stared at him, eyes wide.
"You— you're awake—"
He wasn't.
Not fully.

His eyes were unfocused, glowing faintly, drifting between worlds.
He whispered:
"...don't... touch... them..."
The Hunters regrouped instantly — adjusting, recalibrating, shifting their stance to counter the ghostlight.
Kaelren stepped in front of the Unwritten, sword raised.
"Stay behind me."
The Unwritten blinked slowly, breath trembling.
"...I... remember... fire..."
Elyndra grabbed his hand. "Don't push it. You're not strong enough."
He looked at her — really looked — as if seeing her through layers of fog.
"...you... pulled me back..."
She nodded, tears burning in her eyes. "Always."
The Hunters advanced again.
The Unwritten tried to rise — ghostlight flickering violently, unstable, dangerous.
Kaelren pushed him gently back down.
"Rest. We'll handle this."
The Unwritten's eyes fluttered.
"...don't... let them... take me..."
Kaelren's voice was steady.
"They won't."
The Unwritten exhaled — a shuddering breath — and collapsed back into unconsciousness.
The ghostlight dimmed.
The Hunters surged.
And the squad closed ranks around him.

CHAPTER TWENTY-SEVEN — THE WALL THAT GAVE WAY

The Hunters surged.
Steel clashed. Ghostlight flared. The catacombs shook with every impact.
Kaelren blocked a downward strike, his ribs screaming as the force drove him to one knee. Bren roared and slammed his hammer into a Hunter's side, sparks exploding as obsidian armour cracked but didn't break. Lysa fired point-blank into a mask — the arrow splintered uselessly.
Rynn held the line with his shield, teeth gritted, Talla bracing behind him, spear darting between gaps in the Hunters' formation.
Jorren flickered in and out of shadow, blades flashing like whispers.
Elyndra stood over the Unwritten, lantern blazing, breath ragged.
"We can't hold them!" Bren shouted.
"We don't have to," Kaelren growled. "We just need—"
A Hunter slammed into him, sending him skidding across the stone.
"—a way out!"
As if the Realms themselves heard him, the ground trembled.
A deep, resonant crack echoed through the catacombs.
Everyone froze.
Even the Hunters hesitated.
Elyndra's lantern flared violently. "Something's shifting—"
The wall behind them split.
A jagged fracture tore across the stone, dust raining down in choking clouds. The crack widened, groaning like a wounded beast.
Rynn's eyes widened. "That's not natural."
Talla grabbed his arm. "I don't care. It's an exit."

Kaelren staggered to his feet, sword raised. "Move! Now!"
The Hunters recovered instantly, lunging forward as the squad scrambled toward the widening break.
Bren swung his hammer in a brutal arc, knocking two Hunters back. "Go! I'll cover—"
"No!" Kaelren grabbed his arm. "We stay together!"
The wall split again — a thunderous crack — and a slab of stone collapsed inward, revealing a narrow passage beyond, lit by faint ghostlight.
Elyndra's breath caught. "That's… that's a Lantern Path."
Lysa stared. "In Emberhold?"
"No time!" Kaelren shouted. "Move!"
Jorren vanished into the new passage first, scouting ahead.
Rynn and Talla followed, half dragging each other. Lysa slipped through next, bow ready.
Bren shoved Kaelren toward the gap. "Go!"
Then he grabbed the Unwritten, hauling him over his shoulder despite the agony in his ribs.
Elyndra stayed until the last moment, lantern blazing in a desperate arc that forced the Hunters back a single step.
"Elyndra!" Kaelren shouted.
She turned—
A Hunter lunged.
Kaelren's heart stopped.
The Unwritten stirred.
Ghostlight flickered.
And a pulse of pale fire erupted from his hand — weak, unfocused, but enough to stagger the Hunter mid-strike.
Elyndra dove through the gap.
Bren followed, dragging the Unwritten with him.
Kaelren was the last to enter, slamming his shoulder into the collapsing stone as he passed.
The wall gave way.
Stone crashed down behind them, sealing the passage in a thunderous roar.
Silence. Dust. Darkness.
The squad collapsed in a heap, coughing, shaking, bleeding.
Bren lowered the Unwritten gently to the ground.

Elyndra leaned against the wall, lantern dimming to a faint glow.

Bren wheezed. "Well… that was subtle."

Lysa laughed breathlessly. "We're alive. That's enough."

Rynn squeezed Talla's hand. "Barely."

Jorren stepped out of the shadows, eyes scanning the new tunnel.

"They'll dig through," he said quietly. "We bought time. Not safety."

Kaelren nodded.

"Then we keep moving."

Elyndra lifted her lantern, its ghostlight reflecting off the walls of the narrow passage.

"This isn't just a tunnel," she whispered. "It's a forgotten Lantern Path."

Kaelren looked at her. "Where does it lead?"

Elyndra swallowed.

"Somewhere the Council can't follow."

The Unwritten stirred again, whispering through cracked breath:

"…they're still coming…"

Kaelren tightened his grip on his sword.

"Then we don't stop."

And the squad pressed deeper into the ghostlit passage, leaving the Hunters — and Emberhold — behind.

CHAPTER TWENTY-EIGHT — THE GHOST ROAD

The passage stretched ahead of them like a vein of pale fire carved through the stone. Ghostlight drifted along the walls in slow, swirling currents, as if the tunnel itself were breathing.
Elyndra lifted her lantern.
The ghostlight responded.
It bent toward her — not like light, but like memory recognizing a familiar shape.
Kaelren frowned. "This isn't a normal tunnel."
"It's not a tunnel at all," Elyndra whispered. "It's a Lantern Path."
Bren grunted. "Thought those only existed in Spiritveil."
"They do," Elyndra said. "Which is why this shouldn't be here."
Lysa stepped closer to the wall, watching the ghostlight ripple away from her fingertips. "Then how are we walking it?"
Elyndra hesitated.
Her lantern dimmed.
"Because of him."
They all looked at the Unwritten — unconscious, pale, ghostlight flickering beneath his skin like a heartbeat trying to remember its rhythm.
Kaelren's voice was low. "He opened it?"
"No," Elyndra said. "He is the reason it opened."
The ghostlight pulsed, as if agreeing.
Rynn swallowed. "So the Path is reacting to him?"
"Not reacting," Elyndra murmured. "Recognizing."
Talla shivered. "Recognizing what?"
Elyndra didn't answer.
Because she didn't know.
Not fully.
Not yet.

As they walked, the ghostlight shifted beneath their feet — not solid, not liquid, something in between. The air hummed with faint whispers, like distant voices speaking through water.

Jorren kept glancing behind them. "Hunters won't follow us in here."

Kaelren nodded. "Good."

"But something else might," Jorren added.

No one argued.

The Path felt alive.

Watching.

Waiting.

Elyndra's lantern flickered again, and she stumbled.

Kaelren caught her.

"You're burning out."

"I'm fine," she lied.

Her lantern dimmed further.

The squad's gear wasn't faring much better.

Bren's hammer was cracked along the haft. Lysa's bowstring was frayed. Rynn's shield was split nearly in half. Talla's spear tip was bent. Kaelren's sword was chipped and dull. Jorren's blades were nicked and uneven.

They were armed with scraps.

And the Hunters had been wearing obsidian armour forged by Emberhold's elite.

Lysa looked at her ruined bow. "We can't fight like this."

Bren snorted. "We can barely walk like this."

Rynn glanced at Elyndra. "Spiritveil weapons... do they exist?"

Elyndra nodded slowly.

"Yes."

Talla's eyes widened. "Can we get them?"

Elyndra hesitated.

"Spiritveil weapons aren't forged," she said softly. "They're remembered."

The squad stared at her.

Kaelren frowned. "Meaning?"

Elyndra lifted her lantern.

The ghostlight around them brightened — not in response to her, but to the Unwritten.
"Spiritveil weapons are echoes," she said. "Fragments of what once was. They appear only when memory calls them."
Bren blinked. "So... we can't just pick them up?"
"No," Elyndra said. "They choose their wielder."
Lysa looked down the ghostlit corridor. "And will they choose us?"
Elyndra looked at the Unwritten.
"I don't know."

The Spiritveil Armoury
The tunnel widened suddenly, opening into a vast chamber carved from pale stone. Ghostlight drifted like mist across the floor, swirling around ancient pedestals half buried in the ground.
Weapons rested on them.
Not metal. Not wood. Not anything mortal hands could shape.
They were silhouettes of weapons — outlines made of memory and ghostlight, shimmering like half-remembered dreams.
A spear of frost-blue light. A bow of drifting shadow. A hammer made of molten gold. A shield carved from a forgotten oath. Twin blades that flickered like candle flames. And a sword that hummed with a heartbeat.
The squad froze.
Bren whispered, "Are those... real?"
Elyndra shook her head.
"They're not real," she said. "They're true."
Kaelren stepped forward, breath catching.
"Spiritveil armoury."
Elyndra nodded.
"Only those the Path accepts can take them."
Lysa swallowed. "And if it doesn't accept us?"
Elyndra looked at the Unwritten — ghostlight flickering beneath his skin, calling the Path into existence.

"Then it will accept him," she whispered. "And through him... maybe it will accept you."

Kaelren tightened his grip on his broken sword.

"Then let's find out."

CHAPTER TWENTY-NINE — THE PATH REMEMBERS

The ghostlit chamber breathed around them, the air humming with a low, ancient resonance. The weapons shimmered on their pedestals like half-remembered dreams, their shapes flickering in and out of existence.
Kaelren took a step forward—
And the Path moved.
Not the floor. Not the walls. The *memory* of the place shifted, folding around them like a living veil.
Ghostlight surged beneath their feet, rising in a sudden wave that swallowed the chamber whole. The squad staggered, reaching for each other, but the light tore them apart — not physically, but through something deeper, like their minds were being pulled through different threads of the same tapestry.

Kaelren
He blinked and found himself standing in fire.
Flameborne's capital burned around him, molten rivers glowing beneath a sky split by shadow. He smelled ash. Heard screams. Felt the weight of a sword in his hand.
A figure stepped from the flames — his father, or the memory of him, or something wearing his shape.
The echo spoke without moving its lips.
"Will you carry a burden you do not understand?"
Kaelren tightened his grip. "Yes."
The fire dissolved.

Lysa
She stumbled through a forest of whispering runes, shadows darting between the trees. She raised her bow, but the shadows multiplied, circling her, taunting her.
Her breath shook.
"Can you strike without certainty?" the forest whispered.

She closed her eyes. Drew. Released.
The shadow vanished.
The forest dissolved.

Bren
He stood before towering stone giants carved with Emberhold's laws. His hammer felt impossibly heavy, dragging his arm toward the ground.
The giants leaned in, their carved eyes glowing.
"Will you break what you were taught to uphold?"
Bren roared and lifted the hammer anyway.
The giants bowed.
The stone dissolved.

Rynn and Talla
They stood together on a narrow bridge of ghostlight suspended over an endless void. The bridge trembled beneath them, flickering like a dying flame.
Talla slipped — Rynn caught her hand instantly, pulling her close.
"Will you trust each other when the ground falls away?"
The bridge solidified beneath their feet.
The void dissolved.

Jorren
He walked through a corridor of mirrors, each one reflecting a different version of himself — assassin, traitor, coward, killer. The reflections whispered accusations he had buried long ago.
"Will you face the truth of what you are?"
Jorren drew his blade and shattered the mirrors one by one.
The corridor dissolved.

Elyndra
She stood in a sea of drifting lanterns, each one glowing with a memory she had carried for centuries. One lantern floated toward her, brighter than the rest.

Inside it, she saw him — the Unwritten — broken, lost, calling.
"Will you guide him even if he never remembers you?"
Her hand trembled.
She touched the lantern.
The sea dissolved.

Together Again

The chamber snapped back into focus, ghostlight swirling around them like a storm calming after a single breath. The squad stood in a loose circle, shaken, breathless, changed.
The weapons glowed brighter.
Not as objects. As answers.
The spear of frost-blue light drifted toward Talla, settling into her hands like it had always been there. The bow of drifting shadow curled into Lysa's grip, whispering softly. The molten gold hammer floated to Bren, its weight perfect. The oath-carved shield formed around Rynn's arm, fitting like a promise. Twin flame blades circled Jorren before settling at his sides. And the heartbeat sword drifted toward Kaelren, pulsing once as if recognizing him.
Elyndra watched, lantern dim but steady.
Then the chamber brightened.
A final shape shimmered into existence above the Unwritten — a silhouette of a hammer made of pure ghostlight, its edges flickering like a memory trying to take form.
It hovered.
Waiting. Not choosing. Remembering.
Elyndra's breath caught. "It knows him."
Kaelren shook his head, voice soft with awe.
"No… it remembers him."
The ghostlight hammer pulsed once — a heartbeat, a promise, a warning — then faded back into the Path, not gone, only sleeping.
The chamber fell silent.
The squad stood armed with weapons that were not forged but chosen.
And the Path whispered through the ghostlight:

Go.
The Hunters were coming.
And now the squad was ready.

Kaelren's Restoration
Kaelren exhaled, the heartbeat sword warm in his hand.
Then he froze.
The ache in his ribs — the stabbing, grinding pain he had carried for days — was gone.
He pressed a hand to his side.
No pain.
He lifted his tunic, expecting bruises, cracked skin, blood.
Nothing.
Not a mark. Not a bruise. Not even a scar.
His breath caught.
"Kaelren?" Lysa asked, noticing his stillness.
He shook his head slowly, disbelief softening his voice.
"I… I'm healed."
Bren blinked. "What? How?"
Kaelren looked at the ghostlit floor, at the fading shimmer of the Path, at the sword pulsing gently in his hand.
"I don't know," he whispered. "But the Path… it didn't just test us."
He touched his ribs again, stunned.
"It restored us."
Elyndra's lantern brightened, just a fraction.
"The Path chose you," she murmured. "All of you. It would not let its chosen walk into the dark broken."
Kaelren tightened his grip on the heartbeat sword.
Strength surged through him — real, steady, whole.
For the first time since Emberhold fell into chaos, he felt ready.

CHAPTER THIRTY — THE FIRST TOUCH OF POWER

The echo of the Path's final whisper still hung in the air.
The weapons hovered in the ghostlit chamber, humming softly — not with sound, but with memory. Then, one by one, they settled into the hands of the squad.
And everything changed.
Bren was the first to react.
He stared at the molten-gold hammer in his grip, eyes wide, jaw slack. The weapon felt weightless and impossibly heavy at the same time — like holding a star that had decided to trust him.
"By the Realms..." he breathed. "I could break a mountain with this."
He swung it experimentally.
A shockwave of golden sparks rippled through the chamber, rattling the stone.
Bren froze.
Then grinned.
"Oh, I like this."
Lysa held her new bow as if afraid it might vanish. The shadow-string hummed under her fingers, vibrating with a low, living resonance. When she drew it, the bow formed an arrow of pure darkness — silent, perfect, deadly.
She exhaled.
"This... this isn't a weapon," she whispered. "It's a promise."
Rynn lifted his shield — the oath-carved barrier of ghostlight that had formed around his arm. It felt warm, alive, like a heartbeat pressed against his skin. When he braced it, the ghostlight flared outward, forming a translucent barrier twice its size.
Talla tapped it with her spear.
The shield didn't budge.
Rynn laughed — a breathless, disbelieving sound. "I could hold a breach with this."

Talla spun her frost-blue spear, the air around it shimmering with cold. Every movement left a trail of crystalline light, like she was carving winter into the world. She blinked at it, stunned.

"It moves with me," she whispered. "Like it knows what I'm going to do before I do it."

Jorren tested his twin flame blades, flicking them through the air. They responded instantly — weightless, fluid, almost eager. Each strike left a streak of ember-light that faded slowly, like the memory of fire.

He tilted his head, impressed.

"These aren't blades," he murmured. "They're instincts."

Kaelren lifted his sword — the heartbeat blade. It pulsed once in his hand, syncing with his own heartbeat, steadying it. The edge shimmered with a faint, rhythmic glow, as if remembering battles he had never fought.

He swallowed.

"This is… Flameborne craftsmanship," he whispered. "But purer. Older."

Elyndra watched them, lantern dim but steady, a small smile tugging at her lips.

"You were chosen," she said softly. "The Path remembers strength. It remembers courage. It remembers sacrifice."

Bren hefted his hammer again, eyes shining. "These are better than anything Emberhold ever forged."

"Better than anything any Realm forged," Elyndra corrected gently.

Lysa looked around the chamber, awe softening her features. "We're actually going to survive this."

Rynn nodded. "We're more than a squad now."

Talla smiled — small, but real. "We're a story."

Jorren sheathed his blades, the ghostlight flickering along their edges. "Let's make it a good one."

Kaelren looked at each of them — at the weapons glowing in their hands, at the fire in their eyes, at the hope rising in their chests.

For the first time since the breach, he felt something he hadn't dared to feel.

Confidence.

He turned toward the tunnel ahead.

"Let's move," he said. "Before the Hunters catch up."

Bren slammed his hammer against his palm. "Let them try."

The ghostlight around them brightened, as if the Path itself approved.

And the squad — armed, chosen, reborn — stepped forward into the unknown.

CHAPTER THIRTY-ONE — THE PATH BREAKS

The ghostlight dimmed.
Not slowly. Not gently. Like a candle being pinched out by an unseen hand.
Kaelren felt it first — a tremor beneath his boots, a shiver through the air, the faintest crackle of instability.
"Elyndra," he murmured. "Something's wrong."
Her lantern flickered violently. Too violently.
"The Path is collapsing," she whispered. "It wasn't meant to stay open this long."
A deep groan rolled through the chamber — stone grinding against stone, memory grinding against reality. The walls rippled like water struck by a stone.
Bren tightened his grip on his new hammer. "Time to go."
Jorren was already moving. "This way."
The squad sprinted down the narrowing corridor, ghostlight swirling around their feet like mist trying to hold them back. The Path shuddered again, cracks of darkness splitting through the glowing walls.
Rynn shielded Talla as debris rained down. Lysa fired an arrow of shadow into a collapsing arch, the impact buying them a heartbeat of stability. Bren smashed through a falling slab of stone with a roar. Kaelren carried the Unwritten, who drifted in and out of consciousness, ghostlight flickering weakly beneath his skin.
Elyndra stumbled, lantern dimming. Kaelren caught her arm.
"Stay with us!"
"I'm trying—" Her voice broke as the Path lurched sideways, nearly throwing them off their feet.
The ghostlight surged ahead of them, forming a final, desperate tunnel — a last memory holding itself together by sheer will.
Jorren pointed. "There! Move!"
They ran.

The Path behind them collapsed in a roar of shattering light, the sound like a thousand lanterns breaking at once.
The ghostlight tunnel narrowed, flickered, then—
Burst open.
Cold air slammed into them. Real air. Night air.
They stumbled out onto solid ground, tumbling into dirt and grass and the sharp scent of pine.
Kaelren rolled, shielding the Unwritten with his body. Bren hit the ground hard and laughed breathlessly. Lysa gasped at the sky. Rynn and Talla clung to each other. Jorren landed in a crouch, blades drawn. Elyndra collapsed to her knees, lantern guttering.
Behind them, the Lantern Path sealed shut with a soft sigh — like a memory finally allowed to rest.
For a heartbeat, everything was still.
Then Kaelren looked up.
And his blood ran cold.
"Everyone," he whispered. "On your feet."
The squad followed his gaze.
Beyond the tree line, beyond the broken outer wall of Emberhold, the valley stretched into darkness.
And that darkness moved.
A tide of Voidborn — hundreds, maybe thousands — swarmed across the landscape like a living shadow. Their bodies twisted and shifting, their eyes burning with cold hunger. The ground trembled beneath their advance.
Lysa's breath hitched. "That's... that's an army."
Talla clutched her spear. "We can't fight that."
Bren's hammer glowed brighter. "We don't have to fight all of them. Just the ones that reach us."
Jorren stepped forward, eyes narrowing. "They're heading for Emberhold."
Elyndra's lantern flickered weakly. "No... they're heading for him."
Kaelren looked down at the Unwritten — pale, trembling, ghostlight pulsing like a dying star.
He tightened his grip on his sword.
"Then we keep moving."

The Voidborn shrieked in the distance — a sound like metal tearing, like a Realm dying, like the end of all things. The squad stood together, weapons glowing with Spiritveil memory.

Chosen. Armed. Outnumbered beyond reason.

Kaelren exhaled.

"Welcome to the real fight."

And they ran.

CHAPTER THIRTY-TWO — THE BREAKING OF THE SQUAD

They ran.
Through the shattered tree line. Across the broken outer wall. Into the wilds beyond Emberhold.
The night air was sharp and cold, filled with the distant shrieks of Voidborn tearing across the valley. The ground trembled beneath their feet — not from their own footsteps, but from the swarm behind them.
Kaelren carried the Unwritten, every breath a stab of pain in his ribs. Elyndra ran beside him, lantern flickering weakly, her steps uneven. Bren thundered ahead, hammer blazing. Lysa, Rynn, Talla, and Jorren fanned out, weapons glowing with Spiritveil memory.
But the Voidborn were faster.
Too fast.
A shriek split the night — high, metallic, hungry.
Lysa glanced back. "They're gaining!"
Bren cursed. "How? We're moving as fast as—"
The ground erupted behind them.
A Voidborn burst from the earth — a massive, many-limbed creature of shadow and bone, its eyes burning with cold hunger. It lunged, claws tearing through the soil.
Kaelren shouted, "Scatter!"
They didn't think. They didn't plan. They just moved.
The squad split in different directions as the creature slammed into the ground where they'd been standing. Kaelren and Elyndra veered left, the Unwritten limp in Kaelren's arms. Bren and Lysa sprinted right, the hammer and bow blazing. Rynn and Talla were forced straight ahead, the creature cutting them off from the others. Jorren vanished into the shadows, blades drawn.
The Voidborn swarm poured over the ridge like a living tide.

Kaelren skidded to a stop. "Rynn! Talla!"

Rynn turned, shield raised. "Go! We'll draw them off!"

Talla shook her head violently. "No! Stay together!"

But the swarm surged between them — a wall of shadow and claws and shrieking hunger.

Kaelren tried to push through, sword raised, but Elyndra grabbed his arm.

"Kaelren— stop! You'll die!"

"I'm not leaving them!"

"You don't have a choice!"

The Voidborn pressed closer, forcing them back. Rynn and Talla were already being driven toward the ravine ahead, the ground crumbling beneath their feet.

Rynn shouted, "We'll find you! Just go!"

Talla's voice cracked. "Kaelren— please— keep him safe!"

Kaelren's heart tore.

He took a step forward—

A Voidborn slammed into him, knocking him to one knee. The Unwritten nearly slipped from his arms. Elyndra's lantern flared, blasting the creature back, but she staggered, nearly collapsing.

"Kaelren!" she gasped. "We have to move!"

He looked at Rynn and Talla — their silhouettes shrinking as the swarm pushed them toward the ravine.

"Talla!" Rynn shouted. "Jump!"

"I can't—"

"Jump!"

They leapt.

The ravine swallowed them.

Kaelren screamed their names, but the sound was drowned by the Voidborn shrieks.

Bren and Lysa were nowhere to be seen — lost in the chaos, fighting their own desperate battle somewhere in the dark.

Jorren flickered into view for a heartbeat, eyes wide, blades dripping with ghostlight.

"Kaelren— go! I'll find the others!"

Then he vanished again, swallowed by the shadows.

Kaelren stood frozen, torn in every direction.

Elyndra grabbed his face, forcing him to look at her.
"Kaelren," she whispered, voice trembling. "If they die, it will be for nothing if he dies too."
He looked down at the Unwritten — pale, unconscious, ghostlight flickering weakly beneath his skin.
The Voidborn shrieked again, closer now.
Kaelren swallowed hard.
Then he nodded.
"Run," he said.
And they ran.
Into the forest. Into the dark. Into the unknown.
Behind them, the squad — his family — was scattered across the valley, separated by the swarm, each fighting their own battle in the night.
The Realms had split them apart.
And nothing would ever be the same.

CHAPTER THIRTY-THREE — THE COMMANDER WHO REMAINED

The fortress walls shook again.
Thraeln pushed through the smoke-filled corridor, boots slipping on shattered lantern glass as Emberhold roared under the Voidborn assault. The screams outside were getting closer — too close — echoing through the stone like the fortress itself was crying out.
He burst into the inner courtyard.
Chaos.
Hunters fought in tight formations, shields locked, blades flashing. Soldiers dragged the wounded toward the lower vaults. Councillors shouted orders no one listened to.
Lanterns flickered violently, their flames guttering in the wind of the Voidborn shrieks.
Thraeln's jaw tightened.
This was what happened when leadership vanished.
Kaelren was gone. Stripped of command. Branded a traitor. Driven out with his squad.
And now Emberhold was paying the price.
A Hunter sprinted toward him, armour cracked, mask flickering.
"Sir! The Council demands your presence—"
A Voidborn slammed into the courtyard wall, sending cracks spiderwebbing across the stone.
Thraeln didn't even look at the Hunter.
"No."
The Hunter hesitated. "Sir?"
"I said no. The Council lost the right to command the moment they exiled the only people who understood what was coming."
The Hunter straightened.
"Then who leads us?"
Thraeln stepped forward, drawing his blade.

"I do."

The courtyard stilled.

Not completely — the Voidborn still shrieked, the walls still shook — but the soldiers around him paused, turning toward him like iron filings drawn to a magnet.

A young soldier stumbled up, bleeding from a cut across his brow.

"Commander Kaelren is gone," he said, voice shaking.

"We... we don't know what to do."

Thraeln grabbed him by the shoulders.

"You fight. You hold the line. You protect the people behind these walls. That is what Emberhold does."

The soldier nodded, breath steadying.

Thraeln released him and turned to the Hunters.

"Form a shield wall at the inner gate. No Voidborn gets past you."

They moved instantly.

He pointed to the soldiers.

"Evacuate civilians to the lower vaults. Anyone who can't fight goes below. Anyone who can fight joins me."

A Councillor burst into the courtyard, robes torn, face pale.

"Commander Thraeln! You cannot give orders without—"

Thraeln didn't slow down.

He grabbed the Councillor by the front of his robes and slammed him against the wall.

"Your authority ended the moment you exiled Kaelren," he growled. "Now get out of my way."

The Councillor slid to the ground, stunned.

Thraeln stepped into the centre of the courtyard, raising his sword high.

"EMBERHOLD!" he roared.

The soldiers turned.

The Hunters turned.

Even the terrified civilians paused.

Thraeln's voice cut through the chaos like a blade.

"We hold this fortress. We hold this Realm. We hold until the last ember dies."

A roar rose from the courtyard — fierce, desperate, unified.

The Voidborn surged through the broken gate.
Thraeln pointed his sword at them.
"WITH ME!"
And he charged.

CHAPTER THIRTY-FOUR — THE EDGE OF THE WORLD

The forest spat them out like a mouth exhaling its last breath.
Kaelren stumbled through the final line of trees and skidded to a halt, boots grinding into loose gravel. Elyndra nearly collided with him, catching herself on a twisted root. The Unwritten hung limp in Kaelren's arms, breath shallow, ghostlight flickering beneath his skin like a dying ember.
And before them—
The world fell away.
A sheer cliff dropped into a vast valley of black stone and wind-torn grass. Far below, a river carved a silver scar through the darkness. And beyond that, rising like a broken crown against the night sky—

Emberhold burned.
Flames licked the outer walls. Lanterns shattered in bursts of dying light. Voidborn swarmed over the battlements like ants over a corpse.
Elyndra's breath caught. "No…"
Kaelren couldn't speak.
He had seen Emberhold under siege before. He had seen breaches. He had seen death.
But he had never seen the fortress losing.
Behind them, the forest shook with the thunder of Voidborn claws tearing through the earth. Shrill, metallic shrieks echoed through the trees — closer now, too close.
Elyndra turned, lantern trembling in her hand. "They're almost here."
Kaelren shifted the Unwritten's weight, trying to keep his grip steady.
"We can't go back," he said.
"We can't go forward either," Elyndra whispered, staring at the cliff. "Not with him."

Kaelren looked down.

The Unwritten's eyes fluttered open — unfocused, glowing faintly.

"...falling..." he murmured. "...not again..."

Kaelren's heart clenched. "Hey. Stay with me."

The Unwritten's gaze drifted toward the burning fortress. His voice cracked.

"...I... did that...?"

"No," Elyndra said sharply, stepping closer. "No. You didn't. That's not you."

But the Unwritten's breath hitched, ghostlight pulsing in a frantic rhythm beneath his skin.

"...they're coming..."

The forest behind them exploded.

Voidborn burst through the tree line — dozens of them, maybe more — their bodies twisting in impossible shapes, eyes burning with cold hunger. They shrieked as they spotted the three figures at the cliff's edge.

Kaelren drew his Spiritveil blade with his free hand. The sword pulsed once, syncing with his heartbeat.

Elyndra raised her lantern, its flame flaring weakly.

Kaelren glanced at her. "We can't fight all of them."

"I know."

"We can't outrun them."

"I know."

"We can't jump."

Elyndra swallowed. "I know."

The Voidborn surged forward.

Kaelren stepped in front of Elyndra and the Unwritten, sword raised, breath steadying despite the terror clawing at his throat.

"If this is where we fall," he said quietly, "we fall together."

Elyndra shook her head.

"No."

She stepped beside him.

"We don't fall."

Her lantern flared — brighter than before, brighter than it should have been, brighter than she had strength for. The

flame stretched upward, ghostlight swirling around it like a storm.
The Voidborn hesitated.
Just for a heartbeat.
Kaelren felt the air shift.
"What are you doing?" he whispered.
Elyndra didn't answer.
She lifted the lantern higher.
The flame roared.
The cliff beneath them trembled.
The Voidborn shrieked.
And the Unwritten — eyes half open, voice barely a breath — whispered:
"…not this time…"
Ghostlight erupted beneath them.
The cliff cracked.
The world dropped.
And the three of them fell into the darkness below.

CHAPTER THIRTY-FIVE — THE LONG FALL

The cliff didn't just collapse.
It peeled away.
Stone sheared off in massive slabs, sliding beneath their feet like ice breaking on a thawing lake. Kaelren felt the ground tilt, then lurch, then vanish entirely as the entire ledge tore free from the mountainside.
For a heartbeat, they weren't falling.
They were riding the cliff as it broke.
The slab of stone tilted downward, grinding along the cliff face, throwing sparks as it scraped against jagged outcroppings. The sound was deafening — a grinding roar that drowned out Elyndra's scream and the Voidborn shrieks above.
Below them, the valley opened wide.
And now Kaelren saw the river clearly — not a distant glimmer, but a violent silver ribbon tearing through the black stone far below. He had glimpsed it earlier, but only now did he understand the truth.
The drop was lethal.
The river wasn't calm.
It churned violently, swollen by storm runoff and the collapse of the upper cliffs. White water foamed around boulders the size of houses. The current tore through the valley like a living thing.
"We're sliding into it!" Elyndra shouted, voice raw with terror.
Kaelren tightened his grip on the Unwritten, trying to brace himself against the shifting stone. The slab tilted further, faster, the angle steepening until they were no longer sliding—

They were falling.
The stone dropped out from under them, shattering against the cliff wall as they plunged into open air.

Wind tore at Kaelren's cloak. Elyndra spun beside him, lantern tumbling from her grasp. The Unwritten slipped from Kaelren's arms—
And that was when the ghostlight changed.
It didn't flare.
It ruptured.
A pulse of pale fire burst from the Unwritten's chest, expanding outward in a perfect sphere of shimmering light. It hit Kaelren like a hammer, knocking the breath from his lungs and hurling him sideways.
"Elyndra!" he shouted, reaching for her.
Another pulse followed — colder, sharper, spiralling around the first like a twisting helix. The air warped. The fall distorted. The world bent.
The ghostlight wasn't reacting to the fall.
It was reacting to the Voidborn.
They had reached the cliff's edge above, their shrieks echoing down the ravine. Their presence pressed against the Unwritten's fractured spark, forcing it into a violent, uncontrolled surge.
The pulses collided.
Light and shadow twisted together, forming a swirling vortex — not a portal, not magic, but a violent distortion of memory and ghostlight, pulled into a spiral by the Unwritten's unstable identity.
The vortex caught Elyndra first.
She screamed as the ghostlight wrapped around her, yanking her sideways, pulling her into a stream of shimmering light that tore her away from Kaelren's reach.
"Kaelren!" she cried.
He reached for her—
The vortex shifted.
It grabbed the Unwritten next, dragging him downward in a streak of pale fire. His body spun, ghostlight trailing behind him like a comet's tail.
Kaelren lunged after him—
The river rose up beneath him.
Cold. Black. Raging.
He hit the water like a stone.

The world exploded into darkness and pressure and pain. The current seized him instantly, dragging him under, spinning him through churning foam and jagged rocks.
He tried to surface.
The river pulled him deeper.
And then—
Not water.
Not darkness.
A memory.
Not his.
A voice whispered through the void:
"…Kaelren…"
The river twisted around him, pulling him deeper, deeper, deeper—
And the world split.

CHAPTER THIRTY-SIX — THE MEMORY THAT DROWNS

Cold swallowed him whole.
The river dragged him under, spinning him through darkness so thick it felt like drowning in ink. His lungs burned. His limbs thrashed. But the current wasn't water anymore — it was pulling, not flowing.
Pulling him somewhere he didn't want to go.
Ghostlight flickered in the depths, pale threads drifting like drowned fireflies. They wrapped around his wrists, his throat, his chest — not choking, but guiding. Dragging him deeper.
The roar of the river faded.
The cold faded.
The world blinked.
And Kaelren stood on black stone.
Dry. Breathing. Alive.
But not free.
A battlefield stretched before him — a wasteland of ash and broken banners, lit by a sky the colour of dying embers. The air stank of smoke and old blood. The wind carried distant screams that never reached the ground.
Kaelren's stomach twisted.
He knew this place.
He had sworn never to return to it — not even in memory.
"No…" he whispered.
A figure knelt in the centre of the ruin.
A man. Armoured. Crowned. Still.
Too still.
Kaelren's breath caught in his throat.
The king's armour was cracked, blackened, half-melted. His cloak hung in tatters. His crown — once bright gold — was now a twisted, scorched ruin fused to his skull.
And his skin—

Kaelren's heart lurched.
His skin was ashen, stretched too thin, clinging to bone.
His lips were cracked. His eyes were sunken hollows.
A corpse.
A dead king kneeling in the ashes of a dead Realm.
"No," Kaelren whispered. "You're gone. You're gone. You're gone."
The corpse king didn't move.
Kaelren took a step back.
The corpse king twitched.
Just a tiny movement — a jerk of the head, a crack of bone, a sound like dry branches snapping.
Kaelren froze.
The corpse king lifted his head.
Slowly. Wrongly. As if invisible strings were pulling him upright.
His eyes opened.
Not glowing. Not alive.
Just empty sockets filled with faint, dying embers — embers that flickered in time with Kaelren's heartbeat.
Kaelren staggered backward.
"No. No, this isn't real. You're dead. I saw— I saw—"
The corpse king rose.
Not smoothly. Not like a man.
Like something remembering how to stand.
His joints cracked. His spine bent at impossible angles. His head lolled to the side before snapping upright again.
Kaelren's breath hitched.
"Stay back," he whispered.
The corpse king stepped forward.
Kaelren tried to move. His legs refused.
The corpse king stepped again.
The battlefield trembled.
The sky dimmed.
The air thickened with a pressure Kaelren remembered all too well — a crushing weight that had once driven him to his knees.
But this wasn't the Harrowed King.
This was worse.

This was the memory of the king he loved — twisted, hollowed, puppeted by something far beyond death.
The corpse king stopped a few paces away.
Close enough for Kaelren to see the cracks in his skull.
Close enough to smell the cold rot of ghostlight-burned flesh.
Close enough to hear the faint rattle of breath that should not exist.
The corpse king leaned forward.
His voice was a whisper dragged across broken glass.
"Kaelren."
Kaelren's heart stopped.
The corpse king's jaw cracked open wider than it should, bone splitting, teeth grinding.
"You failed me."
Kaelren shook his head violently. "No— no, I tried— I—"
The corpse king stepped closer.
The world bent around him.
The sky cracked. The ground rippled. The air folded inward like a collapsing lung.
Kaelren fell to his knees, clutching his head as the pressure built — the same crushing weight he had felt the day this memory was born.
The corpse king crouched in front of him, movements jerky and unnatural.
His dead hand reached out.
Cold fingers brushed Kaelren's cheek.
Kaelren flinched as frost spread across his skin.
The corpse king whispered:
"You will choose again."
The battlefield shattered.
Kaelren fell through it.
Fell through memory. Fell through darkness. Fell through himself.
And somewhere far above, beyond the collapsing vision, beyond the river, beyond the cliff—
A voice called his name.
Not the king's.
Someone alive.
Someone trying to pull him back.

But the dead king's whisper followed him into the dark.
"Again."

CHAPTER THIRTY-SEVEN — THE FRACTURED SELF

The vortex swallowed him whole.
Ghostlight tore through the Unwritten's body, ripping him away from Kaelren and Elyndra. His limbs twisted in the current of light, his vision shattering into a thousand flickering shards.
He tried to breathe. He had no lungs.
He tried to scream. He had no voice.
He tried to remember. He had no memories.
The vortex spun faster, pulling him inward, deeper, downward into a place that wasn't a place at all — a hollow between Realms, a wound in the world where ghostlight and Void bled together.
The Unwritten hung suspended in the centre of it.
Weightless. Voiceless. Nameless.
And then—
A whisper.
Not from outside.
From inside.
"...**Voyager**..."
The word echoed through him like a bell struck underwater.
He didn't know it. He didn't understand it. But it felt like it belonged to him.
The vortex pulsed.
Light fractured.
And suddenly he was standing on a bridge of broken memory — a long, narrow span of ghostlight stretching across an endless abyss.
He looked down.
There was no body.
He was a shape of light. A silhouette. A suggestion of a man.
He lifted a hand.
It flickered.

He tried to speak.
His voice came out in three overlapping tones — one young, one old, one hollow.
"...who... am... I...?"
The bridge trembled.
Shadows rose from the abyss — not creatures, not forms, just echoes of people he didn't know:
A woman crying. A soldier kneeling. A child reaching upward. A king falling. A lantern shattering. A crown breaking.
Each image flickered across his body like reflections on water.
He reached toward one.
His hand passed through it.
The echo whispered:
"You were someone."
Another rose.
"You were many."
A third.
"You are nothing."
The bridge cracked beneath him.
The Unwritten staggered, ghostlight flickering violently.
He felt himself unraveling.
Piece by piece. Memory by memory. Identity by identity.
He was falling apart.
He was falling—
A hand caught his wrist.
Warm. Steady. Real.
The Unwritten looked up.
Elyndra stood on the bridge, lantern-spark burning fiercely in her chest, ghostlight swirling around her like a shield.
Her voice cut through the Void like a blade:
"You are not nothing."
The echoes recoiled.
The bridge steadied.
The Unwritten stared at her, confused, flickering.
"...how... did you... find me...?"
Elyndra tightened her grip.
"I followed your spark."

"...I... don't... have one..."
"You do," she said softly. "You always did."
The Void roared beneath them.
The echoes screamed.
The bridge began to collapse.
Elyndra pulled him close, ghostlight flaring around them.
"Hold on," she whispered. "I'm not letting you go."
The Void surged upward.
The bridge shattered.
And Elyndra dragged the Unwritten into the light.

The Memory That Breaks Through
Light swallowed them.
Not warm. Not gentle.
A violent tearing brightness that ripped the bridge apart and hurled them upward through the collapsing fracture.
Elyndra held him tight, ghostlight flaring around her like a shield. The Unwritten clung to her without understanding why — without understanding anything — flickering in and out of shape as the Void tried to pull him back.
"Stay with me!" she shouted, voice raw.
He tried.
He really tried.
But something inside him was breaking.
A crack. A split. A seam tearing open.
And through that seam—
A memory slipped out.
Not a full one. Not even a clear one.
Just a moment.
A sound.
A voice.
A hand gripping his shoulder — firm, steady, familiar.
A man's voice, low and commanding, speaking a single word:
"Rise."
The Unwritten gasped.
The fracture shuddered violently, reacting to the memory like a wound touched by fire.

Elyndra felt it too — the ghostlight around her flared in shock.

"What was that?" she whispered.

The Unwritten's form flickered, stabilizing for a heartbeat.

"**…someone… spoke to me…**"

"Who?"

He shook his head, ghostlight dripping from his fingers like liquid light.

"**…I don't… know…**"

The fracture roared.

The Void surged upward, trying to reclaim him.

Elyndra pulled him closer, lantern-spark burning white hot.

"Hold on," she whispered fiercely. "You're coming back."

The memory echoed again — faint, distant, but unmistakable:

"**Rise.**"

The Unwritten's eyes widened.

He whispered the word back, voice trembling:

"**…I… knew that voice…**"

The fracture collapsed.

Light exploded.

And Elyndra dragged him out of the Void.

CHAPTER THIRTY-EIGHT — THE RIVER TAKES THEM

The river didn't wait for them.

The moment the cliff gave way, the water surged upward like a living thing, swallowing Rynn and Talla before either could scream. The impact knocked the air from Rynn's lungs, the cold biting so deep it felt like knives under his skin.

He surfaced once — just long enough to gasp.

"Talla—!"

A wave slammed into him, dragging him under.

The current was monstrous. Not a stream. Not a river. A flood, swollen by the collapsing cliffs and the storm above. It spun him violently, smashing him against submerged rocks, tearing at his cloak, ripping the breath from his chest.

He fought upward again, kicking hard, breaking the surface—

"Talla!" he choked.

He saw her — a flash of dark hair, a hand reaching, eyes wide with terror as the current dragged her sideways toward a jagged outcropping.

Rynn lunged toward her.

The river disagreed.

A whirlpool formed between them, a spiralling column of white water that yanked him backward. His fingers brushed hers — just for a heartbeat — before the current tore them apart.

"Rynn!" she screamed.

He tried to swim toward her.

The river spun him the other way.

"Talla!" he roared, voice breaking.

She vanished behind a wall of churning foam.

Rynn thrashed, kicking, clawing at the water, trying to fight the current — but the river was stronger. It dragged him

downstream, tumbling him through rapids that felt like falling down a staircase made of stone.
His head struck something hard.
The world flashed white.
He sank.
Cold wrapped around him like a fist.
His limbs slowed. His breath thinned. His heartbeat echoed strangely in his ears.
He tried to swim.
His body refused.
He tried to shout.
Water filled his mouth.
He tried to reach for Talla.
His hand drifted uselessly in the dark.
The river pulled him deeper.
Deeper.
Deeper—
Until the water wasn't water anymore.
It was memory.
The cold thickened. The pressure grew. The darkness shifted into something familiar — something he had spent years trying to bury.
A shoreline. A storm. A boy screaming. A hand slipping from his grasp.
Rynn's eyes widened.
"No," he whispered into the dark. "Not this. Not again."
The river twisted around him, pulling him into the memory he feared most.
The water brightened — not with light, but with lightning, flashing through the depths like veins of fire.
And suddenly—
He was standing on the shore.
Not a man.
A boy.
Barefoot. Soaked. Shivering.
Rain hammered the lake. Wind tore at the trees. Thunder cracked overhead.
And beside him—
A smaller boy.

His brother.
Wide-eyed. Terrified. Clutching Rynn's hand with white knuckles.
"Rynn," the boy whispered. "Don't let go."
Rynn's breath hitched.
He remembered this storm. He remembered this night. He remembered the promise he made.
"I won't," he whispered, even though the boy couldn't hear him. "I swear I won't."
But the memory didn't care.
The lake surged.
A wave crashed over them, knocking both boys off their feet. Rynn scrambled up, grabbing his brother's wrist, pulling him toward the rocks—
Lightning struck the water.
The shockwave hit like a hammer.
Rynn was thrown backward. His brother was ripped from his grasp.
"NO!" Rynn screamed.
He lunged forward, reaching, clawing at the water, trying to grab the small hand slipping beneath the surface.
Their fingers brushed.
Just for a heartbeat.
Then the current tore them apart.
His brother's face vanished beneath the waves.
Rynn dove after him.
The water swallowed him whole.
He kicked downward, lungs burning, eyes stinging, reaching into the dark—
A shape drifted below him.
Small. Still. Sinking.
Rynn's heart shattered.
"Please," he whispered. "Please, not again—"
He reached.
His fingers brushed his brother's sleeve—
The water froze.
Everything stopped.
The storm. The waves. The lightning. The sinking body.
All of it suspended in a single, impossible moment.

A voice whispered behind him.
Not his brother's. Not Talla's. Not anyone he knew.
"You couldn't save him."
Rynn turned.
The lake was gone.
The storm was gone.
He stood in a void of black water stretching into infinity.
And in front of him—
A figure.
Tall. Shadowed. Unmoving.
Rynn couldn't see its face.
But he felt its presence.
Cold. Heavy. Judging.
The voice came again — closer now, almost gentle:
"You will fail again."
Rynn staggered backward.
"No—"
The figure stepped forward.
The water rippled.
"You couldn't save him."
Rynn shook his head violently. "Stop—"
"You won't save her either."
Rynn froze.
The figure leaned closer.
"Talla will drown too."
The world shattered.
Rynn fell through the memory, through the water, through himself—

CHAPTER THIRTY-NINE — THE ONE LEFT BEHIND

The world cracked.
Talla fell through the silence—
And hit the ground.
Not water. Not stone. Something in between.
A grey plain stretched in every direction, flat and endless, lit by a sky with no sun. The air was still. Too still. Her breath sounded wrong in her own ears — thin, distant, like it belonged to someone else.
She pushed herself upright, chest heaving.
"Rynn?"
Her voice vanished the moment it left her lips, swallowed by the silence.
She tried again, louder.
"Rynn!"
Nothing.
The silence pressed closer, thickening like fog. Her heartbeat echoed in her skull, too loud, too slow.
She took a step.
The ground rippled.
Shapes rose from the grey surface — silhouettes of people she knew, people she trusted, people she had bled beside. They stood in a wide circle around her, unmoving, faceless.
Talla's breath hitched.
"Please," she whispered. "Don't do this."
The silhouettes turned away.
All at once.
Every single one.
Walking outward, leaving her in the centre of the empty plain.
"Stop!" she cried, voice cracking. "Don't leave me!"
They didn't stop.
They didn't slow.
They didn't look back.
The silence whispered:

"You were never worth staying for."
Talla staggered backward, shaking her head violently.
"No. No, that's not true. They care. They—"
The ground split beneath her.
A jagged line tore across the plain, opening into a widening chasm of darkness. The silhouettes walked straight into it, vanishing without hesitation, without fear, without a single glance back.
Talla reached toward them, tears burning her eyes.
"Please! Don't leave me alone!"
The silence answered:
"You always end up alone."
The chasm widened.
The ground crumbled beneath her feet.
Talla fell.
She plummeted into the dark, arms flailing, breath tearing from her lungs. The silence swallowed her scream.
Then—
A hand grabbed her wrist.
Warm. Solid. Real.
Talla gasped and looked up.
Rynn hung above her, half-silhouette, half-memory, his face flickering like a candle in the wind. His grip trembled, but he held on.
"Talla!" he shouted — but his voice sounded wrong, distorted, like it was being dragged through water. "Hold on!"
Her heart surged.
"Rynn!"
She reached with her free hand—
The silence hissed:
"He'll let go."
Rynn's form flickered.
His grip slipped.
"No!" Talla screamed. "Don't— don't leave me!"
Rynn's eyes widened in horror as his fingers slid from her wrist.
"Talla—!"
He vanished.

The silence swallowed him.
Talla fell again, deeper this time, the dark rushing up to meet her like a closing fist.
She curled inward, sobbing, the words tearing from her throat:
"I don't want to be alone."
The silence whispered back:
"You always will be."
The darkness closed around her—
And the nightmare shattered.

CHAPTER FORTY — THE FOREST DEVOURS THEM

The world cracked.
And Bren fell into a memory he had spent years burying.

The Memory of the Mountain
He hit the ground hard — not forest soil, not roots, not leaves.
Stone.
Cold, grey, familiar stone.
Bren staggered upright, breath ragged, hammer still in his grip. The forest was gone. The Voidborn were gone. The ravine was gone.
He stood on a narrow mountain ledge, wind howling around him, snow whipping across his face like shards of glass.
His stomach dropped.
"No," he whispered. "Not here."
But the mountain didn't care.
The storm roared overhead, lightning splitting the sky. The wind tore at his cloak, threatening to rip him from the ledge entirely.
And ahead of him—
A boy clung to the cliff face.
Small. Frail. Bare fingers bleeding as they scraped against the rock.
"Bren!" the boy cried, voice cracking with terror. "Please—!"
Bren's heart stopped.
His brother.
The one he couldn't save.
The one he had sworn he *would* save.
The one he had failed.
"No," Bren whispered, shaking his head. "No, this isn't real. This isn't—"
The boy slipped.

His scream tore through the storm.
"BREN!"
Bren lunged forward, dropping to his knees, reaching with both hands.
"I've got you! I've got you, I swear—!"
Their fingers brushed.
Just for a heartbeat.
Then the wind surged.
The boy's grip broke.
He fell.
Bren screamed, reaching into empty air, his voice ripped away by the storm.
"NO!"
The boy's body vanished into the white abyss below.
The mountain went silent.
Bren collapsed to his knees, hammer slipping from his grasp, breath shaking violently.
"Please," he whispered. "Please, not again..."
A voice answered him.
Not the boy's.
Not Lysa's.
Not anyone living.
"You let him fall."
Bren froze.
The storm parted.
A figure stepped onto the ledge — tall, broad-shouldered, wrapped in furs, face hidden in shadow.
Bren's breath caught.
"Father..."
The figure didn't move.
Didn't breathe.
Didn't blink.
It simply stared at him — a silhouette carved from disappointment.
"You let him fall," the voice repeated, deeper now, colder.
"And you will let her fall too."
Bren's blood turned to ice.
"Don't," he whispered. "Don't say her name."
The figure stepped closer.

"Lysa will fall."
Bren shook his head violently. "No—"
"You will fail her."
"Stop—"
"You fail everyone."
The mountain trembled.
The ledge cracked beneath Bren's knees.
The storm roared back to life, wind screaming around him like a thousand accusing voices.
The figure leaned close, its shadow swallowing Bren whole.
"You are strong," it whispered. "But strength is not enough."
The ledge split.
Bren fell.
Through the storm. Through the mountain. Through the memory. Through himself.
And somewhere far above, beyond the collapsing vision, beyond the forest, beyond the ravine—
A voice called his name.
Not his father's.
Not his brother's.
Someone alive.
Someone fighting to reach him.
But the mountain's whisper followed him into the dark:
"You will fail again."

CHAPTER FORTY-ONE — THE WEIGHT OF COMMAND

The forest dissolved.
The roots. The shadows. The ravine. All of it peeled away like wet paint sliding off stone.
Bren staggered forward—
And found himself standing in a narrow stone corridor lit by flickering lanterns.
The air was thick with dust. The walls trembled. Distant screams echoed through the passage.
Bren froze.
He knew this place.
He had sworn never to return to it.
"No," he whispered. "Not here. Not this."
A voice shouted from deeper in the tunnel.
"Captain! The supports are failing!"
Bren's stomach twisted.
He remembered this. He remembered the panic. He remembered the decision.
He ran.
The corridor opened into a larger chamber — a mining outpost carved into the cliffside, lanterns swaying wildly as the ceiling cracked overhead.
Five soldiers stood there.
His squad.
Young. Tired. Trusting him.
"Captain," one of them said, voice shaking, "we need to fall back."
Bren shook his head.
"We hold this position. Reinforcements are coming."
A tremor shook the chamber.
Dust rained from the ceiling.
Another soldier swallowed hard. "Sir, the supports won't last—"

"We hold," Bren snapped. "We don't abandon our post."
He remembered saying it. He remembered believing it. He remembered thinking he was doing the right thing.
A crack split the ceiling.
A beam snapped.
The chamber roared.
"MOVE!" Bren shouted.
But it was too late.
The ceiling collapsed in a thunder of stone and dust. Bren dove forward, grabbing one soldier and dragging him clear as the chamber caved in.
The others—
He heard their screams. He heard the crunch of stone. He heard the silence that followed.
When the dust settled, Bren clawed at the rubble with bleeding hands, trying to dig them out.
He found a hand.
Then an arm.
Then nothing else.
He screamed until his voice broke.
"Captain…" the surviving soldier whispered behind him. "It wasn't your fault."
Bren didn't answer.
He couldn't.
Because he knew the truth.
He had made the call. He had told them to hold. He had killed them.
A voice whispered behind him.
Cold. Cruel. Close.
"You will fail again."
Bren turned.
A figure stood at the edge of the ruined chamber — tall, shadowed, face hidden, watching him with silent judgment.
Bren's fists clenched.
"Get away from me."
The figure stepped closer.
"You couldn't save them then."
It leaned forward.
"You won't save her now."

The chamber cracked.
The world shattered—
And Bren fell into darkness.

CHAPTER FORTY-TWO — THE QUIET AFTER

The ravine vanished.
The cold. The water. The rocks.
All of it dissolved into a stillness so complete it felt like the world was holding its breath.
Lysa stood in a doorway.
A familiar doorway.
Her doorway.
Her chest tightened.
"No," she whispered. "Not this. Not again."
The house was silent.
Not peaceful. Not calm.
Dead.
Dust floated in the slanted light. The shutters hung crooked. The air smelled of smoke and iron and something she had spent years trying to forget.
Her younger self sat on the floor in the centre of the room — knees pulled to her chest, arms wrapped around her legs, eyes wide and empty.
Frozen. Unmoving. Waiting for someone who would never come.
Lysa stepped inside.
The floor creaked beneath her.
The younger girl didn't react.
Didn't blink. Didn't breathe. Didn't cry.
She just stared at the three shapes on the floor — covered with blankets that did nothing to hide the truth beneath them.
Lysa knelt beside her younger self.
"You were so small," she whispered. "Too small for this."
The girl didn't answer.
She didn't need to.
Lysa remembered everything.
The shouting. The breaking glass. The begging. The silence afterward.

She remembered hiding under the table. She remembered the boots walking past her. She remembered the door slamming shut.
She remembered waiting.
Hours. Maybe days. Time didn't matter.
Nothing mattered.
A floorboard creaked behind her.
Lysa froze.
She remembered this sound.
She remembered thinking the killers had come back.
A shadow filled the doorway.
Tall. Broad-shouldered. Armoured.
The figure stepped inside slowly, carefully — as if approaching a wounded animal.
Lysa's breath caught.
She remembered this moment. She remembered the fear.
She remembered the warmth of the cloak that wrapped around her afterward.
But she had never seen the man's face.
Not then. Not now.
The soldier knelt beside the younger Lysa.
His voice was low, steady, gentle in a way she had never heard before.
"You're safe now."
The girl didn't respond.
Didn't look at him.
Didn't move.
The soldier hesitated — then lifted her into his arms.
Lysa watched, heart pounding.
She remembered the way he shielded her eyes from the bodies. She remembered the way he carried her out of the house. She remembered the way he held her until she stopped shaking.
But she had never known who he was.
Not until much later.
The memory blurred around the edges, the soldier's features dissolving into shadow — but his stance, his presence, the way he held the child…
Lysa whispered:

"...Kaelren?"
A voice answered her.
Not Kaelren's. Not the girl's.
The same cold whisper that haunted the others.
"You will lose him too."
Lysa spun.
The shadow figure stood in the corner — tall, faceless, watching.
"You lost your first family."
Lysa's jaw clenched.
"Don't."
"You will lose this one."
"No."
"You always lose them."
The house darkened.
The covered bodies shifted.
The shapes beneath the blankets grew taller. Broader. Familiar.
Lysa's breath hitched.
"No…"
The figure whispered:
"You will bury them all."
The blankets slipped.
And Lysa screamed—
As the world shattered around her.

The Voidborn closed in.
Dozens. Maybe more. Their claws scraped against stone, their breath hissing like steam escaping cracked metal.
Jorren drew both Veilborn blades.
Ghostlight rippled along their edges — pale, trembling, alive.
He tightened his grip.
"Alright," he muttered. "One at a time. Or all at once. Doesn't matter."
His voice shook.
He hoped they didn't notice.
The creatures crept closer.
Jorren stepped back until his heel hit a fallen pillar. No escape. No cover. No squad. No Kaelren. No Bren. No Rynn. No Lysa. No Elyndra. No Unwritten.
Just him. Just the dark. Just the Void.
He lifted the blades.
The ghostlight flickered.
"Not now," he whispered. "Please. Not now."
A Voidborn lunged.
Jorren spun, blades flashing. One cut through its throat, the other through its chest. The creature dissolved into shadow.
Another leapt.
He ducked, slashed upward, felt the blade bite bone.
Another.
Another.
He fought like a man drowning — fast, desperate, burning through every ounce of strength he had left.
But there were too many.
A claw raked across his back.
He staggered.
Another slammed into his ribs.
He gasped.
His blades dimmed.
"No," he whispered. "Stay with me. Stay—"
The ghostlight sputtered.
Then died.

Darkness swallowed him.
The Voidborn froze.
Then retreated.
Not because they feared him.
Because something else was coming.
Something worse.
Jorren's breath hitched.
The darkness thickened.
Pressed in.
Wrapped around him like cold hands.
And suddenly—
He was standing on a bridge of black stone.
A bridge he knew.
A bridge he had sworn never to see again.
Shadowdeep.
His home. His realm. Falling.
Jorren's knees buckled.
"Oh Shadows… no…"
The sky above Shadowdeep was a swirling vortex of ghostlight and shadow, the Veil tearing open like a wound.
Towers cracked. Bridges collapsed. The great lantern spires flickered and died one by one.
Screams echoed through the streets.
People ran. People fell. People dissolved into drifting ash as the Void consumed them.
Jorren staggered forward, breath shaking.
He remembered this night. He remembered the smell of burning stone. He remembered the sound of the Veil screaming. He remembered the moment the sky broke.
He remembered the Harrowed King.
A tremor shook the bridge.
Jorren turned.
His old squad was there — the Shadowdeep Wardens, cloaks torn, armour cracked, faces pale with terror.
"Jorren!" the captain shouted. "We have to fall back!"
"We can't!" Jorren yelled. "The Veil Gate—"
Another explosion rocked the city.
A tower collapsed in a cascade of stone and ghostlight.
The captain grabbed Jorren's shoulder.

"Shadowdeep is gone!"
Jorren shook his head violently. "No. No, we can still—"
A scream cut through the air.
Not human. Not mortal.
A sound like a dying star.
The Harrowed King stepped through the breach in the Veil.
Jorren froze.
He remembered this moment. He remembered the terror.
He remembered the way the world bent around the King's presence.
Tall. Armoured in obsidian and bone. A crown of broken antlers fused to his skull. Eyes burning with cold, ancient light.
He didn't walk.
He arrived.
The air bowed around him. The stone beneath him cracked. The Veil itself recoiled.
Jorren's blades trembled in his hands.
The Harrowed King raised one hand — slow, deliberate, inevitable — and the ghostlight in the lantern spires guttered and died.
Shadowdeep dimmed.
The King spoke.
His voice was a low, resonant rumble that shook the bridge apart:
"This realm is mine."
The Wardens charged.
They didn't stand a chance.
The King moved like a shadow given form — effortless, unstoppable. His blade carved through ghostlight and steel alike. His presence alone shattered minds.
Jorren watched his squad fall.
One by one.
The medic. The captain. The recruit who always asked him to teach blade tricks.
All gone.
All in moments.
Jorren screamed and charged.

The Harrowed King turned toward him.
Their blades met.
Ghostlight exploded.
Jorren was thrown backward, crashing into the bridge hard enough to crack stone.
He couldn't breathe.
He couldn't move.
He couldn't think.
The King approached.
Slow. Heavy. Inevitable.
He knelt beside Jorren.
His voice was a whisper of cold wind through a graveyard.
"You survived once."
He leaned closer.
"You will not survive again."
The King raised his hand.
The world shattered.
And Jorren fell into darkness.

CHAPTER FORTY-THREE — THE SHATTERED PATH

The world snapped back like a whip.
Bren hit the ground hard, rolling through dust and broken stone. His ribs screamed. His vision blurred. The memory of the collapse — the screams, the bodies, the weight he couldn't lift — clung to him like smoke.
He forced himself upright.
The forest was gone.
In its place lay a jagged wasteland of torn earth and shattered roots, as if something enormous had clawed its way through the world.
"Lysa!" he shouted.
His voice echoed.
No answer.
He gripped his hammer and staggered forward, breath ragged. The ground trembled beneath him. Somewhere in the distance, something shrieked — high, sharp, wrong.
Bren froze.
That wasn't Lysa.
That was a Voidborn.
And it was close.
He moved toward the sound anyway.
Because danger meant someone might be fighting. And someone fighting meant someone alive.
He climbed over a fallen trunk, boots slipping on loose soil—
A flash of ghostlight cut through the fog.
Bren's heart lurched.
"Jorren?"
Another flash — two blades, moving fast.
Bren broke into a run.
He rounded the corner just as a Voidborn lunged at a lone figure. The figure spun, blades carving a perfect arc of pale light—
Bren didn't think.

He roared and swung his hammer, smashing the creature sideways into a boulder.

It dissolved into shadow.

The figure turned.

Jorren.

Alive.

Barely.

His eyes were red. His breath shook. His blades trembled in his hands.

Bren opened his mouth to speak—

Jorren collapsed.

Bren caught him before he hit the ground.

"Easy," Bren muttered. "Easy, lad. I've got you."

Jorren's voice was barely a whisper.

"They're gone... all of them... I saw—"

"I know," Bren said, voice low. "Me too."

Jorren's fingers tightened weakly around Bren's arm.

"Don't leave," he whispered.

Bren swallowed hard.

"I'm not going anywhere."

A branch snapped behind them.

Both men turned.

A silhouette stepped through the fog.

Small. Fast. Bow drawn.

Lysa.

Her eyes widened when she saw them.

"Bren—? Jorren—?"

Her voice broke.

She ran.

She skidded to her knees beside them, hands hovering uselessly over Jorren's trembling form.

"What happened to him?"

Bren didn't answer.

He didn't have to.

Jorren's eyes were open but unfocused, staring at something far away — something only he could see. His breath came in short, broken gasps. His fingers still clutched the hilts of his Veilborn blades like they were the only things anchoring him to the world.

"Jorren," Lysa whispered, touching his cheek. "Hey. Hey, look at me."
He didn't.
He couldn't.
Bren swallowed hard.
He knew this look. He'd worn it once. The day the mine collapsed. The day he killed his own squad with a bad call.
Lysa looked up at him, voice shaking.
"What do we do?"
Bren froze.
Those words. Those exact words.
He heard them again — from years ago — echoing through the collapsing chamber.
Captain, what do we do?
He had answered wrong then.
He had told them to hold.
He had killed them.
His chest tightened. His breath hitched. His vision blurred around the edges.
Not again. Not again. Not again.
A distant shriek cut through the fog.
Voidborn.
Close.
Too close.
Lysa's hand tightened on her bowstring.
"Bren—?"
He couldn't breathe.
He couldn't think.
He couldn't lead.
Not again.
Not after what he saw in the vision. Not after watching his squad die under falling stone. Not after hearing their screams echo in the dark.
His voice came out rough, barely audible.
"We… we run."
Lysa's eyes widened.
"What?"
"We run," Bren repeated, louder this time. "We get Jorren out of here. We regroup. We—"

A second shriek. Closer. Hunting.
Lysa shook her head.
"We can't outrun them. Not carrying him."
Bren's jaw clenched.
She was right.
He knew she was right.
But the other option— The other option was to stand and fight.
To make a call. To take responsibility. To risk losing them.
His hands trembled.
He looked down at Jorren — broken, shaking, barely conscious.
He looked at Lysa — terrified, but steady, waiting for him to choose.
He looked at the fog — shifting, alive, full of approaching death.
And he felt it.
The old weight.
The weight he had sworn he would never carry again.
His voice cracked.
"I can't lead."
Lysa stared at him.
"Bren—"
"I can't," he said, louder, harsher. "I can't make that call again. I can't be the reason—"
A roar tore through the trees.
The Voidborn burst through the fog.
Huge. Fast. Hunting.
Lysa raised her bow.
Jorren stirred weakly.
Bren's heart slammed against his ribs.
This was it.
Fight or run.
Lead or break.
He felt the old fear clawing up his throat—
And then he heard something.
Not a roar. Not a scream. Not a voice.
A memory.
Kaelren's voice.

Leadership isn't about being unafraid. It's about choosing anyway.
Bren's breath steadied.
Just a little.
He stood.
Hammer in hand.
Feet planted.
Shoulders squared.
Lysa looked up at him — hope flickering in her eyes.
"Bren...?"
He exhaled.
Long. Slow. Final.
"We fight."
The Voidborn burst through the fog.
Huge. Fast. Hunting.
Bren stepped forward, hammer raised, planting himself between the monsters and the two people behind him.
"Lysa," he growled, "get him up."
She didn't argue.
She hooked her arms under Jorren's shoulders, dragging him back as Bren charged.
The first Voidborn lunged.
Bren met it head on.
The hammer connected with its jaw in a thunderous crack, sending the creature skidding across the broken earth.
Another leapt from the left — Bren pivoted, swinging in a brutal arc that shattered its ribs.
He felt the old fear clawing at him.
The fear of choosing wrong. The fear of losing them. The fear of being the reason they died.
But he pushed it down.
He swung again.
And again.
And again.
Behind him, Lysa shouted, "Bren— incoming!"
He turned just in time to see a third Voidborn pounce.
Too fast. Too close. Too late—
A shield slammed into the creature's side with bone-cracking force, knocking it off its feet.
Bren blinked.

A figure stumbled out of the fog, shield raised, ghostlight flickering along its rim.
Rynn.
His hair was plastered to his forehead. His eyes were red.
His breath came in ragged, uneven pulls.
But he was alive.
He planted his shield in the ground, using it to steady himself.
"I heard screaming," he rasped. "Figured it was either you... or something worse."
Bren snorted. "Could've been both."
Rynn managed a weak, crooked smile — then lifted his shield again as more Voidborn shrieked in the distance.
Lysa dragged Jorren upright. "We can't hold this!"
Bren tightened his grip on the hammer.
"Yes," he said. "We can."
Rynn stepped beside him, shield glowing faintly.
Lysa nocked an arrow.
Jorren forced himself upright, blades trembling.
The Voidborn charged.
The squad braced.
And then—
A silver streak tore through the fog.
A Voidborn's head snapped sideways as a spear punched clean through its skull.
The weapon ripped free, spinning back into the hands of a small, furious figure who slid into view like a thrown knife.
Talla.
Her eyes were wild. Her stance perfect. Her voice a snarl.
"You idiots better not die before I get a turn."
Bren barked a laugh — short, sharp, disbelieving.
The squad was coming back together.
Piece by piece. Fight by fight. Choice by choice.
The Voidborn hesitated.
Just for a heartbeat.
And in that heartbeat, the air changed.
A pressure rolled through the fog — heavy, cold, commanding.
The Voidborn shrieked and recoiled.

Lysa's breath caught.
Rynn's shield flickered.
Jorren's blades hummed.
Talla whispered, "Oh… he's here."
Footsteps approached.
Slow. Measured. Inevitable.
Kaelren stepped out of the fog.
His cloak was torn. His armour cracked. His eyes burned with a cold, steady fire.
He took in the scene — Bren standing firm, the squad gathered behind him, Voidborn circling.
And he nodded once.
"Good," Kaelren said. "You chose to fight."
Bren exhaled — a long, shaking breath he didn't realize he'd been holding.
For the first time since the collapse, he felt the weight lift.
Not because the danger was gone.
But because he wasn't carrying it alone.
Kaelren drew his blade.
"Let's finish this."

CHAPTER FORTY-FOUR — THE PATH OF ECHOES

The Lantern Path opened beneath Elyndra's feet in a swirl of ghostlight and drifting mist. She stepped out into the shattered forest, the air thick with the scent of torn earth and burning roots.
The world was wrong here.
The Veil had been ripped. The ground trembled with distant impacts. Voidborn shrieks echoed through the trees.
And somewhere ahead — faint, flickering, fragile — she felt them.
The squad.
Alive. Fighting. Barely holding on.
She tightened her grip on her lantern.
Behind her, the man who had fallen through the Gate staggered out of the fading Path.
The Unwritten. The Voyager.
He braced himself against a tree, breath ragged, sweat beading on his brow. His legs trembled beneath him, but he stayed upright.
Barely.
Elyndra moved to steady him.
"Careful," she said softly. "Your spark is still unstable."
He shook his head, jaw clenched. "I can walk."
"You shouldn't."
"I don't care."
His voice cracked — not with anger, but with something deeper. Something like fear. Something like urgency.
Elyndra studied him.
His eyes still glowed faintly with dying runes. His hands trembled. His breath came in uneven pulls. But beneath all that weakness… something pulsed.
A rhythm. A memory. A spark trying to ignite.
She stepped closer. "You're pushing yourself too hard."

He met her gaze — and for the first time, there was clarity in his eyes.

"I saw them," he whispered. "In the visions. The hammer. The shield. The bow. The blades. They're fighting."

Elyndra's breath caught.

"You remember them?"

"No," he said. "But I feel them."

He pressed a hand to his chest, fingers trembling.

"Like a pull. Like a thread. Like I'm supposed to be there."

Elyndra swallowed.

"That's the spark," she said quietly. "It's waking."

He flinched at the word.

"Spark…"

He closed his eyes.

And suddenly—

Flashes.

A Realm of molten rivers. A sky of golden pillars. A storm-fortress chained to lightning. A crown of fire shattering. A hand reaching for him through the Veil. A voice whispering—

Voyager.

His eyes snapped open.

He staggered, gripping a tree to stay upright.

Elyndra caught his arm. "What did you see?"

He shook his head, breath shaking. "I don't know. I don't know what any of it means."

But he did.

Somewhere deep inside, he did.

Elyndra placed a hand on his chest — over the faint, dying runes.

"You are the Voyager," she whispered.

He froze.

The forest went silent.

Even the Voidborn shrieks seemed to fade.

He stared at her, eyes wide, breath caught in his throat.

"The… Voyager?"

Elyndra nodded slowly.

"It's not a name. It's a mantle. A destiny. A spark that refuses to die."

He swallowed hard.

"And me?"

"You are the one who carries it."

He shook his head violently. "No. No, I'm no one. I don't remember anything. I don't even know my own name."

"That's why you're dangerous," Elyndra said softly. "A spark without memory burns wild."

He looked down at his trembling hands.

"I don't want to be dangerous."

"You don't have a choice."

He flinched.

Elyndra softened her voice.

"But you do have a purpose."

He looked up.

"What purpose?"

She turned toward the distant battle — where ghostlight flickered through the trees, where steel clashed, where the squad fought for their lives.

"To reach them," she said. "To stand with them. To survive with them."

He hesitated.

Then nodded.

"Then take me to them."

Elyndra lifted her lantern.

Ghostlight flared.

The forest parted.

And together — the memorywalker and the man without a name — they began to walk.

Slowly. Unsteadily. But forward.

With every step, the Voyager felt something inside him tighten — a thread pulling him toward the fight, toward the squad, toward the moment his spark would finally remember itself.

He stumbled once.

Elyndra caught him.

"You're still weak," she said.

"I'll get stronger."

"You don't have to."

He looked at her.

"Yes," he said quietly. "I do."
The ground trembled.
A distant roar shook the trees.
The battle was close now.
Elyndra lifted her lantern higher.
"Stay with me," she said.
He nodded.
"I'm trying."
And for the first time since he fell through the Gate — he believed he could.

CHAPTER FORTY-FIVE — THE LIGHT THAT REMEMBERS

The forest shook with the sound of battle.

Steel clashed. Voidborn shrieked. Ghostlight flickered like dying stars.

Elyndra pushed through the shattered undergrowth, lantern raised, the Voyager stumbling beside her. His breath came in ragged pulls, each step a battle of its own.

"Almost there," she whispered.

He nodded, jaw clenched, sweat beading on his brow. His legs trembled, but he didn't fall.

Not now. Not when he could feel them.

The hammer. The shield. The bow. The spear. The blades.

Threads pulling him forward.

A family he didn't remember — but somehow belonged to.

A roar tore through the trees.

Elyndra froze.

The clearing opened before them — and the squad was losing.

Badly.

Voidborn swarmed from every direction, claws flashing, jaws snapping. Bren swung his hammer in wide, desperate arcs, but his arms shook with exhaustion. Rynn's shield flared with ghostlight as he blocked another strike, but the impact drove him back a step. Lysa's hands trembled so badly she could barely draw another dark arrow into existence. Talla fought like a cornered animal, spear flashing, but the creatures pressed her relentlessly. Jorren's Veilborn blades dimmed, ghostlight flickering like a dying heartbeat.

Kaelren stood at the centre, holding the line alone — but even he was being pushed back.

They were seconds from being overrun.

The Voyager staggered forward.

"No," he whispered. "No, no, no—"
Elyndra grabbed his arm. "You can't go in there. You'll die."
"They'll die," he rasped. "I can't— I can't let that happen." His voice cracked.
Elyndra looked at him — really looked — and saw the truth.
He didn't know them. He didn't remember them. But he felt them.
The spark inside him did.
She lifted her lantern.
"Then let me open the way."
She stepped into the clearing.
Ghostlight flared.
The lanterns orbiting her ignited in a blinding burst of white-blue radiance. The air rippled. The Voidborn shrieked, recoiling, claws scraping against their own faces as the light seared their senses.
Kaelren shielded his eyes. Bren stumbled back. Lysa gasped. Rynn braced behind his shield. Talla hissed in awe. Jorren blinked through tears.
Elyndra's voice rang out like a bell.
"BEHOLD THE VEIL!"
The light exploded outward.
The Voidborn screamed.
And in that moment — that single, perfect heartbeat — the Voyager stepped past her.
He didn't run. He didn't shout. He didn't raise a weapon. He simply existed.
And the world reacted.
A pulse rippled from his chest — faint at first, then growing, then roaring outward like a shockwave of memory and light.
The runes beneath his skin ignited.
Not bright. Not controlled. But alive.
The pulse hit the Voidborn.
They froze.

Their bodies convulsed. Their forms flickered. Their shadows tore away from them like smoke ripped from a flame.
And then—
They disintegrated.
Not burned. Not shattered. Not slain.
Unwritten.
Erased from existence in a single breath.
Silence fell.
The forest stilled.
The squad stared — stunned, breathless, terrified.
Elyndra lowered her lantern, eyes wide with awe and fear.
The Voyager swayed.
His knees buckled.
Elyndra caught him before he hit the ground.
He looked up at her, eyes glowing faintly, voice barely a whisper.
"I... I did that?"
She nodded slowly.
"Yes."
He swallowed hard.
"Why?"
Elyndra's voice trembled.
"Because you are the Voyager."
He closed his eyes.
And for the first time — the title didn't feel like a lie.
It felt like a memory.

CHAPTER FORTY-SIX — A NAME REMEMBERED

Silence clung to the clearing.
The Voidborn were gone — erased in a single breath. The air still shimmered with the fading echo of the pulse that had torn them apart.
Elyndra knelt beside him, steadying him as he swayed. His breath trembled. His hands shook. But his eyes were open. And he was awake.
Kaelren approached slowly, sword lowered, expression caught somewhere between awe and relief.
"You're... conscious," he said.
The man managed a weak smile. "Mostly."
Bren let out a shaky laugh. "Well, that's better than the alternative."
Lysa elbowed him. "Read the room, Bren."
Rynn planted his shield in the dirt and leaned on it, catching his breath. Talla twirled her spear once, eyes wide with something like respect.
Kaelren crouched in front of him.
"You saved us," he said quietly.
The man swallowed. "I didn't mean to."
"Doesn't matter," Kaelren replied. "You did."
He studied the man's face — the flickering runes beneath his skin, the haunted confusion in his eyes, the spark trying to remember itself.
"So," Kaelren said gently, "what do we call you?"
The man hesitated.
He looked down at his trembling hands, as if the answer might be carved into his skin.
"I... I don't know my name," he admitted. "But I remember something. A word. A title."
Kaelren leaned in. "Tell us."
The man closed his eyes.
A memory surfaced — faint, fractured, but real. A voice calling to him across a burning horizon.

"Voyager," he whispered. "I... I was called the Voyager."
Lysa raised an eyebrow. "That's it? Voyager?"
Bren shrugged. "Could be worse."
Talla smirked. "Could be 'Fell Out of the Sky Guy.'"
Rynn grunted. "Or 'Nearly Got Us Killed.'"
Kaelren ignored them, gaze fixed on the man.
"Voyager," he repeated thoughtfully. "It fits."
But Elyndra stiffened.
Her lantern dimmed, then brightened — a pulse of recognition.
"Not just Voyager," she said softly.
The man looked up at her, confusion tightening his brow. "What do you mean?"
Elyndra stepped closer, voice barely above a whisper. "You were the Eternal Voyager."
The clearing went still.
The runes beneath his skin flickered — not bright, but deep, like an old ember remembering fire.
A breath caught in his throat.
"I... I know that," he murmured, startled by his own certainty. "I don't know how, but... I know that."
A shard of memory cut through the fog — a lantern sea, a broken crown, a name he once refused.
Then it was gone.
Kaelren rose slowly, offering him a hand.
"Eternal Voyager," he said. "That's who you were."
The man took his hand, unsteady but standing.
"And who I might be again," he whispered.
The squad gathered around him — bruised, exhausted, shaken, but alive.
For the first time since he fell through the Gate, something settled inside him.
Not clarity. Not certainty. But direction.
Elyndra stepped forward, lantern dimming softly.
"Welcome back to the Last Realm," she said. "Eternal Voyager."
He exhaled.
And for the first time, the title didn't feel like a burden.
It felt like a memory waiting to wake.

OFFICIAL

CHAPTER FORTY-SEVEN — THE FIRST OMEN

The Void shifted.
Not because the Harrowed King stirred — he had never been still. Not because he awakened — he had not slept since the fall of Shadowdeep. Not because he rose — he had been walking the dead Realms for years, carving his dominion from their ashes.
No.
The Void shifted because something challenged him.
A pulse. A spark. A memory he had believed extinguished.
The Harrowed King halted mid-stride atop a ridge of broken stone, the remnants of a once-living Realm crumbling beneath his boots. His cloak of shadow coiled around him like smoke caught in a storm.
The crown of broken antlers fused to his skull pulsed once with cold blue fire.
He felt it again.
A ripple through the Veil. A flare of ghostlight. A spark refusing to die.
The Eternal Voyager.
Alive. Awake. Returned.
The King's head tilted slightly, as if listening to a distant heartbeat.
Voidborn crawled from the cracks in the stone, drawn to him like insects to a flame. They bowed low, trembling, their forms flickering in fear.
He raised one hand.
The Voidborn shrieked and scattered.
The King stepped forward, obsidian armour groaning like tectonic plates grinding together.
His voice rolled through the dead Realm — low, resonant, ancient.
"So. You live."
The shadows around him twisted, recoiling from the cold fire burning in his eyes.

He turned toward the Last Realm. Toward Emberhold.
Toward the spark that dared to flare in defiance of the Void.
"Then I will come for you."
He began to walk.
And the Void followed.

CHAPTER FOURTY-EIGHT — THE BROKEN PATH HOME

The forest felt different after the battle.
Not dangerous. Not corrupted. Just... unsettled.
As if the world itself was still trying to understand what had happened.
Ghostlight drifted lazily between the branches, catching on leaves and bark like dew. The air hummed with a faint, lingering vibration — the echo of the Voyager's pulse.
Kaelren led them along the old Emberhold trail, his sword drawn but lowered. The others followed in a loose, uneven formation, each of them bruised, exhausted, and silent in their own way.
The Voyager walked between Bren and Elyndra. He was awake, but pale, his breath uneven, his legs trembling with every step. The runes beneath his skin flickered faintly, like embers struggling to stay lit.
"You need rest," Elyndra murmured.
He shook his head. "If I stop, I'll fall."
Bren tightened his grip on the man's arm. "Then don't stop."
They moved deeper into the woods. The path was familiar, but the forest around it had shifted. A fallen tree blocked the trail — one that hadn't been there the day before.
Lysa crouched beside it, running her fingers along the splintered trunk.
"This wasn't storm damage," she said quietly.
Kaelren examined the break. "No. Something pushed it over."
"Voidborn?" Talla asked.
"Maybe," Kaelren said. "Maybe not."
They stepped around the fallen tree and continued. The forest grew denser, the air cooler. The Voyager stumbled once, catching himself on Bren's shoulder.

"Sorry," he muttered.

"You're fine," Bren said. "You're doing better than I would after falling out of the sky."

Lysa snorted. "You'd be dead."

"Probably," Bren admitted.

The Voyager managed a weak smile.

They walked for another hour before the trail curved toward a small clearing. A stone marker stood at its centre — old, weathered, half buried in moss. Beside it lay a broken lantern, its metal frame twisted, its glass shattered.

Elyndra stopped immediately.

"That's Veilborn make," she said softly.

Kaelren approached it cautiously. "Yours?"

"No," Elyndra said. "Older. Much older."

Talla frowned. "Older than Spiritveil?"

Elyndra didn't answer.

The Voyager crouched beside the lantern. As his fingers brushed the metal, a faint spark of ghostlight flickered across its surface. He jerked his hand back, startled.

"What was that?" Bren asked.

"I don't know," the Voyager whispered. "It felt like... recognition."

Elyndra's expression tightened. "Don't touch it again."

Kaelren straightened. "We're not stopping here. Whatever this is, we don't have the strength to deal with it now."

They moved on.

The clearing faded behind them, swallowed by trees and drifting ghostlight. None of them looked back. None of them saw the faint glow that pulsed once more inside the broken lantern — as if something within it had stirred at the Voyager's touch.

The squad pressed forward, the forest growing darker as the sun dipped behind the ridge. Emberhold was still hours away, but the path was familiar, and the worst — as far as they knew — was behind them.

Kaelren glanced over his shoulder at the Voyager.

"Stay with us," he said quietly.

The Voyager nodded. "I'm trying."

OFFICIAL

And they continued toward the Last Realm, unaware that something far beyond the trees had turned its gaze toward them.

CHAPTER FORTY-NINE — THALEN AGAINST THE COUNCIL

The Council chamber doors slammed open so hard they rattled on their hinges.
Captain Thalen stormed out, jaw clenched, fists balled at his sides. The guards along the hallway straightened instinctively — not out of fear, but because Thalen radiated the kind of fury that made even stone stand at attention.
Behind him, muffled voices rose in argument.
"Captain, you will NOT undermine this Council—" "They disobeyed direct orders—" "They endangered the city—"
Thalen didn't slow.
He didn't trust himself to speak without breaking something.
He reached the courtyard before he finally stopped, bracing his hands on the railing overlooking the training yard. His breath came hard. His pulse hammered in his ears.
Mareth approached quietly.
"That bad?"
Thalen let out a harsh laugh. "They want to brand them deserters."
Mareth's eyes widened. "They wouldn't."
"They would," Thalen snapped. "They're terrified. And when the Council is terrified, they start looking for someone to blame."
"And they chose the squad."
"They always choose the ones who actually do something."
Mareth rested a hand on his arm. "You defended them."
"I nearly tore the chamber apart," Thalen muttered.
"Kaelren warned them the Gate was unstable. Lysa saw the runes flicker. Bren heard the whispers. Rynn felt the pressure. Talla saw the ghostlight shift. Jorren—"
He stopped.
Jorren's haunted eyes flashed through his mind.

"They were right to leave," Thalen said quietly. "And the Council was wrong to try to cage them."

Mareth studied him. "You're worried."

He didn't deny it.

"They've been gone too long," he said. "No message. No signal. No sign."

"Kaelren knows what he's doing."

"That's what scares me," Thalen said. "If something went wrong, he'd send someone back. He hasn't."

Mareth hesitated. "Do you think it's the Gate?"

"I don't know," Thalen said. "And the Council doesn't care. They're too busy arguing about protocols and containment and what the Unwritten might be."

He looked toward the Shattered Gate.

It pulsed faintly, ghostlight drifting from its cracks like dying embers.

Thalen's voice dropped.

"They're out there alone. And I can't help them."

Mareth squeezed his arm.

"They'll come back."

Thalen didn't answer.

He wasn't sure he believed it.

But he hoped.

CHAPTER FIFTY— THE SWARM AND THE FOG

Captain Thalen heard the Voidborn before he saw them.
A shriek tore across the valley — sharp, metallic, wrong — rattling the braziers along the battlements. Thalen spun toward the eastern wall, hand already on his sword.
That sound didn't belong anywhere near Emberhold.
He sprinted up the steps.
"Positions!" he barked. "Eyes east!"
Guards scrambled. Arrows lifted. Shields locked.
Then the tree line erupted.
A swarm of Voidborn burst from the forest, shadows with claws, moving in a tide of black and blue flame. They weren't heading for Emberhold. They swept along the valley's edge like a hunting pack.
Thalen's stomach twisted.
"They're chasing something," he muttered.
A guard swallowed. "Sir... the squad went out that way."
Thalen's pulse hammered.
"Kaelren... what have you run into?"
The swarm shrieked again, the sound echoing off the stone walls.
Then came the hiss.
Soft. Low. Wrong.
A thin mist drifted behind the swarm, sliding across the ground like spilled ink. It wasn't thick. It wasn't fast. It wasn't threatening at first glance.
Just... wrong.
Thalen frowned. "Fog? At this hour?"
The guard beside him rubbed his eyes. "Feels... heavy, sir."
Thalen didn't answer.
He watched the fog creep closer, curling around rocks and roots, hugging the earth like a living shadow.
The first guard slumped against the wall.
"Hey!" Thalen grabbed him. "Stay awake!"

The man blinked slowly, unfocused. "Just... tired..."
Another guard yawned. A third swayed. A fourth dropped his spear.
Thalen's heart kicked hard.
"Everyone on your feet!" he shouted. "Wake up!"
But the fog was already brushing the outer stones of Emberhold.
A wave of exhaustion slammed into him — sudden, heavy, suffocating. His vision blurred. His knees buckled.
No. Not now. Not like this.
He forced himself upright.
"Sound the—"
His voice died.
The courtyard shimmered. The sky darkened. The walls melted into shadow.
Thalen blinked hard.
He was standing in Emberhold — but not as it was.
As it had been.
A memory. A nightmare.
A figure stepped from the fog.
Tall. Broad-shouldered. Eyes burning with ambition and grief.
Thalen's breath caught.
"Rhett..."
His brother smiled — the same smile he wore the night he tried to seize the fortress. The night he turned half the guard against their own people. The night Thalen had been forced to—
"No," Thalen whispered. "You're dead."
Rhett stepped closer.
"You killed me."
Thalen staggered back. "I had no choice."
"You always have a choice," Rhett said. "And you chose power."
"That's not true."
Rhett's smile widened.
"Then why are you still afraid of becoming me?"
The fog thickened.
Rhett dissolved into shadow.

And the squad appeared.
Kaelren falling to his knees. Lysa screaming. Bren reaching for him. Rynn's shield dimming. Talla's spear slipping from her fingers. Jorren dragged into darkness.
Thalen roared and swung his sword through the fog.
The vision shattered.
He collapsed to one knee on the battlements, gasping, sweat dripping down his face. The fog drifted away, thinning, dissolving into the night as if it had never been there.
A guard rushed to him. "Captain! Are you—"
"I'm fine," Thalen snapped, though his hands still shook. "What direction did the swarm go?"
"East," the guard said. "Toward the old trail."
Thalen's heart hammered.
Toward the squad.
He stood, gripping the battlement so hard his knuckles whitened.
"Double the watch," he said. "No one leaves the walls."
"But Captain—"
"No one."
He stared into the darkness where the swarm had vanished.
"Kaelren," he whispered. "Lysa. Bren. All of you... please be alive."
The fog had shown him his brother.
Then it had shown him the squad.
And Thalen understood the message.
He had already lost one family.
He would not lose another.

CHAPTER FIFTY-ONE — THE FIRST OMEN

The fog had not fully lifted.
It clung to Emberhold's stones in thin, fading wisps, drifting like the last remnants of a bad dream. The braziers guttered weakly. The courtyard was quiet — too quiet — as if the fortress were still trying to remember how to breathe.
Captain Thalen jolted awake on the battlements with a gasp.
His heart hammered. His hands shook. Sweat clung to his brow.
For a moment he didn't know where he was.
Rhett's voice still echoed in his skull. *You killed me. You failed them. You'll fail again.*
Thalen pressed a hand to his face, forcing the nightmare back into the dark corner where it belonged.
He looked around.
Guards lay slumped against the walls, groggy and confused. A few were stirring. Others blinked at the fog as if unsure whether they were still dreaming.
"What… happened?" one muttered.
Thalen didn't answer.
Because something else was happening.
The air shifted.
A low hum rippled through the courtyard stones — faint at first, then growing, vibrating through the walls, the braziers, the very bones of the fortress.
Thalen's breath caught.
"No," he whispered. "Not now…"
The Shattered Gate pulsed.
Once. Twice. A third time — harder, deeper, like a heartbeat trying to break free of stone.
Ghostlight bled from its cracks, drifting upward in thin, trembling strands.
The First Omen.

The one the Council feared. The one the Lanterns whispered about. The one Thalen prayed he'd never see.
The Gate screamed.
A sound like a thousand memories tearing at once.
Guards clapped hands over their ears. Braziers flared and died. The sky dimmed as if the sun itself recoiled.
Thalen staggered, gripping the battlement.
"Not again," he muttered. "Not another breach…"
But this wasn't a breach.
This was something else.
Something older.
Something waking.
The ghostlight surged upward in a column of pale fire — then collapsed inward, sucked back into the Gate as if the world had inhaled sharply.
Silence followed.
A silence so deep it felt like the world had stopped.
Then—
"CAPTAIN!"
A shout from the western wall.
Thalen spun.
A guard pointed toward the tree line.
Shapes emerged from the forest.
Seven of them.
Thalen's heart lurched.
Kaelren at the front, limping but upright. Lysa beside him, bow in hand. Rynn supporting Talla. Jorren dragging one leg. Bren waving frantically.
And between Bren and Elyndra—
The stranger.
The man with the faint runes beneath his skin. The man who had fallen through the Gate. The man the Council feared. The man Elyndra had called unwritten.
Thalen didn't wait for the gate to be opened.
He ran.
Down the steps. Across the courtyard. Through the fog.
Toward the people he thought he'd lost.
The gate creaked open just as the squad reached it.
Kaelren stepped through first.

Thalen grabbed him by the shoulders.

"You're alive," he said, voice cracking despite himself.

Kaelren managed a tired smile. "Barely."

Thalen pulled him into a rough, brief embrace — the kind only a man who'd nearly lost a brother could give.

Then he turned to the others.

Lysa grinned weakly. "Miss us?"

"Shut up," Thalen said, pulling her into a hug too.

Bren barrelled into him next. "Captain! We saw—"

"I don't care what you saw," Thalen said, voice thick. "You're here."

Then he saw the stranger.

The man stood unsteadily, supported by Elyndra. His eyes were half-lidded, his breath shallow, the runes beneath his skin flickering like dying embers.

Thalen stepped toward him.

"You," he said quietly. "You're the reason the Gate screamed."

The stranger swallowed. "I… don't know."

Elyndra tightened her grip on him. "He needs rest. And Emberhold needs answers."

Thalen nodded slowly.

"Then let's get both."

He looked up at the Shattered Gate.

The ghostlight still trembled along its cracks.

The First Omen had erupted. The squad had returned. And nothing in the Last Realm would ever be the same.

CHAPTER FIFTY-TWO — THE COUNCIL DESCENDS

The courtyard was still trembling from the First Omen when the shouts cut through Emberhold.
"Open the gate!" "They're back!" "Kaelren's squad — they've returned!"
The words hit the Council Hall like a hammer.
Inside, lanterns guttered violently as the five Councillors lurched out of the nightmare fog's grip. Chairs scraped. Scrolls scattered. A brass inkpot rolled across the stone floor.
Councillor Seris clutched the table, breath shaking. "Archivist preserve us... that fog — it wasn't natural."
Councillor Veylan wiped sweat from his brow. "A Void trick. It had to be. I saw—" He stopped, swallowing hard.
High Councillor Arath didn't wait for explanations. He shoved past them, robes half fastened, eyes wild.
"What did the guard shout?" he demanded. "Who returned?"
A young runner burst in, panting. "Kaelren's squad, sir! They're at the gate!"
Arath froze.
"That's impossible," he whispered. "They were exiled. The fog — the swarm — they should have—"
He didn't finish.
Because the truth hung between them like a blade:
They were never meant to come back.
Arath didn't walk. He ran.
The other Councillors followed, stumbling through the corridors, still half caught between waking and nightmare. Their voices rose in frantic argument as they descended the steps.
"They survived the fog—" "They survived the swarm—" "They brought something back—" "We should have sealed the Gate—" "We should have listened to Elyndra—" "We must contain this—"

No one agreed. But they all ran.

Down the stone steps. Across the courtyard. Toward the open gate.

And there they saw them.

Kaelren — battered, bloodied, but standing. Lysa leaning on her bow. Rynn supporting Talla. Jorren limping. Bren waving weakly. Elyndra steadying the man whose skin still flickered with faint, dying runes.

And Captain Thalen — planted before them like a wall of iron, jaw set, eyes burning with a fury he no longer bothered to hide.

Arath skidded to a halt.

"You—" he gasped. "You're alive."

Kaelren raised an eyebrow. "You sound surprised."

Arath flinched. Because the truth was written across his face.

He hadn't expected them to return. He hadn't wanted them to return.

His gaze snapped to the stranger — the same stranger they had exiled with the squad, the one they had hoped the fog would swallow.

The runes beneath the man's skin pulsed once, faint but unmistakable.

Arath recoiled. "He's still alive?"

Elyndra stepped forward, lantern dimming protectively. "He is under my care. And he is not what you feared."

"You brought him back here?" Arath snapped. "After what the Gate did? After the Omen?"

Thalen stepped between them.

"They didn't bring him," he said. "He fell through the Gate. And they saved him. Again."

Arath's jaw tightened. "They were exiled for a reason."

Thalen's voice dropped to a dangerous calm.

"They were exiled because you were afraid."

Silence rippled through the courtyard.

The Councillors exchanged uneasy glances — shame, fear, and political calculation flickering across their faces.

The stranger swayed, breath shallow. Elyndra tightened her grip on him.

Kaelren stepped forward, voice steady despite the exhaustion in his eyes.

"We need answers. And Emberhold needs to hear what we saw."

Arath hesitated.

Then the Shattered Gate pulsed again — a faint, trembling heartbeat that rippled through the courtyard stones.

Everyone froze.

The First Omen was not finished.

Arath swallowed hard.

"Very well," he said. "Bring them inside."

Thalen exhaled — not relief, not victory, but something close to hope.

The squad had returned. The Council had come running. And the Last Realm was about to learn the truth.

CHAPTER FIFTY-THREE — MARETH'S EXAMINATION

The infirmary had never felt so small.
Mareth Hollowhands moved quickly, clearing space on the central cot as Kaelren and Bren carried the Eternal Voyager inside. Lanternlight flickered across his skin, catching on the faint runes that pulsed beneath the surface like dying embers.
"Lay him down gently," Mareth said. "He's barely holding on."
Kaelren nodded, jaw tight. Bren's hands shook as they lowered the man onto the cot.
Elyndra hovered at his side, lantern dimmed to a soft glow. She looked like she wanted to intervene, but Mareth raised a hand.
"Let me work."
Elyndra stepped back, though her eyes never left the Voyager.
Thalen entered next, followed by the Council — Arath, Seris, Veylan, and the others — crowding the doorway like carrion birds pretending to be concerned.
Mareth ignored them.
She pressed her fingers to the Voyager's throat.
His pulse fluttered like a trapped bird.
"Breathing is shallow," she murmured. "Heart unstable. Runes fading."
Arath cleared his throat. "Is he dangerous?"
Mareth didn't look up. "Everything in Emberhold is dangerous. Including you."
Thalen smothered a grin. The Council bristled.
Mareth leaned closer, studying the runes. They weren't carved. They weren't inked. They weren't scars.
They were alive.
Ghostlight flickered beneath them, dim and uneven, as if the man's very spark was trying to remember how to burn. She brushed her thumb across one of the lines.

The rune pulsed weakly.
The stranger flinched.
Mareth froze.
"Did you see that?" she whispered.
Kaelren nodded. "He reacts to touch."
"Not to touch," Mareth said. "To memory."
Elyndra inhaled sharply.
Mareth continued her examination, voice low and steady.
"His body is stable enough. No broken bones. No internal bleeding. But his spark—"
She hesitated.
Thalen stepped closer. "What about it?"
"It's fractured," Mareth said. "Like a lantern with cracked glass. The light's still there, but it's leaking."
Elyndra closed her eyes. "I felt it. In the courtyard."
Arath stepped forward. "Can he wake?"
Mareth shot him a glare. "He's not a prisoner. He's a patient."
"That didn't answer my question."
"It wasn't meant to."
Thalen moved between them. "Back off, Arath. Let her work."
The Councillor swallowed his anger but didn't retreat far.
Mareth placed her hand over the Voyager's chest. The runes beneath her palm flickered, then steadied — just slightly.
"He's fighting," she murmured. "Something inside him is trying to hold on."
The Voyager's breath hitched.
His fingers twitched.
His lips parted.
A whisper escaped — faint, broken, barely a sound.
"…light…"
Elyndra stepped forward instantly. "He's remembering."
Mareth shook her head. "No. He's reaching."
"For what?" Kaelren asked.
Elyndra's voice was soft. "For whom."
The stranger's eyes fluttered open — just a sliver — and ghostlight shimmered beneath them.

He looked at Elyndra.
Not with recognition. Not with confusion. With longing.
Then he collapsed again, breath shuddering.
Mareth steadied him, pressing a hand to his chest.
"He's burning through himself," she said. "If he keeps fighting like this, he'll tear his spark apart."
Thalen's voice dropped. "What do you need?"
"Quiet," Mareth said. "Space. Time. And for the Council to stop breathing down my neck."
Arath bristled. "We have a right to—"
Thalen turned, eyes cold. "You have a right to leave."
Arath opened his mouth — then closed it.
The Council retreated to the doorway, muttering among themselves.
Mareth exhaled and returned her focus to the Voyager.
"Listen to me," she whispered, leaning close. "Whoever you are... whatever you are... you need to stay with us. Emberhold is hanging by threads. Don't make me lose another one."
The runes beneath his skin flickered — faint, but steady.
Elyndra stepped closer, voice barely a breath.
"He hears you."
Mareth didn't look up.
"I know."
She placed both hands over his heart.
"Let's keep him alive long enough to find out why he came."
Outside, the Shattered Gate pulsed again — a faint, trembling heartbeat that rippled through the stones.
The First Omen was still echoing.
And the stranger's spark flickered in answer.

CHAPTER FIFTY-FOUR — WHAT SHOULD NOT BE SEEN

The infirmary was too small for this many people. Mareth worked over the Voyager's trembling form, hands steady despite the chaos around her. Elyndra hovered close, lantern dimmed to a trembling glow. The squad stood in a tight cluster near the wall, pale and exhausted. And the Council crowded the doorway like vultures.
Arath's voice cut through the room. "Kaelren. You said Emberhold needs to hear what you saw. Speak."
Mareth didn't look up. "Not here. Not now."
Arath ignored her. "We don't have the luxury of waiting."
Kaelren exhaled slowly.
He looked at his squad — at Lysa's trembling fingers, Bren's pale face, Rynn's clenched jaw, Talla's haunted eyes, Jorren's shaking hands.
They had all seen it.
And none of them had slept since.
Kaelren stepped forward.
"It happened on the way back," he said quietly. "After the fog. After the swarm. When the forest went silent."
The lanterns flickered.
Arath folded his arms. "Go on."
Kaelren swallowed.
"We found a man standing in a clearing. Perfectly still. Eyes open. Breathing… wrong."
Lysa's voice cracked. "He wasn't there. Not really."
Rynn nodded. "His eyes were empty. Like someone had scooped the person out of him."
Mareth froze mid-motion.
Elyndra's lantern dimmed further.
Kaelren continued.
"We approached him. Slowly. Carefully. And then—"
He stopped.

His breath hitched.
Bren whispered, "His shadow moved."
The Council stiffened.
Kaelren nodded.
"Not with him. Not like him. It moved on its own. Like it was hungry."
Rynn's voice trembled. "It stretched across the ground like a stain. Like a hole in the world."
"And then it rose," Kaelren said. "Not into a creature. Not into a shape. Into… an absence."
The lanterns guttered violently.
Elyndra closed her eyes.
"Oh no," she whispered. "A Herald."
Arath recoiled. "A what?"
Elyndra didn't answer.
Kaelren pressed on.
"It leaned over the man. And he—"
He swallowed hard.
"He screamed without making a sound. His face twisted. His eyes went wide. And then… he forgot."
Seris frowned. "Forgot what?"
Kaelren's voice broke.
"Everything."
Silence fell like a blade.
"He forgot his name. His past. His family. His fear. His hope. His self."
Lysa wiped her eyes. "And then he just… emptied."
Jorren whispered, "He became a shell."
Kaelren nodded.
"And the Herald turned toward Emberhold."
The room went still.
Even the Voyager's runes flickered in response.
Arath's voice shook. "Why would it come here?"
Elyndra finally spoke.
Her voice was barely a breath.
"Because it was following a trail."
Arath frowned. "A trail of what?"
Elyndra looked at the Voyager.
"Memory."

The runes beneath his skin pulsed once — a single, steady heartbeat.

The Council stepped back.

Mareth whispered, "Archivist preserve us…"

Elyndra's lantern dimmed to a trembling ember.

"The First Omen wasn't the Gate," she said. "It wasn't the fog. It wasn't the swarm."

Her eyes lifted to the Council.

"It was the Herald. And it has found the Last Realm."

The Voyager's body jerked violently.

The runes flared.

And the Shattered Gate pulsed in answer.

CHAPTER FIFTY-FIVE — THE COUNCIL'S FEAR

The Council's arguing rose again — sharp, frantic, overlapping voices that made the infirmary feel even smaller.
But Kaelren wasn't listening anymore.
He was watching Jorren.
The young soldier stood near the far wall, half in shadow, hands trembling so violently he pressed them against his thighs to hide it. His breathing was shallow. His eyes unfocused. Sweat beaded along his brow despite the cold.
He wasn't hearing the Council. He wasn't seeing the Voyager. He was somewhere else.
Somewhere far worse.
Kaelren moved toward him quietly, slipping between Mareth's equipment and the Councillors' robes. Jorren didn't notice until Kaelren was right beside him.
"Jorren," Kaelren murmured. "Look at me."
Jorren flinched.
His eyes snapped up — wide, glassy, terrified.
"Captain," he whispered. "I… I'm fine."
He wasn't.
Kaelren gently took him by the arm and guided him toward the corner, away from the others. Jorren didn't resist. He moved like someone half awake from a nightmare.
When they reached the quietest part of the room, Kaelren lowered his voice.
"What's happening to you?"
Jorren swallowed hard.
His throat bobbed once, twice.
Then he whispered:
"I've felt him before."
Kaelren's breath caught.
"The Herald?" he asked.
Jorren shook his head violently.
"No. Him. The King."

Kaelren froze.

Jorren pressed a shaking hand to his forehead, fingers digging into his hair.

"It was years ago," he whispered. "Before Emberhold. Before the squad. Before I even knew what the Void was." His voice cracked.

"I was in Shadowdeep."

Kaelren's jaw tightened.

Shadowdeep was the Realm that didn't fall with fire or screams. It fell with silence.

Jorren continued, voice trembling.

"I was on the northern ridge when it happened. One moment the world was there — the trees, the frost, the lantern glow in the distance — and the next..."

He swallowed hard.

"...the sound went out."

Kaelren frowned. "Sound?"

"All of it," Jorren whispered. "Wind. Birds. My own breath. It was like the world forgot how to make noise."

His eyes unfocused again, staring at something only he could see.

"And then I felt him."

Kaelren steadied him. "Jorren—"

Jorren's voice dropped to a broken whisper.

"He didn't walk through Shadowdeep. He didn't appear. He didn't arrive. He just... was. Like he'd always been there, and the Realm had only just remembered."

A chill crawled up Kaelren's spine.

Jorren continued.

"I didn't see his face. I didn't see his form. I only saw the shadow he cast — a shadow that didn't match anything around it. A shadow that bent the frost. A shadow that made the trees lean away."

His breath hitched.

"And I felt him inside my skull. Like he was peeling me open. Like he was looking for something."

Kaelren tightened his grip. "Jorren—"

"I thought I imagined it," Jorren whispered. "I told myself it was shock. Fear. The Realm collapsing. But when you said the Herald turned toward Emberhold… when Elyndra said the King is coming…"

He shook his head violently.

"I felt the same presence. The same silence. The same… wrongness."

His voice cracked.

"He's coming here. I know it. I can feel it."

Kaelren leaned in, voice steady as iron.

"Listen to me. You survived Shadowdeep. You survived the fog. You survived the Herald. You're here. You're breathing. You're not alone."

Jorren shook his head.

"You don't understand," he whispered. "In Shadowdeep… he didn't see me. But he will now. He'll know I lived. He'll know I remember."

Kaelren's grip tightened.

"Then he'll have to go through me first."

Jorren blinked — a single tear slipping down his cheek. Kaelren squeezed his shoulder.

"You're not facing him alone this time."

Behind them, the Voyager gasped — a sharp, broken sound — and the runes beneath his skin flared like lightning.

The Gate pulsed in answer.

The Council fell silent.

And Jorren whispered, barely audible:

"He's getting closer."

CHAPTER FIFTY-SIX — THE VOYAGER STIRS

The Shattered Gate pulsed again.
A deep, resonant thrum rolled through the infirmary floor and up their bones. The lanterns flickered. The air thinned. Ghostlight trembled along the walls like frightened birds.
The Voyager convulsed.
Mareth reacted first. "Kaelren—!"
Kaelren and Bren lunged to the cot, pinning the man's shoulders as his back arched with impossible force. His muscles trembled, every line of his body drawn tight as a bowstring.
The runes beneath his skin ignited.
Not flickering. Not fading. Burning.
Lines of molten ghostlight raced across his arms, chest, throat — spirals, fractures, constellations that didn't belong to any Realm.
Jorren stumbled backward, hitting the wall hard.
"Shadows guide me—"
His voice cracked.
The Council recoiled. Seris covered her mouth. Veylan whispered something that sounded like a prayer to no one.
Arath's voice shook. "Is he waking?"
"No," Elyndra said.
Her lantern flared violently, ghostlight swirling around her fingers.
"He's remembering."
The Voyager's eyes snapped open.
Just a sliver.
But enough.
Ghostlight poured from them like tears.
His breath came in ragged, broken gasps — each one scraping against something sharp inside him.
His fingers clawed at the air, reaching for something none of them could see.
"—stop—"

Mareth leaned closer. "Stop what? Talk to me."
His head jerked violently to the side.
"—don't— let— it—"
Kaelren tightened his grip. "You're safe. Stay with us."
The Voyager's eyes locked onto him — unfocused, glowing, terrified.
"—not— safe—"
The room went cold.
Elyndra stepped forward, lantern trembling in her hand.
"He's seeing it," she whispered. "He's seeing the Herald."
The Voyager convulsed again.
The runes along his arms flared in a pattern none of them recognized — spirals breaking into fractures, fractures breaking into lines that looked like broken stars.
His voice tore out of him.
"—memory—"
Seris staggered. "Archivist preserve us…"
The Voyager's breath hitched.
His body went rigid.
And then—
He screamed.
Not a human scream. Not a mortal scream.
A sound like a star collapsing. A sound like the Veil tearing. A sound that made the lanterns gutter and the Gate pulse in answer.
Jorren clamped his hands over his ears, eyes wide with terror.
Kaelren held on, jaw clenched, muscles straining.
Thalen staggered but didn't fall.
Elyndra didn't move.
She stepped closer.
"Listen to me," she whispered. "You are here. You are not lost. You are not alone."
The Voyager's eyes snapped toward her.
Recognition flickered.
Not of her face. Not of her name. But of her light.
His hand reached toward her — shaking, desperate.
"—lantern—"
Elyndra's breath caught.

"Yes," she whispered. "I'm here."
Their fingers brushed.
And the ghostlight in the room surged.
Images flashed across the Voyager's eyes — too fast to understand, too bright to hold:
A bridge of black stone cracking beneath his feet. A crown of antlers burning with cold fire. A hammer striking a star. A book with no pages. A shadow drinking memory. A Realm collapsing into ash. A hand reaching for him through the Veil.
He gasped.
His body jerked.
And he collapsed back onto the cot, chest heaving, runes dimming to a faint, trembling glow.
Silence fell.
Heavy. Absolute.
Mareth checked his pulse with shaking hands.
"He's alive," she whispered. "Barely. But alive."
Elyndra didn't look away from him.
"He wasn't waking," she said softly. "He was remembering."
Arath swallowed hard. "Remembering what?"
Elyndra's lantern dimmed.
"Everything the Void tried to erase."
Kaelren exhaled slowly.
Jorren whispered, voice trembling:
"Shadows guide me… he saw the King, didn't he?"
Elyndra didn't answer.
She didn't need to.
The Shattered Gate pulsed again — a deep, resonant heartbeat.
And the Voyager's fingers twitched in answer.

CHAPTER FIFTY-SEVEN — THE MEMORY THAT SHOULD NOT RETURN

The Voyager's fingers twitched.
Once. Twice. Then curled into a trembling fist.
Elyndra inhaled sharply.
"He's slipping again."
Her lantern brightened, ghostlight swirling around her wrist like a living ribbon. She stepped toward the cot, eyes fixed on the Voyager's face — the flickering runes, the shallow breaths, the faint tremor beneath his skin.
Kaelren moved instinctively to block her path.
"Elyndra, wait—"
She brushed past him, voice steady but strained.
"If I don't go in now, he'll fall into the Herald's pull. And if that happens, we lose him."
The lantern flared.
The air thickened.
The Shattered Gate pulsed again — a slow, heavy heartbeat that made the floor vibrate beneath their boots.
Jorren pressed himself against the wall, whispering, "By the shadows…"
Elyndra placed her hand over the Voyager's heart.
Ghostlight surged.
The infirmary dimmed as if the light itself were being pulled inward.
Kaelren felt the shift before anyone else.
A ripple. A warmth. A pressure behind his eyes.
He staggered.
"Kaelren?" Bren reached for him. "Captain—?"
But the world was already dissolving.
The lanterns blurred. The walls melted into shadow. The Gate's pulse faded into silence.
And suddenly—
He was standing in sunlight.

Warm stone beneath his boots. Golden banners fluttering overhead. The scent of spiced bread drifting on the breeze.
A courtyard.
Familiar.
Forgotten.
And beside him stood the Flameborn King.
Not in ceremonial armour. Not on a throne. Not as a ruler. Just as the man Kaelren had known his whole life.
Tall. Broad-shouldered. Laughing. A simple training tunic. A grin that could light a hall.
"Kaelren," the King said, clapping him on the shoulder.
"You're gripping that spear like it owes you money."
Kaelren flushed. "Sorry, si—"
The King barked a laugh.
"'Sir'? Since when do you call me that? You sound like your father."
Kaelren's chest tightened.
Of course. His father — the General — had been the King's closest friend. Kaelren had grown up under this man's shadow and smile.
The King nudged him with an elbow.
"Come on. I want to show you something."
They crossed the courtyard to where a young recruit struggled with a training hammer nearly as tall as he was. The boy's stance was wrong, his feet too close together, his arms shaking with effort.
"Tallen!" the King shouted, voice carrying across the yard. "Shift your stance! You're fighting the hammer, not wielding it!"
The boy — Tallen, earnest and overeager — froze, then shuffled his feet awkwardly.
"Like this, Your Majesty?"
The King grinned. "Better. Now lift."
Tallen tried.
The hammer rose.
Barely.
But it rose.
The King beamed like Tallen had just lifted a mountain.
Kaelren couldn't help smiling.

211

OFFICIAL

"You always see the best in them," he said quietly.
The King shrugged. "Someone must. Your father says the same thing. The world is cruel enough without us adding to it."
Tallen wobbled, nearly dropped the hammer, then caught it again.
"I'm doing it!" he shouted, voice cracking.
"You are," the King said warmly. "And tomorrow you'll do it better."
Kaelren felt something warm bloom in his chest — a feeling he hadn't felt in years.
The King turned to him, expression softening.
"You're a good man, Kaelren. Better than you think. One day, you'll lead them. And they'll follow you because they trust you — not because they fear you."
Kaelren swallowed hard.
The King smiled.
"Come on. Before Tallen drops that thing on his foot and your father blames me."
The memory shattered.
Kaelren gasped, stumbling back into the infirmary.
Elyndra was still bent over the Voyager, lantern blazing, ghostlight pouring from her hand into his chest. Her eyes were closed, her breathing shallow — she was deep inside. She didn't notice Kaelren at all.
Jorren did.
"Captain?" he whispered. "What happened?"
Kaelren wiped his eyes quickly, before anyone could see.
"Nothing," he said. "Just... a memory."
A good one. A forgotten one. A piece of his heart he didn't know he'd lost.
The Voyager jerked beneath Elyndra's hand.
The lantern flared.
The Gate pulsed again — louder, heavier, closer.
And Elyndra whispered, voice strained:
"I'm in."

CHAPTER FIFTY-EIGHT — THE FRACTURED SPARK

Ghostlight swallowed Elyndra whole.
One heartbeat she was in the infirmary, her hand pressed to the Voyager's chest.
The next—
She was falling.
Not through darkness. Not through air. Through **memory**.
Shards spiralled around her like broken mirrors:
A lantern drifting through Spiritveil fog. A hammer striking molten starmetal. A sky citadel chained to lightning. A river of magma beneath a burning city. A titan sleeping beneath ice. A book with no pages. A crown of fire collapsing into ash. A Realm dissolving into nothing.
She hit the ground—
Except it wasn't ground.
It was a surface made of light, rippling like water, shifting beneath her feet.
Elyndra steadied herself.
"Voyager?" she whispered.
A figure stood ahead of her.
The Voyager.
Exactly as he was in the waking world.
But flickering.
Not into different ages — he had none. Not into different bodies — he had only one.
But into **different lives**.
A scholar, ink staining his fingers as he wrote in a book with no pages — *Lightforge*. A soldier, armour scorched by a war no Realm remembered — *Stormreach*. A wanderer, dust on his boots from a desert that no longer existed — *Metalcrown's outer wastes*. A healer, blood on his hands from a stranger he could not save — *Spiritveil's lantern paths*. A ghostlight walker drifting through memories — *Spiritveil again*. A Realm-walker stepping through a Gate that no

longer stood — *the Ascension era*. A Shardborn silhouette surrounded by collapsing possibility — *the Unstable Shard*. A Soulforged echo lifting a hammer of starmetal and flame — *the First Spark's memory*.

All the same man. All the same age. All the same face.

Elyndra's breath caught.

"You've lived so many lives…"

The Voyager didn't react.

He didn't see what she saw.

His form flickered again — scholar, soldier, wanderer, healer — each one a life he had lived, a burden he had carried, a role he had worn.

But his eyes were blank.

Empty.

He whispered:

"I don't remember."

Elyndra stepped closer.

"You're not supposed to. These are echoes. The spark remembers what the mind cannot."

The scholar echo wrote furiously in a book with no pages. The soldier echo stood guard over a burning gate. The wanderer echo walked alone across a desert of broken glass. The healer echo held a dying stranger in his arms. The Soulforged echo lifted a hammer glowing with the First Spark.

Elyndra felt her heart twist.

"You've been so many things…"

The Voyager trembled.

"I don't know who I am."

The world around them dimmed.

The rippling light beneath her feet turned black.

Elyndra reached out, lantern glowing softly.

"You are all of them. And none of them. You are the one who survived."

The soldier echo turned, eyes hollow.

"No," he said. "I am the one who was unmade."

A shockwave tore through the space.

Elyndra staggered, shielding her lantern as ghostlight exploded outward.

When the light cleared—
All the echoes were gone.
Only the Voyager remained.
Kneeling. Shaking. Hands pressed to the ground.
Elyndra moved toward him.
"Look at me," she whispered. "You're safe."
He lifted his head.
Ghostlight streamed from his eyes like tears.
"No," he whispered. "Not here."
The world cracked.
A sound like stone splitting. A sound like a Realm collapsing. A sound like a scream swallowed by the Void.
Elyndra grabbed his shoulders.
"Tell me what you see."
The Voyager's voice broke.
"I see the moment I was unmade."
The world shattered.

CHAPTER FIFTY-NINE — THE UNMAKING

The world shattered.
Light fractured into a thousand spiralling shards, each one reflecting a different Realm, a different sky, a different future that never came to pass.
Elyndra fell through them.
Not physically. Not bodily. Through **memory**.
Through the moment the Voyager was unmade.
The light around her twisted, bent, and then—
It became a Realm.
A Realm that should not exist. A Realm that lasted only moments in creation.
The Unstable Shard.
Its landscape rippled like liquid thought. Mountains rose and collapsed in the same breath. Rivers flowed upward. Stars flickered in and out of existence like dying candles.
Reality had no anchor here.
And in the centre of it—
The Voyager stood.
Exactly as he was now.
Same age. Same face. Same form.
Because he had never been anything else.
Elyndra whispered, "This is where you were born…"
The air trembled.
The Voyager didn't turn.
He stared at the horizon, where the sky was tearing open — not with darkness, but with **possibility collapsing**.
The Shard was dying.
It had been dying since the moment it formed.
Elyndra stepped closer.
"What happened to you here?"
The Voyager's voice was barely a breath.
"I remember… heat."
The ground beneath them rippled like molten glass.
"I remember… sound."

A distant ringing — like a hammer striking starmetal — echoed across the collapsing Realm.
"I remember... light."
A flare of radiance burst across the sky, blinding and beautiful and wrong.
"And then..."
His voice broke.
"...I remember nothing."
The sky split open.
Not into darkness.
Into **Void**.
Not emptiness. Not shadow. Not death.
Awareness.
A vast, ancient, formless consciousness pressing against the edges of the dying Realm.
The Void did not speak.
It did not need to.
Its presence was a pressure behind the eyes, a weight on the soul, a cold hand closing around the spark of identity.
Elyndra staggered.
The Voyager fell to his knees.
The Void reached for him.
Not physically. Not with hands.
With **unmaking**.
The air around him warped. His outline flickered. His spark screamed — not in sound, but in memory.
Elyndra reached for him.
"Hold on—"
The Void pressed harder.
The Voyager's voice cracked.
"It took something from me."
Elyndra's lantern flared violently.
"What did it take?"
The world shook.
The sky tore wider.
The Void pressed closer.
And the Voyager whispered:
"My name."
The Realm convulsed.

The ground split open. The sky collapsed inward. The light shattered into spirals of broken possibility.

Elyndra grabbed him, pulling him close, anchoring him with ghostlight.

"Stay with me—"

But the Void was already inside him.

Not possessing. Not corrupting.

Erasing.

The Voyager screamed — a sound of memory tearing, identity collapsing, a soul being rewritten by silence.

His spark flickered.

His eyes went blank.

His voice broke into a whisper:

"I was someone…"

The Void swallowed the rest.

The Shard collapsed.

Light imploded.

Memory dissolved.

And Elyndra was thrown backward through the fracture—

—back into the ghostlight —back into the spark —back into the present

As the last echo of his voice whispered:

"…and then I wasn't."

CHAPTER SIXTY — THE RETURN TO THE BODY

Elyndra hit the world like a falling star.

Her body arched off the floor, ghostlight bursting from her mouth in a silent scream. The lantern in her hand flared white-hot, guttered, then flared again — as if fighting something she had dragged back with her.

"Elyndra!" Kaelren lunged forward, catching her before her head struck the stone.

Her eyes were open.

But she wasn't seeing the room.

She was seeing the collapse of a Realm. She was seeing the moment the Voyager was unmade. She was seeing the Void reach for him.

Her voice came out as a whisper of pure terror.

"Don't let it take him…"

Kaelren held her tighter.

"Elyndra. Elyndra, look at me."

Her breath hitched.

Her pupils snapped into focus.

She gasped — a sharp, broken sound — and clutched Kaelren's tunic with trembling fingers.

"He doesn't know," she whispered. "He doesn't know what he lost."

Kaelren swallowed hard.

"What did you see?"

Before she could answer—

The Voyager convulsed.

Every lantern in the infirmary flared at once.

The runes beneath his skin ignited in a pattern none of them had ever seen — not spirals, not fractures, not constellations.

Something older.

Something closer to the First Spark.

Mareth stumbled backward. "By the Realms—"

The Shattered Gate pulsed.

Once. Twice. A third time — harder, deeper — shaking dust from the rafters.

Jorren pressed himself against the wall. "It's reacting to him—"

"No," Elyndra whispered, still half inside the memory. "It's answering him."

Kaelren turned sharply.

"Answering what?"

Elyndra looked at the Voyager — really looked — and her face went pale.

"He called out."

The room went still.

Even the lanterns seemed to hold their breath.

Arath's voice trembled. "Called out to who?"

Elyndra shook her head slowly.

"Not who."

Her lantern flickered.

"What."

The Voyager's back arched.

His mouth opened in a soundless cry.

Ghostlight poured from his eyes like tears.

And then—

He inhaled.

A sharp, ragged, living breath.

Mareth's hands flew to her mouth.

"He's waking—"

"No," Elyndra said, voice trembling. "Not waking."

Kaelren stepped closer, heart pounding.

"Then what is he doing?"

Elyndra's lantern dimmed to a single trembling ember.

"He's remembering."

The Voyager's fingers twitched.

His lips parted.

And for the first time since he fell through the Shattered Gate—

He spoke.

One word. One syllable. A fragment of a name stolen from him. A sound older than the Realms. A sound the Void tried to erase.

The Voyager whispered:

"—Kael…"

The room froze.

Kaelren's breath caught in his throat. Elyndra's eyes widened in horror.

"No," she whispered. "Not that memory. Not yet."

The Shattered Gate pulsed again — violently this time — as if something on the other side had heard the name. And answered.

CHAPTER SIXTY-ONE — THE NAME THAT SHOULD NOT BE SPOKEN

The room froze.
The lanterns stopped flickering. The air stopped moving. Even the dust motes hung suspended, as if the world itself had forgotten how to breathe.
Kaelren stared at the Voyager, heart hammering in his chest.
"…Kael…?"
It wasn't a full name. Not even half a name. Just a syllable.
But it hit Kaelren like a blow.
He stepped back without meaning to.
"Why," he whispered, "why would he say my name."
Elyndra's hand shot out, gripping his wrist with surprising strength.
"No," she said sharply. "Not your name. Not you."
Kaelren blinked. "What are you talking about."
But Elyndra wasn't looking at him.
She was looking at the Voyager.
And she was terrified.
"Kaelren," she whispered, "that wasn't your name he spoke. It was a memory of a name. A name that begins the same way."
Kaelren's stomach dropped.
"You're saying—"
"I'm saying," Elyndra cut in, "that he remembered something he was never meant to remember."
The Shattered Gate pulsed.
Once. Twice. A third time — violently — sending a crack racing up the stone arch.
Arath stumbled backward. "The Gate— it's destabilizing."
Jorren pressed himself against the wall. "Something's pushing through—"

"No," Elyndra said, voice trembling. "Something is listening."
The lanterns guttered.
The temperature dropped.
A pressure filled the room — not a presence, not a voice, but a *noticing*. As if something vast and ancient had turned its attention toward Emberhold.
Kaelren drew his blade without thinking.
"What did he call."
Elyndra shook her head.
"He didn't call anything. He remembered something. And the Void heard it."
The Voyager convulsed.
His back arched. His fingers clawed at the air. Ghostlight poured from his eyes like tears.
Mareth rushed forward. "Hold him—"
Kaelren and Bren pinned him to the cot as his body shook with impossible force.
The runes beneath his skin ignited again — but this time, they weren't random.
They formed a pattern.
A spiral. A fracture. A crown. A flame.
Elyndra's breath caught.
"No," she whispered. "Not that memory. Not now."
Kaelren looked at her sharply.
"What does it mean."
Elyndra swallowed hard.
"It means he's remembering the one person he should never remember."
The Shattered Gate pulsed again — a deep, resonant thrum that rattled the lanterns.
A hairline crack split the arch.
Arath shouted, "The Gate is responding to him."
"No," Elyndra said, voice barely audible. "It's responding to the name."
Kaelren's grip tightened on the Voyager's shoulders.
"What name."
Elyndra looked at him with eyes full of sorrow.
"The name he lost."

The Voyager's lips moved.
A whisper escaped.
Not a word. Not a name. A sound like a memory trying to claw its way back into existence.
"—Kael...ra—"
The Shattered Gate screamed.
A sound like metal tearing. A sound like a Realm collapsing. A sound like the Void pressing its face against the Veil.
Elyndra lunged forward, slamming her lantern against the floor.
Ghostlight exploded outward, forming a barrier of shimmering white flame.
"STOP."
The Gate's pulse faltered.
The crack froze.
The pressure in the room eased — barely.
Elyndra knelt beside the Voyager, her voice trembling.
"Don't speak it," she whispered. "Not here. Not now. Not with the Gate open."
The Voyager's eyes fluttered.
He whispered one last broken syllable.
"—Kael...ra—"
Elyndra slapped her hand over his mouth.
The lantern flared.
The Gate went silent.
The room collapsed into stillness.
Kaelren stared at her, breath shaking.
"What," he whispered, "did he almost say."
Elyndra closed her eyes.
And for the first time since she arrived in Emberhold—
She looked afraid.
"His name," she said softly. "Or the beginning of it."
Kaelren swallowed.
"And why is that dangerous."
Elyndra opened her eyes.
She didn't say the truth — *because the Void remembers it too.*
She said:

"Because if he speaks it before he's ready… the Void will come for him."

The Shattered Gate pulsed once more — a slow, hungry heartbeat.

And somewhere beyond it…

Something answered.

CHAPTER SIXTY-TWO — THE SCREAM THAT ANSWERS

The Herald froze mid-stride.
Something shifted in the fabric of the Last Realm — a tremor, a memory, a wound reopening. His head snapped toward Emberhold as if yanked by an invisible chain. For a heartbeat he stood perfectly still, spine rigid, eyes wide with a recognition he should not have possessed.
Then his body arched.
And the scream tore out of him.
It wasn't a sound meant for mortal ears. It was metal shearing apart. It was a Realm collapsing in on itself. It was the Void remembering hunger.
The sky split under the force of it.
Across the dead plains, the ground convulsed. Fissures ripped open, spilling shadows like blood. Winged shapes burst from the clouds in a frenzy. Crawling horrors dragged themselves from the dust, limbs bending wrong, jaws unhinging as they shrieked in answer.
They didn't hesitate. They didn't choose. They swarmed. Drawn to the echo of a single fractured syllable. Drawn to the spark that had dared to speak it. Drawn to **Kael—**
The Herald lifted his head, voice a rasp of ash and memory.
"He remembers."
And the Voidborn surged toward Emberhold like a tide of living night.
The Shattered Gate buckled as if struck from within. Runes spasmed. Ghostlight bled from the seams. Cracks spider-webbed across the arch, pulsing in time with something that was not a heartbeat.
Arath staggered back from the Gate. "Something's forcing its way through—"
Elyndra's lantern flared violently.
"No," she whispered. "It's coming for him."

The Voyager collapsed back onto the cot, the half-spoken syllable still trembling on his lips.
Kaelren didn't hesitate. He drew his Veil blade, ghostlight rippling along the edge.
"Positions!"
The fortress shuddered under the first impact. Dust rained from the rafters. Lanterns swung wildly. A second blow followed — harder — then a third that cracked the outer wall.
Bren charged toward the breach, war hammer raised. Rynn braced beside the doorway, shield glowing with Veil light. Talla spun her spear, the tip leaving a trail of white fire. Lysa climbed a fallen pillar, bow already drawn. Jorren sprinted ahead, twin blades flashing. Mareth knelt beside a wounded guard, hands glowing with desperate urgency.
The fourth impact shattered the wall.
A jagged hole tore open, and the first wave of Voidborn spilled through — shrieking, writhing, clawing at the stone.
Elyndra's breath caught.
"The Herald heard him."
Kaelren's grip tightened.
"Heard what."
"The beginning of the name," she whispered. "The Void remembers it. The Herald remembers it. They all do."
The Voidborn surged.
Kaelren stepped forward.
"Hold the line."
Bren's hammer crashed into the first creature, ghostlight exploding on impact. Rynn slammed his shield into another, sending a shockwave of pale fire through its body. Talla's spear punched through a shadow beast's chest. Lysa's arrows streaked like falling stars. Jorren carved through the swarm with lethal precision. Mareth dragged the wounded to cover, hands trembling with effort.
Elyndra stood over the Voyager, lantern blazing, ghostlight forming a protective circle around them both.
The Shattered Gate pulsed again — not in warning.
In answer.
The Second Omen had begun.

CHAPTER SIXTY-THREE — THE SECOND OMEN

The fortress gates buckled under the next wave.
Voidborn shadows poured through the cracks. Winged horrors dove from above. Crawling shapes swarmed the battlements. The air filled with shrieks and ghostlight and the thunder of collapsing stone.
Kaelren cut down a Voidborn lunging for Mareth. Jorren pivoted, twin blades crossing in a scissor strike. Bren smashed another into the ground. Rynn held the line, shield braced. Talla spun her spear in a blazing arc. Lysa's arrows rained down like white fire.
But this wave was different.
It wasn't wild. It wasn't chaotic. It was **directed**.
Every creature turned its head the same way — toward the Voyager.
Elyndra's lantern flared brighter, ghostlight spilling across the floor in frantic pulses.
"Stay back!" she cried, her voice echoing with Spiritveil's power.
A wave of ghostlight burst outward, forcing the nearest Voidborn to recoil. Their bodies hissed where the light touched them, shadows peeling like burnt skin.
But they didn't retreat.
They circled.
Waiting.
Listening.
The Gate pulsed again — violently — as if something on the other side had heard the syllable the Voyager whispered.
And answered.
A deep vibration rolled through the stones beneath their feet. Dust drifted from the rafters. The lanterns hanging from the beams flickered wildly, their flames bending toward the Gate as if pulled by an unseen tide.

Arath stumbled backward, eyes wide. "It's reacting to him. To the stranger. To the—"

"The Voyager," Elyndra snapped, her lantern blazing. "Say his name."

Arath flinched as if struck.

Kaelren didn't look away from the battle. "Elyndra — what does this mean."

Elyndra swallowed, her voice trembling despite her effort to steady it.

"It means the Second Omen is here."

The words hung in the air like a death sentence.

A low groan echoed through the fortress walls — not stone, not wind, but something older. Something waking.

Kaelren's grip tightened on his blade. "What does the Second Omen do."

Elyndra's eyes lifted toward the ceiling, toward the sky beyond it.

"It means the sky is about to bleed."

But she wasn't finished.

She stepped closer to the Voyager, lantern trembling in her hand.

"And it means the Herald is no longer searching."

Her voice dropped to a whisper.

"He's coming."

The Gate convulsed — a violent, shuddering lurch that sent cracks racing across the arch. Ghostlight bled from the seams in frantic pulses, each one brighter than the last.

The Voidborn shrieked in unison.

Not in hunger.

In anticipation.

Kaelren felt the temperature drop. Frost formed along the edges of his blade. His breath misted in the air.

Jorren's eyes widened. "Captain... the air—"

"I know," Kaelren said.

The fortress groaned again, louder this time. A sound like a heartbeat — but wrong. Too slow. Too heavy. Too ancient.

Elyndra's lantern dimmed, then flared violently.

"The Second Omen marks the moment the Void stops whispering," she said.

A crack split the sky above the fortress — a thin, jagged line of red light.

"And starts screaming."

The Voidborn surged.

Kaelren raised his blade.

"Hold the line."

And the sky began to tear.

CHAPTER SIXTY-FOUR — THE SKY BLEEDS

The first drop fell like molten iron.
It hissed as it struck the stone, burning a hole straight through the battlement. Another drop followed. Then another. Then the sky tore open entirely, spilling a curtain of crimson light that fell in burning streaks.
The air tasted like iron and smoke and something older — something wrong.
Talla stared upward, her voice barely a breath. "Veil... please..."
But the prayer drowned beneath the roar of the Voidborn. They hit the walls like a living storm.
The north side collapsed first. Stone exploded outward as shadows poured through the breach, shrieking with a hunger that felt ancient. Thalen met them head-on, Veil axe blazing, carving a path through the first wave. Hale slammed his shield into a lunging horror, ghostlight rippling across the impact.
Behind them, two young recruits — Mira and Torren — tried to hold the line.
They never stood a chance.
A winged Voidborn dove straight into Torren, talons punching through his chest. Mira screamed his name, thrusting her spear wildly, but another creature latched onto her arm and dragged her toward the swarm.
"TORREN!" she sobbed, reaching for him even as Thalen yanked her back.
Torren's scream cut off like a candle snuffed.
Mira's voice broke into a sound that wasn't a scream, wasn't a sob — something hollow, something lost.
Thalen shoved her behind him. "MOVE!"
But she kept reaching for the place where Torren had been, fingers trembling, as if she could pull him back from nothing.
She couldn't.

No one could.

The South Wall Falls
Rynn braced his shield against the gate, ghostlight trembling across its surface. Three Voidborn slammed into him at once. His boots slid. His shield cracked.
"Rynn!" Bren roared, sprinting toward him.
A creature leapt onto Rynn's back. He screamed — a raw, human sound — as Bren tore it off and smashed it into the ground.
Rynn collapsed to his knees, shaking, breath ragged.
"I'm— I'm fine—" he lied.
He wasn't.
Mareth slid beside him, hands glowing, voice trembling.
"Stay still— please— stay still—"
But the bleeding sky made the shadows stronger. Faster. Hungrier.
And the fortress was breaking.

The Moment That Shatters Them
Jorren was everywhere at once.
Twin blades flashing. Feet gliding across stone. Every movement precise, controlled, beautiful.
He fought like someone who had already accepted death — but refused to let it take anyone else first.
Kaelren saw it. He always saw it.
"Jorren! Fall back!" he shouted.
But Jorren didn't fall back.
He stepped forward.
He cut down three Voidborn in a single breath, spun, severed a fourth—
And the sky screamed.
A winged Voidborn dropped from above, talons extended.
Lysa's voice tore from her throat. "JORREN!"
He turned — too late.
The creature struck him with the force of a falling star. Its talons punched into his chest. His body jerked. His breath caught.
His blades fell from his hands.

Kaelren sprinted toward him, shouting something wordless, something broken — something that didn't sound like a captain. It sounded like a man losing someone he loved.
Talla hurled her spear. It clipped the creature's wing. The Voidborn crashed to the ground, dragging Jorren with it. Bren was there in an instant, hammer rising, smashing the creature's skull.
But Jorren wasn't moving.
Kaelren dropped to his knees beside him.
"Jorren— Jorren, look at me—"
Jorren's eyes fluttered. He tried to breathe. Failed. Tried again.
His hand lifted — shaking — reaching for Kaelren's arm. Kaelren grabbed it, gripping tight, refusing to let go.
Jorren's voice came out cracked, barely a whisper.
"...I was finally... gonna tell you..."
Kaelren leaned closer, heart pounding. "Tell me now. Jorren, tell me—"
Jorren swallowed, blood on his lips.
"...about... before Emberhold..."
His eyes flicked toward the bleeding sky, toward the Voidborn tearing through the walls.
"...about him..."
Kaelren froze.
"Who?"
Jorren's breath hitched — a sound of pain and memory colliding.
"...the Harrowed King..."
Kaelren's stomach dropped.
Jorren's fingers tightened weakly around his wrist.
"...you need to... beware him..."
His voice cracked.
"...he wasn't always... like that..."
A tear slid down Kaelren's cheek.
"Jorren—"
Jorren's eyes unfocused for a moment, drifting somewhere far away — somewhere Kaelren couldn't follow.
"...I thought... I'd never have to see him again..."

His breath shuddered.

"…guess I was right…"

His hand slipped from Kaelren's grip.

His chest stilled.

And the world went silent.

Kaelren didn't move.

Didn't breathe.

Didn't blink.

He just stared at Jorren's face, as if waiting for him to finish the sentence he'd been holding for years.

Talla sobbed behind him — a sound that cracked. Lysa collapsed to her knees, bow falling from her hands. Rynn whispered a broken prayer. Mareth covered her mouth, shaking. Bren bowed his head, hammer trembling.

Even Thalen — unshakeable, unbreakable Thalen — closed his eyes.

Elyndra whispered, "The Second Omen always takes someone. But this… this is cruel."

Kaelren rose slowly, blood on his hands, grief burning like fire in his chest.

He lifted his blade.

And when he spoke, his voice was not a shout.

It was a promise.

"They will pay for him."

The sky bled harder.

The Gate pulsed like a dying heart.

And the Herald drew closer.

CHAPTER SIXTY-FIVE — THE GATE BREAKS

The sky bled harder as Jorren's body cooled on the stone. Kaelren didn't remember standing. He didn't remember lifting his blade. He only remembered the sound of Jorren's last breath — the way it had hit him like a blade between the ribs — and the hollow, ringing silence that followed. There was no time to grieve. The Second Omen didn't allow grief.

The courtyard shook as another wave of Voidborn slammed into the walls. Crimson rain hissed against the stone, each drop burning like acid. The air tasted of iron and smoke and something older — something wrong.

"Kaelren!" Elyndra shouted over the roar. "The Gate — it's failing!"

He turned just in time to see the runes carved into the Shattered Gate flicker, dim, and crack. Ghostlight sputtered like a dying flame. The arch trembled as if something inside it was clawing to get out.

But Kaelren couldn't reach it.

Three Voidborn lunged at him at once, claws scraping across his armour. He drove his Veil blade through the first, spun, severed the second, and slammed his shoulder into the third — but they kept coming.

Everywhere he looked, the squad was drowning.

Bren was pinned beneath a collapsed archway, hammer swinging in brutal arcs as Voidborn crawled over the rubble toward him. Rynn knelt behind a shattered shield, whispering a prayer he couldn't remember the words to. Talla fought with one hand pressed to her bleeding ribs, teeth gritted against the pain. Mareth dragged a wounded soldier away from the Gate, tears streaking her face. Lysa stood atop a broken pillar, drawing and releasing dark arrows as fast as she could breathe — each one forming like a shard of night, streaking into the swarm below. She wasn't running out. She was running down.

And Mira — little Mira Halden — clutched a spear she barely knew how to hold, shaking so hard she could barely stand. She had seen Jorren die. She had seen the squad break. She had seen Kaelren fall to his knees beside the body of a man she barely knew but everyone loved.

If he could die… If they could break… What chance did she have?

"Mira!" Talla shouted, blocking a Voidborn that lunged for her. "Stay behind me!"

"I'm trying!" Mira cried, voice cracking. "I'm trying—"

She thrust her spear forward — clumsy, desperate — and by some miracle, the tip pierced a Voidborn's throat. It dissolved into smoke, leaving her staring at her own trembling hands.

"I killed it," she whispered. "I—"

A shadow fell over her.

Not a Voidborn.

Something worse.

The Herald.

He stood at the far end of the courtyard, half shrouded in bleeding light, half shrouded in his own darkness. His presence bent the air around him. The ground seemed to sag beneath his feet. The world dimmed.

Mira's breath hitched. Her spear slipped from her fingers. She didn't know him. But she knew what he was.

Everyone did.

Thalen saw her freeze. He saw the Herald's gaze settle on her. And something inside him snapped.

He shoved Mira behind him and roared — a sound torn from the bottom of his soul.

"YOU DON'T TOUCH HER!"

He charged.

But Kaelren didn't see it. Not yet.

He was locked in a brutal struggle with the Voidborn, his Veil blade flashing in desperate arcs. One creature clung to his back, claws digging into his armour. Another snapped at his throat. A third lunged for Mareth, forcing him to intercept.

"Kaelren!" Mareth cried. "I can't— I can't hold—"
"I'm coming!" he shouted, but he wasn't.
He couldn't.
And the Voyager — the one who had cleared entire fields of Voidborn before — was nowhere.
"Where is he?" Lysa gasped between shots. "Where is the Voyager? He should be— he should be—"
"He's not coming!" Bren roared. "Forget him!"
But they couldn't.
Because if the Voyager wasn't coming...
Then no one was.
The Gate screamed.
A shockwave of ghostlight blasted outward, throwing everyone off their feet. Kaelren hit the ground hard. Bren crashed beside him. Lysa slammed into a pillar. Talla rolled across the stone, coughing blood.
Mira hit the ground with a cry, hands over her ears.
The Gate's arch split down the centre.
A crack opened — wide, jagged, glowing with impossible darkness.
Not shadow. Not absence. Not night.
Void.
A cold wind poured through the fracture, carrying whispers that scraped across the mind like broken glass.
Mira screamed, "MAKE IT STOP—!"
Thalen dragged her back again. "Don't listen! DON'T LISTEN!"
But the whispers were everywhere.
Inside their skulls. Behind their eyes. Under their skin.
Elyndra's lantern flickered violently as she turned toward the sound of Thalen's roar.
Her eyes widened.
"THALEN, NO!"
He didn't hear her.
"THALEN!" she screamed again, voice cracking. "YOUR WEAPON CAN'T HURT HIM!"
Thalen didn't stop.
He didn't even slow.

He swung his steel axe in a wide arc, sparks flying as it carved through the air. The Herald moved to intercept — but Thalen twisted, redirected, and slammed the axe into the Herald's side with a roar that shook the courtyard.

The blow would have split a warhorse in half. It would have shattered stone. It would have killed anything born of flesh.

The Herald staggered.

Just a fraction.

Just enough for Thalen to see it.

He grinned — bloody, wild, triumphant.

"Not so untouchable after all."

Elyndra's voice broke.

"ONLY VEIL WEAPONS CAN AFFECT HIM!"

Kaelren froze mid-strike.

His heart lurched.

His stomach dropped.

He spun toward Thalen — toward the Herald — toward the impossible fight unfolding behind him.

"THALEN!" he shouted, voice raw. "STOP—!"

He ran.

But he was too far. Too slow. Too late.

The Herald caught the axe.

Not between two fingers.

With his whole hand.

He held it there, unmoving, as Thalen strained, muscles bulging, teeth gritted, veins standing out along his neck.

Thalen roared and pushed harder.

The Herald didn't move.

Not an inch.

Then — with a sound like the world cracking — the Herald squeezed.

The steel axe shattered.

Fragments scattered across the stone.

Thalen stared at the broken haft in his hands.

Not in disbelief. Not in fear.

In fury.

"You think that stops me?"

He dropped the haft and swung his fist.

It connected with the Herald's jaw.
The impact echoed.
The Herald's head snapped to the side.
For a moment — a single, impossible moment — the Herald turned to look at him.
Not with annoyance. Not with anger.
With recognition.
As if acknowledging:
You are worth killing properly.
The Herald raised his hand.
Thalen didn't flinch.
He stood tall. He stood proud. He stood like a man who had held the line his entire life.
"Come on then," he growled. "Do it."
The Herald's hand pressed against his chest.
Thalen gasped — a sound torn from the bottom of his soul — as the Herald pulled.
Not flesh. Not blood.
Memory.
Thalen's eyes widened. His breath hitched. His knees buckled.
Mira screamed, "THALEN—!"
He turned his head toward her — barely — eyes already fading.
"...little runner..."
His voice was a ghost.
"...don't... forget... yourself..."
Then the Herald pulled the last of him away.
And Thalen collapsed — empty, hollow, unmade.
Not killed.
Erased.
Kaelren reached him two seconds too late.
Two seconds that would haunt him forever.
The world slowed. The sound faded. The courtyard blurred.
Kaelren saw Thalen's body on the stone.
And time cracked open.

He saw himself years ago, staggering through Emberhold's gate, bleeding, hunted, half dead. Guards shouting. Steel drawn. Suspicion thick in the air.

And Thalen — younger, broad-shouldered, steady as a mountain — stepping between Kaelren and the blades.

"Hold," he barked. "He's Flameborn, not Voidborn. Look at him — he's dying."

Thalen kneeling beside him. Lifting his head. Saying the words that saved him:

"You're safe now. You're in Emberhold."

Kaelren remembered the arena. The day he earned the title of Leading Commander. The day he faced Thalen in the ring.

Thalen had fought like a storm — relentless, powerful, unyielding. Kaelren had fought like a man with nothing left to lose.

When Kaelren finally disarmed him, pinning him to the sand, Thalen had stared up at him — chest heaving, pride wounded — and then he'd laughed.

"Damn you, Flameborn," he'd said. "You earned it."

He had stood first. He had offered Kaelren his hand. He had shouted to the watching soldiers:

"THIS IS YOUR COMMANDER!"

And now he was gone.

The Herald turned toward Kaelren.

And the world seemed to shrink.

Elyndra's voice trembled as she whispered:

"The Second Omen is complete."

Kaelren lifted his Veil blade with shaking hands.

"What's the Third."

Elyndra looked at him with hollow eyes.

"The Third Omen," she said, "is when he speaks."

The Herald opened his mouth.

And the world held its breath.

CHAPTER SIXTY-SIX — WHEN THE HERALD SPEAKS

The courtyard was still trembling from Thalen's fall when Kaelren rose.
He didn't feel the pain in his ribs. He didn't feel the blood running down his arm. He didn't feel the weight of the Veil blade in his hand.
He only felt the absence.
Thalen's absence.
The Herald stood where Thalen had fallen, a silhouette of impossible darkness, the bleeding sky bending around him as if he were the centre of gravity. The crack in the Gate pulsed behind him, widening with every heartbeat, whispering with a voice that scraped across the mind like broken glass.
Kaelren stepped forward.
He didn't shout. He didn't roar. He didn't speak.
He simply moved — a man with nothing left to lose.
The Herald watched him approach, head tilted, as if studying a creature that didn't understand its own insignificance.
Kaelren swung.
The Veil blade struck the Herald's arm — and the Herald recoiled, a ripple of distortion shuddering through his form. Kaelren pressed forward, teeth gritted, blade flashing repeatedly, each strike fuelled by grief and fury and the desperate need to make this thing bleed.
But the Herald was faster.
A single backhand — effortless, almost bored — sent Kaelren flying across the courtyard. He hit the stone hard enough to crack it, breath torn from his lungs. His vision blurred. His ears rang. His memories flickered like dying lanterns.
He tried to rise.

He couldn't.
The Herald stepped toward him.
And the squad moved.
Lysa fired first — a dark arrow streaking through the air, slamming into the Herald's shoulder with a burst of shadow fire. The Herald staggered a fraction, turning toward her with a slow, unnatural grace.
Talla sprinted in next, spear glowing with ghostlight as she thrust it into the Herald's side. The impact sent a shockwave through the courtyard, knocking Voidborn off their feet.
Rynn followed, shield raised, slamming into the Herald with a roar that tore his throat raw. Bren broke free of the rubble, hammer swinging in a brutal arc that cracked the stone beneath the Herald's feet. Mareth, shaking, sent a burst of healing light into Kaelren's chest, dragging him back from the edge of oblivion. Mira — terrified, trembling — grabbed a fallen spear and charged with a cry that was more fear than courage.
For a moment — a single, impossible moment — they stood together.
A wall. A family. A force.
The Herald tilted his head.
And then he spoke.
The sound wasn't a word. It wasn't a voice.
It was a **shockwave**.
A blast of resonance that tore through the courtyard like a storm of invisible blades.
Lysa was thrown from her pillar, crashing into the stone below. Talla was hurled backward, her spear skittering across the ground. Rynn's shield shattered completely, sending him sprawling. Bren slammed into the rubble he'd just escaped, coughing blood. Mareth collapsed, hands over her ears, screaming. Mira curled into a ball, sobbing as her memories flickered like dying stars.
Kaelren was thrown across the courtyard again, slamming into the wall hard enough to crack the stone.
The Herald stepped forward.
Unstoppable. Unbroken. Unimpressed.

The Third Omen had begun.
Kaelren forced himself to his knees, vision swimming. He saw the squad struggling to rise. He saw the Herald advancing. He saw the Gate behind him, the crack widening, the Void pouring through.
And something inside him snapped.
"TOGETHER!" he roared, voice breaking. "NOW!"
They didn't hesitate.
Lysa fired a dark arrow that struck the Herald's leg, staggering him. Talla swept low, grabbing her spear and driving it into the Herald's knee. Rynn slammed into the Herald's side, forcing him off balance. Bren brought his hammer down with a roar that shook the courtyard. Mareth sent a burst of ghostlight into Kaelren's blade. Mira — shaking, terrified — threw her spear with everything she had.
Kaelren rose.
He sprinted.
He leapt.
He brought the Veil blade down with all the strength left in him.
The blade struck the Herald's chest — and for the first time, the Herald fell.
Not far. Not hard.
But enough.
Enough to make him recoil. Enough to make him retreat. Enough to make him dissolve into shadow and pull back toward the Gate.
The Voidborn froze.
Then followed him.
One by one. Then in a flood. A tide of darkness retreating into the crack.
The Herald's form flickered, distorted, and vanished into the Void.
The courtyard fell silent.
The squad collapsed.
Kaelren dropped to his knees, breath shaking, vision blurred.
They had survived.

Barely.

But the Gate still glowed with impossible darkness. The crack still widened. The whispers still crawled across the stone.

The Third Omen had begun.

And the Harrowed King was coming.

CHAPTER SIXTY-SEVEN — THE BREATH AFTER THE STORM

The Void retreated like a tide pulled by an unseen moon. One moment the courtyard was a battlefield of screams and steel and shadow. The next, it was silent.
Too silent.
The last of the Voidborn dissolved into smoke as they followed the Herald back through the widening crack. The Gate pulsed once, twice, then dimmed to a low, sickly glow — like a dying heart still beating out of spite.
Kaelren stood in the centre of the courtyard, chest heaving, Veil blade hanging limp at his side. He didn't move. He didn't speak.
He stared at the place where Thalen had fallen.
The stone was still warm.
Behind him, the squad slowly gathered themselves.
Rynn limped toward a wall and slid down it, staring at nothing. Talla pressed a shaking hand to her ribs, whispering a prayer through clenched teeth. Bren wiped blood from his mouth, eyes red with fury he didn't know where to put. Lysa sat on the broken pillar, bow across her lap, hands trembling uncontrollably. Mareth knelt beside a wounded soldier, but her magic flickered, unstable, her breath uneven.
And Mira—
Mira broke.
She didn't scream. She didn't sob. She didn't collapse.
She just... folded.
Her knees buckled, and she sank to the stone, hands clamped over her ears, rocking back and forth as if trying to shake the Herald's voice out of her skull.
"I can't remember," she whispered. "I can't— I can't remember— I can't—"
Elyndra rushed to her, lantern flickering weakly.

"Mira, look at me. Look at me."

"I can't remember my brother's face," Mira choked. "I can't— I can't— he's gone— he's—"

Her voice cracked into a sound that wasn't human. Elyndra flinched — not from the sound, but from something else. Something distant. Something only she could hear.

For a heartbeat her eyes unfocused, as if she were staring through Mira, through the courtyard, through the world itself. Her lantern flickered violently, casting two shadows behind her — one kneeling beside Mira, one kneeling beside someone unseen.

Then the shadows snapped back into one.

Kaelren didn't turn. He didn't move.

He just stared at the stone.

THE COUNCIL ERUPTS

By the time they reached Emberhold's inner hall, the council was already waiting — shaken, pale, terrified.

The moment the squad entered, the shouting began.

"What happened out there." "Why did the Gate break." "How did the Herald enter the Realm." "Where is the Voyager." "Why wasn't he fighting." "He's cleared entire fields before — why wasn't he here." "Has he abandoned us." "Has he betrayed us."

Elyndra stepped forward, lantern held tight — but her grip trembled, as if she were holding onto two worlds at once.

"He hasn't betrayed anyone," she snapped. "He's not ready. He's not—"

"Not ready?" a councillor barked. "He's the most powerful weapon Emberhold has."

"He's a child," Elyndra shot back. "A child with a burden no one should carry. You don't throw him at the Herald. You don't throw him at the Void. You don't—"

"We needed him!" another shouted. "Thalen is dead because he wasn't there."

The words hit the squad like a physical blow.

Lysa flinched. Bren's jaw clenched. Talla's eyes filled with tears she refused to let fall. Mira curled tighter into herself, shaking.

Kaelren didn't move.

He stood at the centre of the hall, silent, still, staring at the floor as if the stone itself held the answer to a question he couldn't bear to ask.

The council kept shouting.

"Where is he." "Why didn't he come." "Why didn't you summon him." "Why didn't he save Thalen." "Why didn't he save any of you."

Elyndra tried again — but her voice wavered, layered with something distant.

"He's not ready—"

Her lantern flickered violently. Her pupils dilated. For a heartbeat she wasn't looking at the council at all.

She was looking at someone else. Somewhere else.

Then she blinked hard, dragging herself back into her body.

"Then what good is he?" someone shouted. "What good are any of you." "Emberhold is falling." "The Third Omen has begun." "We are out of time."

The shouting grew louder. Angrier. More desperate.

Kaelren's hands curled into fists.

The room vibrated.

No one noticed.

Not yet.

The council kept shouting.

"Where was the Voyager." "Where was your commander." "Where was Kaelren when Thalen fell." "Why didn't he stop it." "Why didn't he—"

The stone beneath Kaelren's boots cracked.

The lanterns flickered.

The air tightened.

Elyndra's eyes widened — she felt the shift even through the haze of the other mind she was holding together.

"Stop," she whispered. "Everyone— stop—"

But they didn't.

They kept shouting. Kept accusing. Kept tearing open wounds that hadn't even begun to bleed.

Kaelren lifted his head.
Slowly.
His eyes were hollow.
Dead.
And then he spoke.
Not loudly. Not angrily.
Just with a voice that carried through the hall like a blade drawn from a sheath.
"Silence."
The word hit the room like a shockwave.
The lantern flames snapped straight. The air stilled. Every voice died mid-breath. Even the stone seemed to hold itself still.
Kaelren stepped forward.
One step.
Then another.
The council shrank back.
He didn't shout. He didn't roar. He didn't threaten.
He simply spoke again — quiet, controlled, terrifying.
"You will not speak of Thalen again in my presence unless you speak of him with honor."
No one breathed.
"You will not question the Voyager again. He is a child. And he is not your weapon."
A councillor opened his mouth.
Kaelren's gaze cut him down.
"And you will not," he said, voice dropping to a whisper that felt like a storm about to break, "ever question my command again."
The hall was silent.
Utterly silent.
Elyndra swayed — just slightly — as if the weight of two worlds pressed down on her shoulders.
Kaelren turned away.
The crack in the Gate pulsed in the distance.
The Third Omen had begun.
And Emberhold was running out of time.

The screams from Emberhold never reached him at first. Down in the chamber beneath the fortress — a place carved from old stone and older secrets — the Voyager sat with his back pressed to the wall, knees drawn tight to his chest. His fingers dug into his temples as if he could hold his skull together by force alone. The air trembled with distant thunder, the kind that came from magic tearing itself apart, but he barely registered it.

The lantern beside him flickered, its light stretching and shrinking across the runes etched into the walls. Those runes pulsed like a heartbeat.

A weak one. A failing one.

He squeezed his eyes shut.

And the visions came instantly.

A field of bodies beneath a sky split open. A shadow descending. A voice scraping across the world like a blade dragged over bone.

He saw himself standing alone in the center of that field, hands glowing with impossible light, Voidborn collapsing around him like puppets with their strings cut.

And behind them — watching — the Herald.

The vision shattered.

Another took its place.

The Gate cracking. The Void pouring through. The Harrowed King stepping into the Realm. Kaelren kneeling in blood. Mira screaming. Thalen's empty body on the stone.

He saw it all. He felt it all. Even though he wasn't there.

His breath hitched. He pressed his palms harder against his skull.

"Not again... not again... not again..."

But the darkness didn't listen.

It whispered.

Voyager...

He flinched, curling tighter.

"Stop— please— stop—"

The whisper grew louder, layered with countless voices, each one colder than the last.

You are not ready.
"I know," he whispered.
You will break.
"I'm trying—"
You will fail.
"I'm trying!"
His voice cracked, echoing off the stone.
The chamber door creaked.
He didn't look up.
Elyndra stepped inside.
Her lantern was dim, its flame trembling like a candle in a storm. Her face was pale, drawn, exhausted — not from the climb down the stairs, but from something deeper. Something that stretched her thin across two worlds.
She closed the door behind her, sealing out the distant echoes of shouting from the council hall. For a moment she simply stood there, watching him shake, watching the runes pulse weakly around him.
Then she knelt beside him.
Her hand hovered over his shoulder, trembling.
He didn't lift his head.
"I heard him," he whispered. "The Herald. I heard him from here."
Elyndra swallowed.
"Yes."
"I felt him," he said, voice trembling. "He was calling to me."
She placed her hand on his shoulder — and for a heartbeat, her lantern flickered violently, casting two shadows behind her.
One kneeling beside him. One standing in a hall full of shouting voices.
Then the shadows snapped back into one.
"He wasn't calling you," she said softly. "He was hunting you."
The Voyager's breath caught.
"If you had gone out there," Elyndra continued, "if you had faced him now… he would have taken you. He would

have broken you. And then he would have used you against us."

He squeezed his eyes shut.

"I saw Thalen die."

Elyndra's breath faltered — not here, but somewhere else, in another room, in another moment.

"I saw it," he whispered. "I wasn't there, but I saw it. I felt Kaelren break. I felt Mira's mind slip. I felt the Gate crack."

He finally looked up.

His eyes were wet.

"I should have helped them."

Elyndra shook her head.

"You would have died."

"I should have died with them."

"No." Her voice sharpened — conviction layered over fear. "You are the only one who can face the Harrowed King. You cannot die now. You cannot break now. You cannot go to them until you are ready."

The Voyager's voice was barely a breath.

"I'm scared."

Elyndra pulled him into her arms.

"I know."

He trembled against her.

"I can feel him," he whispered. "Even now. The Herald. He's still here. He's waiting for me."

Elyndra closed her eyes.

"The Third Omen has begun," she said. "And when the time comes... you will have to face him."

The Voyager's voice cracked.

"I'm not ready."

Elyndra held him tighter.

"You will be."

But her voice shook.

Because she wasn't sure.

Not anymore.

CHAPTER SIXTY-EIGHT — THE QUIET THAT FOLLOWS

Silence clung to the council chamber like smoke.
Kaelren's command still hung in the air, vibrating faintly in the stone, in the lanterns, in the bones of everyone present.
No one dared move. No one dared breathe too loudly.
Even the torches along the walls dimmed, as if afraid to draw attention.
Kaelren stood with his back to the council, shoulders rigid, jaw clenched. The Veil blade at his side hummed faintly, reacting to the tension in him — to the storm he was barely containing.
Behind him, the squad hovered in a loose, broken cluster.
Rynn leaned heavily against a pillar, sweat beading on his brow. Talla kept one arm around Mira, who trembled in small, uncontrollable spasms. Lysa's bow lay across her lap, her fingers twitching as if still firing arrows. Bren's fists were clenched so tightly his knuckles had gone white.
Mareth's magic flickered weakly around her hands, the glow unstable.
And Elyndra—
Elyndra swayed.
Just slightly.
Just enough for Kaelren to notice.
Her lantern flickered in uneven pulses, casting two shadows behind her again — one standing in the council hall, one kneeling beside someone unseen. The shadows merged, split, merged again.
A few councillors saw it.
They paled.
Kaelren turned his head just enough to see her out of the corner of his eye.
"Elyndra," he said quietly. "You're overextending."
She blinked hard, as if pulling herself back into her body.

"I'm fine," she whispered.
She wasn't.
Her voice carried an echo — a faint, distant resonance that didn't belong to this room. Her pupils dilated, unfocused for a heartbeat, as if she were listening to someone far below the fortress, someone in pain.
Kaelren stepped toward her.
The council flinched.
"Elyndra," he repeated, softer this time. "Release him."
Her breath hitched.
"I can't," she murmured. "Not yet. He's... he's barely holding on."
A ripple of fear passed through the council.
One of the elders swallowed hard. "You mean the Voyager is—"
"Alive," Elyndra snapped, sharper than she intended.
"Alive because I am with him."
Her lantern flickered violently.
"And because he is not here."
The implication hung in the air like a blade.
If he had been here... If he had faced the Herald... If he had stepped into the courtyard...
He would have been taken.
Kaelren turned fully now, facing the council with eyes that no longer looked hollow — they looked carved from stone.
"You demanded answers," he said. "Here they are."
He pointed to Elyndra.
"She is standing in this room while holding the Voyager's mind together in another. She is fighting two battles at once. And you dare accuse her of negligence."
A councillor opened his mouth.
Kaelren's gaze cut him down before he could speak.
"You dare accuse him of cowardice."
Silence.
"You dare accuse us of failure."
The room shrank around him.
Kaelren stepped closer to the council table, the stone beneath his boots still cracked from his earlier outburst.

"You sit in this hall and shout," he said. "We bled in the courtyard. Thalen died in my arms. Mira nearly lost her mind. The Herald walked through our walls as if they were smoke."

He leaned forward.

"And you think your fear gives you the right to question us."

The elder councillor trembled.

"We… we only want to protect Emberhold."

Kaelren's voice dropped to a whisper.

"Then listen."

The room held its breath.

"The Third Omen has begun. The Herald will return. And when he does, he will not come alone."

A chill swept through the hall.

Kaelren straightened.

"You will give us time to regroup. Time to bury our dead. Time to prepare the Voyager. Time to stabilize Mira. Time to repair the Gate."

He paused.

"And you will stay out of our way."

No one argued.

No one dared.

Elyndra exhaled shakily, her lantern dimming as she eased some of the strain on her mind. The second shadow behind her faded — though not entirely.

Kaelren turned away from the council.

"Come," he said to the squad. "We're done here."

They followed him out — limping, shaking, broken, but together.

As the doors closed behind them, the council finally breathed again.

And in the silence that followed, one truth settled over Emberhold like a shroud:

The Third Omen had begun. And nothing would ever be the same.

CHAPTER SIXTY-NINE — THE WEIGHT THEY CARRY

The doors of the council chamber slammed shut behind them, muffling the last trembling echoes of Kaelren's command. The hallway outside was dim, lit only by a few guttering lanterns that cast long, wavering shadows across the stone.
No one spoke.
No one even breathed loudly.
They walked until they reached the outer hall — a wide, empty space overlooking the courtyard where the battle had taken place. The shattered stones below were still stained with the remnants of Voidborn smoke. The air still tasted of iron and ash.
And the place where Thalen had fallen was still visible.
Still warm.
The squad stopped.
As if pulled by the same invisible thread.
Rynn leaned heavily against a pillar, sliding down until he sat on the cold floor, his shield arm hanging uselessly at his side. His breath came in ragged pulls, each one sounding like it hurt.
Talla lowered Mira gently onto a bench, brushing a trembling hand through the girl's hair. Mira curled into herself, knees to her chest, eyes unfocused. She rocked slightly, whispering something too soft to hear.
Lysa sat on the floor beside the broken railing, bow across her lap. Her fingers still twitching. She stared at the courtyard with a hollow expression, jaw clenched so tightly it trembled.
Bren paced.
Back and forth. Back and forth. Back and forth.
His fists opened and closed, opened and closed, still wanting to release the anger inside him.

Mareth knelt beside Rynn, her hands glowing faintly as she tried to heal the bruises and fractures, she could reach — but her magic flickered, unstable, her breath uneven. She wiped her eyes with the back of her wrist, pretending it was sweat.

Kaelren stood apart from them all.

He didn't sit. He didn't lean. He didn't speak.

He stared out at the courtyard, at the place where Thalen had fallen, at the stone that still held the shape of his body.

His hands were shaking.

He didn't try to hide it.

No one did.

It was Lysa who broke first.

Her breath hitched — once, twice — and then she pressed both hands over her mouth as a sob tore out of her. She curled forward, shoulders shaking, bow clattering to the floor beside her.

Talla reached for her, pulling her close, and Lysa collapsed into her arms, crying into her shoulder.

Bren stopped pacing.

He stood there, fists clenched, chest heaving, eyes burning with tears he refused to let fall.

"He shouldn't have died," Bren whispered. "He shouldn't have— he shouldn't—"

His voice cracked.

He punched the wall.

Hard.

The stone cracked under his fist.

He didn't stop.

He hit it again. And again. And again.

Mareth grabbed his arm, tears streaming down her face.

"Bren— stop— please— stop—"

He froze.

Then he sank to his knees, head bowed, breath shaking. Rynn wiped his face with the back of his hand, but the tears kept coming.

"He saved Mira," Rynn whispered. "He saved all of us. And I— I couldn't— I couldn't reach him."

Mira lifted her head.

Her voice was small. Broken.
"He called me little runner."
Talla's breath caught.
Mira pressed her hands to her ears.
"I can't remember his face," she whispered. "I can't— I can't remember— I can't—"
Kaelren turned.
Slowly.
He walked toward her, each step heavy, as if the weight of the world hung from his shoulders. He knelt in front of her, gently taking her hands away from her ears.
"Mira," he said softly. "Look at me."
She did.
Barely.
Her eyes were glassy, unfocused, full of terror.
Kaelren swallowed hard.
"Thalen loved you," he said. "He was proud of you. He died protecting you. That is the truth. That is what you hold onto."
Mira trembled.
"I can't remember his face."
Kaelren's voice broke.
"Then I will remember it for you."
Mira collapsed into him, sobbing into his chest.
Kaelren held her.
Held her like she was the last fragile thing in a world made of breaking glass.
The squad watched.
And for the first time since the battle ended, Kaelren let the tears fall.
When Mira finally quieted, Kaelren stood.
He looked at each of them — Rynn, Talla, Bren, Lysa, Mareth — and something in his eyes had changed.
Not hardened.
Not cold.
Resolved.
"We bury him at dawn," Kaelren said. "With honour. With fire. With the rites of Emberhold."
No one argued.

No one could.

"And then," Kaelren continued, voice steady despite the tremor beneath it, "we prepare."

"For what?" Lysa whispered.

Kaelren looked toward the Gate.

Toward the crack pulsing with sickly light.

Toward the darkness waiting beyond it.

"For the Herald's return," he said. "And for the King who follows."

The squad fell silent.

Not out of fear.

Out of understanding.

Out of grief sharpened into purpose.

Out of love for the man they lost.

And the man who still stood.

OFFICIAL

CHAPTER SEVENTY— THE ECHOES BELOW

The stairwell to the lower chambers was cold. Not the natural cold of stone, but the kind that seeped into the marrow — the kind that came from magic stretched thin, from minds pulled in too many directions, from grief pressing down on the world like a weight no one could lift.

Kaelren descended first.

His steps were heavy, deliberate, each one echoing off the walls like a slow heartbeat. Elyndra followed behind him, lantern dim, her breath uneven. The squad remained above, tending to Mira, tending to each other, tending to wounds no healer could reach.

The deeper they went, the colder it became.

Kaelren didn't speak.

Elyndra didn't either.

Not until they reached the final landing — the door to the Voyager's chamber just ahead, faint light flickering beneath it.

Elyndra reached out, touching Kaelren's arm.

"Before we go in," she whispered, "you need to understand something."

Kaelren turned, eyes sharp.

"I understand enough."

"No," she said softly. "You don't."

Her lantern flickered — and for a heartbeat, Kaelren saw it again:

Two shadows behind her. Two presences. Two worlds pulling at her mind.

"He's not weak," Elyndra said. "He's not young. But his mind... it's unshielded. Open the way a child's is. He feels everything. Too much. Too fast."

Kaelren's jaw tightened.

"And Thalen is dead."

The words hung between them like a blade.

Elyndra closed her eyes.

"I know."
Kaelren stepped closer, voice low.
"He died buying us time. He died protecting Mira. He died because the Herald walked through our walls like smoke. And the one person who could have stopped him—"
"Could not," Elyndra whispered.
Kaelren's voice sharpened.
"Would not."
Elyndra flinched.
"He would have been taken," she said. "The Herald was hunting him. If he had stepped into that courtyard, he would have been unmade. And then he would have been used against us."
Kaelren didn't answer.
He didn't need to.
The grief in his eyes said everything.
Elyndra swallowed.
"His power awakened before his mind learned how to bear it," she said. "He has no walls. No filters. The Void hits him harder than any of us. I'm holding him together by threads."
Kaelren looked at the door.
"Then let's see him."
He pushed it open.
The chamber was dim, lit only by the trembling lantern beside the man curled against the far wall. His knees were drawn up, his hands pressed to his temples, breath shaking.
He looked up the moment the door opened.
Not because he heard it.
Because he had heard *them*.
Every word. Every accusation. Every fear. Every grief-soaked whisper.
Kaelren froze.
The Voyager's eyes were red, wet, wide with something between terror and shame.
"You think I should have been there," he whispered.
Kaelren didn't answer.
"You think I let Thalen die."
Elyndra stepped forward. "He didn't mean—"

"Yes," the Voyager said, voice cracking. "He did."
Kaelren exhaled slowly.
"Thalen died because the Herald is stronger than anything we've faced," he said. "Not because of you."
The Voyager shook his head.
"You don't believe that."
Kaelren's jaw tightened.
Elyndra knelt beside the Voyager, placing a hand on his shoulder.
"You heard too much," she whispered.
"I hear everything," he said. "I hear the Herald. I hear the Gate. I hear the Void whispering my name. I hear the council shouting. I hear Mira crying. I hear Kaelren breaking."
Kaelren flinched.
The Voyager looked up at him.
"I saw Thalen die," he whispered. "I saw it in my head. I felt it. I felt you fall to your knees. I felt Mira's mind slip. I felt the Gate crack. I felt everything."
His voice trembled.
"And I wasn't there."
Kaelren stepped closer.
"You would have died."
"I should have died with them."
Kaelren's voice sharpened.
"No."
The Voyager blinked.
Kaelren knelt — slowly, painfully — until he was eye level with him.
"You don't die for us," Kaelren said. "You live for us."
The Voyager's breath hitched.
Kaelren continued, voice low, steady, heavy with grief and truth.
"Thalen didn't die because you weren't there. He died because he chose to stand between Mira and the Herald. He died because he was a soldier. He died because he was brave. He died because he loved us."
The Voyager's eyes filled again.
Kaelren's voice softened.

"And he died so you wouldn't have to."
Silence.
Heavy. Thick. Sacred.
The Voyager looked down at his hands.
"My mind isn't right," he whispered. "It's... open. Raw. I can't shut anything out."
Elyndra squeezed his shoulder.
"That's why I'm here," she said. "That's why I'm with you. That's why I'm in two places at once. I won't let you face this alone."
The Voyager trembled.
Kaelren stood, offering his hand.
"Come with us," he said. "Not to fight. Not yet. Just... come."
The Voyager hesitated.
Then he reached out.
And took Kaelren's hand.

CHAPTER SEVENTY-ONE — WHEN WORLDS MEET

They climbed the stairs slowly.
Kaelren walked a half step ahead, not touching the Voyager, but close enough that if the man faltered, he could steady him. Elyndra followed behind, lantern dim, her breath uneven — her mind still stretched between two worlds.
The Voyager moved carefully, each step deliberate. His balance wasn't gone, but his focus was fractured. Every sound — every echo, every distant footfall, every whisper of wind — made him tense, as if the world itself were too loud.
His mind was open. Raw. Unshielded.
And the world pressed in on him from all sides.
When they reached the upper hall, the squad was still there.
Rynn slumped against a pillar, eyes half closed. Talla knelt beside Mira, murmuring soft reassurances. Lysa sat on the floor, bow across her lap, staring at nothing. Bren leaned against the wall, fists bruised and bloodied. Mareth hovered near them all, magic flickering weakly around her hands.
They looked up as Kaelren entered.
Then they saw him.
The Voyager stopped.
So did the squad.
Silence stretched between them — thick, heavy, trembling.
Kaelren stepped aside, giving the Voyager space to stand on his own.
No one moved.
No one breathed.
It was Lysa who broke the stillness.
"...you're alive."
The Voyager swallowed.
"I... yes."

Lysa rose slowly, her legs unsteady. She took a step toward him — then hesitated, as if afraid she might break him by getting too close.

"You weren't there," she said, voice cracking. "We thought— we thought—"

"I know," he whispered.

Rynn pushed himself upright, wincing.

"You heard us," he said. Not accusing. Just tired.

The Voyager nodded.

"I hear everything."

Bren's jaw tightened.

"Did you hear Thalen die."

Elyndra inhaled sharply.

Kaelren turned, ready to intervene.

But the Voyager lifted a hand — not to defend himself, but to steady his own shaking breath.

"Yes," he said. "I saw it. I felt it. I felt all of you."

Mira looked up.

"You felt me."

The Voyager's eyes softened.

"Yes."

Mira stood — slowly, shakily — and walked toward him. Talla reached out as if to stop her, but Mira shook her head.

She stopped a few feet away.

"You felt me break," she whispered.

The Voyager nodded.

"I felt the Herald's voice tear through your mind. I felt your memories slip. I felt your fear. I felt your grief. I felt… everything."

Mira's eyes filled.

"Then why didn't you come."

The question hit him like a blade.

He opened his mouth — then closed it again.

Kaelren stepped forward, but the Voyager raised a hand.

"I didn't come," he said quietly, "because if I had… the Herald would have taken me. And then he would have used me to kill all of you."

Silence.

Mira's breath hitched. Lysa covered her mouth. Rynn bowed his head. Bren looked away, jaw trembling. Talla wiped her eyes. Mareth whispered, "By the Veil…"
The Voyager continued, voice shaking.
"My mind isn't like yours. It's… open. Raw. I can't shut anything out. The Herald's voice hits me harder than any blade. If I had stepped into that courtyard, he would have broken me. And then I would have become the weapon that killed you."
He looked at each of them — Rynn, Talla, Bren, Lysa, Mareth, Mira.
"I didn't stay away because I didn't care," he whispered. "I stayed away because I cared too much."
Mira took another step toward him.
Then another.
Then she threw her arms around him.
The Voyager froze — startled, overwhelmed — then slowly, hesitantly, he returned the embrace.
Mira trembled against him.
"I'm glad you're alive," she whispered.
The Voyager's breath shook.
"So am I."
One by one, the others approached.
Rynn placed a hand on his shoulder. Talla touched his arm gently. Mareth gave a small, trembling nod. Lysa wiped her eyes and stepped closer. Even Bren, after a long moment, muttered, "Don't scare us like that again."
The Voyager looked at them — all of them — and something inside him shifted.
For the first time since the visions began, since the Herald whispered his name, since the Gate cracked…
He didn't feel alone.
Kaelren watched them, something softening in his expression.
Elyndra exhaled, her lantern finally steadying.
The squad stood together — bruised, broken, grieving — but united.
And the Voyager stood among them.

Not as a weapon. Not as a burden. Not as someone to be protected.
But as one of them.

CHAPTER SEVENTY-TWO — THE WALK TO DAWN

The armoury was quiet when they entered — not the silence of peace, but the heavy, aching stillness that follows a night of screaming. Dawn's first light crept through the high windows, pale and hesitant, brushing the racks of armour with a cold, metallic sheen.
No one spoke.
They didn't need to.
They moved through the room like ghosts, each drawn to their own ritual, their own way of preparing to say goodbye.
Rynn unbuckled his battered chestplate with slow, deliberate movements, setting each piece down as though it might shatter if he let it fall too quickly. His breath hitched once — barely — before he forced it steady again.
Talla drifted toward him, her steps soft, almost uncertain. She reached for the strap at his shoulder, fingers brushing his skin.
"You're bleeding again," she murmured.
Rynn didn't look up. "It'll stop."
Talla's hand tightened, gentle but firm. "You don't have to pretend."
He finally met her eyes. Something passed between them — grief, fear, the fragile understanding that they could lose each other just as easily as they lost Thalen. Talla stepped closer, resting her forehead against his for a single, trembling breath.
Kaelren paused in the doorway, watching them. He said nothing. He simply nodded once, a quiet acknowledgment, and moved on.
Across the room, Lysa sat on a low bench, Thalen's broken bow across her knees. She ran her fingers along the frayed string, tracing the place where it had snapped. Her eyes were red, but dry now — the kind of dry that comes after too many tears. She whispered something under her breath,

a promise meant only for him, then rose and slung her quiver over her shoulder.

Bren stood near the wall, tightening the wraps around his bruised knuckles. He pulled them taut, then tighter still, as if the pressure might hold him together. His gaze drifted to Thalen's empty scabbard hanging on the far wall.

"Should've been me," he muttered.

Kaelren stopped beside him. "No," he said quietly. "It shouldn't."

Bren didn't answer. But he didn't argue.

Mareth adjusted the clasp of her healer's cloak, her hands glowing faintly with magic that flickered like a candle in wind. She touched the pendant at her throat — the one Thalen used to tease her about — and held it for a long moment before letting it fall.

Mira sat on a stool, staring at her trembling hands. Talla knelt beside her again, fastening the straps of her light armour.

"I can do it," Mira whispered.

"I know," Talla said softly. "But you don't have to."

Mira nodded, swallowing hard.

Near the far wall, Elyndra stood close to the Voyager. He was upright, but unsteady — his balance intact, his mind frayed. Every sound made him tense, every echo made him flinch. Elyndra kept a hand near his arm, lantern dim but steady, anchoring him to the world.

Kaelren approached them. "You're sure he's ready."

Elyndra nodded once. "He needs to be with us. And... he wants to be."

The Voyager met Kaelren's eyes. "I can walk," he murmured. "Just... stay close."

"We will," Kaelren said.

When they were ready, they gathered at the armoury door — not in formation, not as soldiers, but as people bound by loss.

Rynn and Talla stood side by side, shoulders brushing. Lysa held Thalen's broken bow. Bren carried the torch. Mareth steadied Mira. Elyndra walked beside the Voyager, her

lantern casting a thin ribbon of ghostlight along the floor. Kaelren stood at the front, silent, resolute.
Together, they walked through Emberhold's halls.
Soldiers bowed their heads as they passed. Apprentices stepped aside, eyes lowered. Even the walls seemed to quiet themselves. The Voyager walked among them, each step careful, the world still too loud around him — but he stayed with them. He stayed present.
Kaelren led them.
His steps were steady, but his mind drifted — not to the courtyard ahead, not to the pyres waiting in the cold morning air, but to a memory that rose unbidden, warm and sharp, like a blade catching sunlight.
He saw the old training yard again. Not the scarred one they used now, but the quiet one — sunlit, peaceful, the air filled with the soft clack of wooden blades. He remembered standing there, younger but already carrying the weight of command, sweat dripping down his brow as he practiced alone.
The King had approached without guards.
"Your stance is too rigid," he'd said, stepping into the ring. Kaelren had straightened, startled. "Your Majesty—"
"Kaelren," the King interrupted gently, "if I wanted ceremony, I'd have brought half the court."
He'd taken a wooden sword from the rack, testing its weight with a faint smile.
"Show me."
Kaelren had obeyed, moving through the forms. The King watched with a warmth Kaelren rarely saw — not distant, not regal, but proud. When Kaelren finished, the King stepped closer and adjusted his grip.
"Your father held his blade the same way," he said softly. "Too tight. Like he was trying to hold the world together with his hands."
Kaelren had almost smiled. Almost.
"You don't have to carry everything alone," the King had said. "Not while I'm here."

For a heartbeat — just one — Kaelren felt warmth bloom in his chest. A rare, fragile thing. A memory untouched by blood or betrayal.

The corridor opened into the courtyard.

Cold morning light spilled across the stone, catching on the twin pyres standing side by side. The air was still, too still, as if the world itself were holding its breath.

The squad slowed.

Rynn's steps faltered. Talla's hand found his. Lysa pressed Thalen's broken bow tighter to her chest. Bren's jaw clenched. Mareth wiped her eyes. Mira froze. Elyndra's lantern dimmed. The Voyager stopped beside her, breath trembling as he looked at the shrouds.

Kaelren walked forward alone.

He stopped between the two pyres, his breath visible in the cold air. For a moment, he didn't move. Didn't speak. Didn't breathe.

He just looked at them.

Jorren. Thalen. Two brothers. Two graves. Two pieces of himself carved out in the span of days.

His throat tightened.

He reached out — first to Jorren's shroud, then to Thalen's armour — fingertips brushing the cold fabric, the cold metal.

"I'm sorry," he whispered.

The others gathered behind him, forming a loose circle around the pyres. The Voyager stood among them, head bowed, grief flickering across his face like a memory he didn't know he had.

Kaelren inhaled slowly. He opened his mouth to speak. To honor them. To name them. To give them the farewell they deserved.

But the world didn't let him.

A tremor rippled through the courtyard.

Soft at first. Barely noticeable. Like a heartbeat beneath the stone.

Kaelren froze.

Another tremor — stronger — cracked through the ground, rattling the pyres, sending ash drifting into the air.

Elyndra's lantern flared violently. Her eyes widened.
"No…" she whispered. "Not now… not during this…"
The Voyager staggered, clutching his head as the pulse tore through him. Elyndra caught his arm, steadying him — then her expression changed.
Fear. Urgency. Recognition.
She grabbed his shoulders.
"Listen to me," she whispered sharply. "Run. Go back to your chambers. Now."
The Voyager blinked, dazed. "Elyndra—"
"Go!" she hissed. "If you stay here, it will find you."
Kaelren turned, eyes widening. "Elyndra—?"
"Get him out!" she snapped. "Before it locks onto him!"
The Gate pulsed.
A deep, sickening thrum rolled across the courtyard, vibrating through their bones. The runes carved into the arch flickered, dimmed, then flared with a harsh, unnatural light.
The Voyager stumbled backward, breath ragged, then turned and ran — not out of fear, but because he finally understood:
If he stayed, they would all die.
Elyndra watched him go, lantern blazing.
Kaelren turned toward the Gate. His grief hardened into something sharp. Something ready. Something dangerous.
The Gate pulsed again — louder, deeper, like a dying heart trying to beat its way back to life.
A crack of darkness split across its surface.
Elyndra's voice broke.
"It's waking."
Kaelren stepped forward, Veil blade rising.
The burial would have to wait. The dead would have to wait. The Gate was calling.
And the world was about to break again.

OFFICIAL

CHAPTER SEVENTY-THREE — THE CALL BACK TO WAR

The Gate pulsed.
A low, sickening thrum rolled across the courtyard, rattling the pyres and scattering ash into the cold morning air. The dawn light flickered as if something enormous had passed between it and the world.
Kaelren didn't look back at Jorren or Thalen.
He couldn't.
"Rest time's over," he said quietly.
The words cut through the courtyard like a blade.
For a moment, no one moved.
The squad stood frozen in the half-light, caught between grief and instinct, between the weight of the dead and the threat of the living. The cold air stung their lungs. The pyres crackled softly behind them. The Gate hummed like a dying star.
Then the world seemed to slow.
Kaelren felt his heartbeat first — a heavy, deliberate thud that echoed in his ears. Another. Another. Each one louder, sharper, until it drowned out the wind and the crackling pyres.
Rynn inhaled sharply, the breath misting in the cold air and hanging there too long. Talla's fingers tightened around her spear. Lysa's arrow trembled on the string. Bren's hammer rose inch by inch. Mareth's magic flickered. Mira's eyes widened. Elyndra's lantern flared.
Kaelren blinked.
And the courtyard dissolved.

THE MEMORY OF FIRE
Heat slammed into him.
Not Emberhold's cold dawn — but the blistering, suffocating heat of Flameborn fire. The sky above him burned red, streaked with smoke and ash. The ground

shook beneath his boots as the Void tore through the Veil, spilling horrors into the world.
He was there again.
Younger. Bloodied. Breathless.
Standing shoulder to shoulder with the King.
The King's armour glowed with Veil light, cracked and scorched but unbroken. His cloak whipped in the burning wind. His eyes — gods, his eyes — were steady, fierce, alive.
Around them, soldiers faltered.
Some cried out. Some prayed. Some stared at the Void with hollow terror.
Kaelren remembered the fear. The choking, paralysing fear.
And then the King raised his voice.
Not loud. Not booming.
But clear — cutting through the roar of fire and screams like a blade through smoke.
"Look at me."
The soldiers turned.
"Look at me," the King repeated, louder now, his voice carrying across the battlefield.
Kaelren felt his younger self straighten beside him.
The King lifted his sword — cracked, glowing, trembling with Veil light.
"This is not the end," he said. "This is the moment we were born for."
The fire roared. The Void shrieked. The sky bled.
But the King's voice rose above it all.
"We stand here because no one else can. We stand here because the world needs us. We stand here because if we fall—"
He pointed his sword toward the breach, toward the impossible darkness spilling through.
"—then everything falls."
Kaelren felt the words burn into him, branding themselves into his bones.
The King stepped forward, eyes blazing.
"So hear me now."
He lifted his sword high.

"If this is our last dawn—"
The soldiers held their breath.
"—then let it be the dawn we chose."
A roar rose from the ranks — raw, desperate, defiant.
Kaelren felt it again. The fire in his chest. The certainty.
The courage born not from hope, but from purpose.
The King turned to him — to the younger Kaelren — and placed a hand on his shoulder.
"Stand with me."
Kaelren had nodded.
And together, they charged into the fire.

THE RETURN TO NOW
The vision shattered.
Kaelren gasped, stumbling as the cold air of Emberhold slammed back into his lungs. The Gate pulsed again, the crack widening with a sound like stone screaming.
But something inside him had changed.
The fear was still there. The grief was still there. The weight of Jorren and Thalen still pressed against his ribs.
But beneath it — deeper — something else stirred.
The King's voice.
If this is our last dawn… then let it be the dawn we chose.
Kaelren lifted his Veil blade.
His heartbeat steadied.
He stepped forward.
"Together," he said — not as a command, but as a vow.
The squad tightened around him.
Rynn braced his shield, breath steadying. Talla lowered her stance, spear angled toward the Gate. Lysa drew her arrow, eyes sharp despite the tears. Bren planted his feet, hammer ready. Mareth whispered a prayer under her breath, magic gathering in her palms. Mira swallowed her fear and raised her spear. Elyndra's lantern blazed, ghostlight swirling like a storm.
The Gate screamed.
And the war began again.

THE FIRST WAVE

The Gate ruptured.

A blast of cold darkness exploded outward, slamming into the courtyard like a shockwave. The pyres flickered. Ash spiralled into the air. The ground cracked beneath their boots.

And then the first wave came through.

Not a horde. Not a swarm.

Just one.

A single Voidborn stepped through the crack — tall, skeletal, its limbs too long, its joints bending wrong, its skin a shifting mass of shadow and bone. Its head tilted, listening to something only it could hear.

Its eyes — if they were eyes — glowed with a faint, sickly blue.

It moved.

Fast.

Too fast.

Kaelren barely had time to shout before it lunged, claws slicing through the air toward Rynn. The impact slammed into his shield with a sound like metal screaming. Rynn staggered, boots skidding across the stone.

Talla was already there.

She drove her spear into the creature's side, ghostlight flaring on impact. The Voidborn shrieked — a high, tearing sound that made Mira flinch and Mareth gasp.

Lysa's arrow flew.

It struck the creature's shoulder, shadow bursting outward like ink in water. The Voidborn twisted, limbs contorting, and lunged again — this time toward Lysa.

Bren intercepted it with a roar, hammer crashing into its spine. The blow sent the creature skidding across the courtyard, limbs flailing, body twisting unnaturally as it tried to right itself.

Kaelren moved.

He didn't think. He didn't hesitate. He simply stepped into the creature's path and brought his Veil blade down in a clean, brutal arc.

The blade struck true.

The Voidborn convulsed, its form flickering between shadow and bone, between shape and nothingness. It let out one last, broken shriek before collapsing into a smear of smoke that dissolved into the cold air.
Silence followed.
A thin, trembling silence.
Mira exhaled shakily. Rynn steadied himself. Talla wiped blood from her cheek. Lysa lowered her bow, breath ragged. Bren spat onto the stone. Mareth pressed a hand to her chest. Elyndra's lantern dimmed, then steadied.
Kaelren didn't lower his blade.
He stared at the Gate.
The crack was still widening. The runes were still dimming. The air was still trembling.
"That wasn't the wave," he said quietly.
The Gate pulsed again.
Harder. Deeper.
And the second wave began to push through.

CHAPTER SEVENTY-FOUR — THE SECOND WAVE

The Gate pulsed again.
This time the sound wasn't a tremor or a crack — it was a deep, dragging inhale, as if something on the other side had finally found its breath. The air thickened. The cold deepened. Every breath tasted of metal and ash.
Kaelren felt the shift before the others did.
A pressure. A weight. A wrongness.
His heartbeat thudded once, hard enough to shake his ribs. Then again.
Then again — faster, sharper, until it drowned out the world.
He lifted his blade.
The others tightened around him, drawn into formation not by command, but by instinct — by the same pulse of dread that crawled up their spines.
The crack across the Gate widened.
Darkness spilled through it like smoke underwater, swirling, thickening, taking shape. The runes flickered violently, ghostlight bleeding from their edges. The stone beneath their feet vibrated like a drumskin.
Kaelren inhaled.
The world slowed.
Rynn braced his shield, breath steadying. Talla lowered her stance, spear angled toward the Gate. Lysa's arrow hovered, the string pulled taut against her cheek. Bren planted his feet, hammer rising. Mareth whispered a prayer, magic gathering in her palms. Mira swallowed her fear and raised her spear. Elyndra's lantern blazed, ghostlight swirling like a storm — but her face was pale, strained, sweat beading at her temples.
She was losing her grip on the Voyager. Kaelren saw it. He said nothing.
There was no time.
The Gate screamed.

And the second wave surged.

THE FLOOD

They came all at once.
Not one. Not a handful.
A rush.
Dozens of Voidborn poured through the Gate in a single, writhing mass — limbs too long, jaws unhinged, bodies flickering between bone and shadow. They hit the courtyard like a flood, shrieking with hunger and memory and something older than either.
Kaelren didn't shout orders.
He didn't need to.
The squad moved as one.
Rynn met the first creature with his shield, the impact ringing through the courtyard like a bell. The force drove him back a step — then Talla was there, spear flashing past his shoulder, driving into the creature's throat. It dissolved into smoke, and Rynn surged forward again, shield raised, teeth bared.
Lysa's arrow streaked overhead, a shard of shadow that buried itself in the chest of a Voidborn leaping for Bren. The creature twisted mid-air, shrieking, and Bren's hammer came up to meet it, smashing it into the stone with a crack that echoed off the walls.
Mareth's hands glowed as she pulled Mira behind her, then thrust a burst of ghostlight into the face of a Voidborn that had slipped past the front line. The creature reeled, its form flickering — and Mira, shaking but steady, drove her spear into its heart.
Elyndra staggered.
Her lantern flickered violently, ghostlight sputtering.
Kaelren saw her knees buckle.
"Elyndra!" he shouted.
She didn't answer.
Her eyes were unfocused — as if part of her mind was somewhere else entirely.
Somewhere deep below Emberhold. Somewhere holding the Voyager together by sheer force of will.

Kaelren's stomach twisted.
Not now. Not now. Not now.
A Voidborn lunged for him — tall, skeletal, its jaw splitting open in a scream that scraped across his mind. Kaelren stepped into the strike, blade flashing in a clean, brutal arc. The creature split in two, dissolving before it hit the ground.
Another came from the left. Another from behind. Another from the right.
Kaelren moved like a man who had already died once and refused to do it again.
Rynn slammed into his side, shield raised, blocking a blow meant for Kaelren's ribs. Talla swept low, cutting the creature's legs out from under it. Lysa's arrow pinned it to the stone before it could rise.
They were a circle. A storm. A heartbeat.
Every motion fed the next. Every strike opened a path. Every breath kept someone alive.
But the wave didn't stop.
It grew. It thickened. It pressed harder.
Mira screamed as a Voidborn nearly tore her from Mareth's grasp. Bren roared as three creatures slammed into him at once. Lysa's quiver emptied faster than she could draw. Rynn's shield cracked down the centre. Talla's spear splintered. Elyndra's lantern flickered again — dimmer this time.
Kaelren's chest burned. His arms shook. His breath tore.
But he didn't stop.
He couldn't.
Not while the Gate kept widening. Not while the darkness kept pouring through. Not while the world kept breaking.

THE EDGE OF COLLAPSE

The courtyard was a blur of motion and screams and ghostlight. The pyres flickered violently, ash swirling through the air like snow. The dawn dimmed. The cold deepened.

Kaelren cut down another Voidborn — then another — then another — but for every one that fell, two more took its place.

Rynn stumbled. Talla caught him. Lysa's bowstring snapped. Bren's hammer slipped from his grasp. Mareth's magic sputtered. Mira froze, eyes wide with terror. Elyndra collapsed to one knee, lantern dimming to a faint, trembling glow.

Kaelren's heart lurched.

"Elyndra!"

She didn't respond.

Her lips moved soundlessly. Her eyes were glassy.

She was losing him. The man below. The one she was holding together.

Kaelren's throat tightened.

Not now. Not now. Not—

A Voidborn slammed into him, claws raking across his armour. He staggered, blade slipping from his grasp. The creature lunged again — jaws wide, shrieking.

Rynn threw himself between them, shield raised.

The impact shattered the shield completely.

Rynn screamed.

Talla drove her broken spear into the creature's skull, ghostlight flaring.

Kaelren gasped for breath.

The world spun.

The Gate pulsed again.

Harder. Deeper.

The crack widened. The runes dimmed. The air trembled.

And then Kaelren felt it.

Not a presence. Not a mind. Not a creature.

A memory.

A voice he had heard only once before — the voice that had killed Thalen.

His blood ran cold.

"No..." he whispered. "No, not him..."

The darkness inside the Gate shifted.

Gathered.

Focused.

And Kaelren understood.
The Herald was coming back.
The Gate cracked open wider.
And something stepped toward the light.

CHAPTER SEVENTY-FIVE — THE HERALD RETURNS

He emerged like a shadow peeling itself from the darkness — tall, skeletal, wrapped in a shifting cloak of void-smoke. His face was a mask of bone and shadow, his eyes two hollow pits of blue fire.
But it wasn't his form that froze the squad.
It was the memory.
Thalen's body collapsing. The Herald's hand pressed to his chest. The light leaving his eyes. The helplessness that followed.
Kaelren's breath caught. His vision blurred. His heart pounded so hard it hurt.
The Herald tilted his head, studying him with a curiosity that felt like a knife pressed to the throat.
"You survived," he murmured. "How disappointing."
Kaelren's grip tightened on his blade. "Stay behind me," he said.
But the squad didn't move.
They couldn't.
The Herald stepped forward — slow, deliberate, predatory. Frost spread across the stone with every step.
Rynn tried to lift his arm to defend himself, but the muscles spasmed from exhaustion, refusing to obey. Talla gasped, stumbling backward. Lysa reached for another arrow — only to find her quiver empty. Bren's hammer slipped from numb fingers. Mareth's magic sputtered out. Mira froze entirely, eyes wide with terror. Elyndra collapsed, lantern dimming to a faint, trembling glow.
The Herald lifted a hand.
Voidlight gathered in his palm — cold, hungry, alive.
Kaelren stepped forward. "Face me."
The Herald smiled.
"You are not the one I came for."
The Voidlight flared.
Kaelren's heart stopped.

He knew who the Herald meant. Who the Herald wanted. The man Elyndra was barely holding together below the fortress. The man who had not yet risen. The man who was not ready.

The Herald raised his hand higher.

"Let me take him," he whispered. "And I will make your deaths painless."

Kaelren roared and charged.

The Herald didn't even look at him.

A wave of Voidlight slammed into Kaelren's chest, hurling him backward across the courtyard. He hit the stone hard, breath torn from his lungs, vision exploding with stars.

The Herald turned toward the Gate. Toward the sanctum below. Toward the man he wanted.

Elyndra screamed, clutching her head as the tether snapped taut.

Kaelren forced himself to his knees. "No—!"

The Herald raised his hand to strike.

And then—

From deep below Emberhold...

A pulse. A tremor. A heartbeat.

Something woke.

Something powerful. Something furious. Something held together by sheer will and a single lantern's light.

The Herald froze.

His head snapped toward the fortress.

Kaelren's breath caught.

Elyndra gasped, eyes widening. "He's waking," she whispered.

The Herald's smile vanished. The Voidlight in his hand flickered.

And for the first time since stepping through the Gate...

The Herald looked afraid.

CHAPTER SEVENTY-SIX — THE VOYAGER AWAKENS

The sanctum was dark.
Not the darkness of night, or shadow, or stone — but the deep, suffocating dark of a mind unraveling. The air was cold. The walls hummed with faint, fractured echoes. Ghostlight flickered weakly from the runes carved into the floor, pulsing in uneven rhythms like a dying heartbeat.
The Voyager lay at the centre of the chamber.
Unmoving. Breathing shallowly. Skin pale with exhaustion. Veins threaded with faint lines of blue light that pulsed in time with the Gate above.
He wasn't asleep. He wasn't unconscious.
He was caught — suspended between waking and breaking, held together by a single thread of will and the last scraps of Elyndra's strength.
Her voice whispered faintly through the chamber, a trembling echo of her mind reaching for his.
Hold on... please... hold on...
But her voice was fading. Her lantern was dimming. Her strength was failing.
And the Herald's return tore through the tether like a blade.
The Voyager's eyes snapped open.
He gasped — a sharp, ragged breath that tore through his chest like fire. His back arched. His hands clawed at the stone. His vision exploded with light and memory and pain.
Thalen's scream. Jorren's last breath. Kaelren's grief. The Herald's voice. The Gate's pulse. The squad's fear. Elyndra's pain. The world breaking.
It all hit him at once.
He choked on it. He drowned in it.
He felt Thalen die again — felt the moment the light left him, felt the void tear through the courtyard, felt the helplessness of not being there.
He felt Jorren's final words echo through Kaelren's mind.

He felt Kaelren's heart cracking under the weight of everything he carried.
He felt the Herald's presence above — cold, hungry, triumphant.
He felt the Gate widening.
He felt the world tipping toward ruin.
And he felt Elyndra's voice — faint, trembling, breaking.
I can't hold you... I'm sorry... I'm so sorry...
The tether snapped.
The chamber shook.
The Voyager screamed.
He forced himself upright.
Every muscle trembled. Every breath burned. Every heartbeat felt like it might tear him apart.
But he stood.
He stood because he had to. He stood because they needed him. He stood because he had failed them once already — and he would not fail them again.
He staggered toward the stairs.
The sanctum walls pulsed with ghostlight as he passed, reacting to the unstable power radiating from him. The runes flickered violently. The air crackled. The stone trembled beneath his feet.
He climbed.
One step. Then another. Then another.
Each one felt like lifting the weight of the world.
Halfway up, he collapsed against the wall, breath tearing from his lungs.
He saw Thalen's face. He saw Jorren's smile. He saw Kaelren's grief. He saw the Herald's hand reaching for the Gate.
He pushed himself up again.
He climbed.
The screams above grew louder.
The Herald's voice cut through the air like a blade. Kaelren roared in defiance. Elyndra cried out in pain.
The Voyager reached the final step.
He stepped into the courtyard.
Chaos.

Voidborn corpses dissolved into smoke across the stone. The pyres flickered violently. The dawn was gone — swallowed by the Gate's widening maw. The squad lay scattered, broken, barely standing.

Rynn was on one knee, shield shattered. Talla held him upright, blood running down her arm. Lysa clutched her snapped bow, eyes wide with terror. Bren staggered, hammer lost. Mareth knelt beside Mira, trying to shield her with trembling hands. Elyndra lay collapsed, lantern dim, breath shallow.

And Kaelren —

Kaelren stood alone.

Blade raised. Chest heaving. Eyes burning with grief and fury.

Facing the Herald.

The Herald turned.

His hollow blue eyes widened.

"You," he hissed.

The Voyager didn't answer.

He didn't speak. He didn't breathe.

He simply raised his hand.

The Herald lunged.

Voidlight flared.

The Voyager stepped forward — and the air shattered.

A pulse of raw, unstable power burst from him, rippling across the courtyard like a shockwave. The stone cracked. The pyres flared. The Gate flickered.

The Herald froze mid-strike.

His body convulsed. His form flickered. His scream tore through the air — high, broken, furious.

"No—! You are not— you cannot—!"

The Voyager's eyes burned with white-blue fire.

He clenched his fist.

The Herald's body twisted, contorted, unraveling into strands of Voidlight that writhed and screamed and clawed at the air.

The Voyager whispered — voice low, steady, final:

"Enough."

The Herald erased.

Gone. Not killed. Not defeated.
Erased.
Silence followed.
A stunned, trembling silence.
The squad stared at the Voyager — shocked, relieved, horrified.
Kaelren lowered his blade, breath shaking.
Elyndra gasped, tears streaming down her face.
The Voyager swayed.
His vision blurred.
His knees buckled.
Kaelren reached for him—
But the Voyager collapsed before he could catch him.
The courtyard held its breath.
The Herald was gone. The Voyager lay unconscious. And the Gate pulsed again.

CHAPTER SEVENTY-SEVEN — THE HARROWED KING ARRIVES

The Gate pulsed.
Not a tremor. Not a scream.
A heartbeat.
Deep. Slow. Final.
The courtyard froze.
Ash hung motionless in the air. The pyres stilled mid-flicker. Even the wind seemed to hold its breath.
Kaelren felt the stillness settle over him like a burial shroud.
Something was coming.
Something older than the Void. Something stronger than the Herald. Something he had prayed — begged — never to face again.
His heartbeat stuttered.
And then the vision struck.
It didn't whisper. It didn't warn.
It tore into him.
He was back in Flameborn.
The sky burning red. The breach tearing open. The King — his King — fighting like a storm.
And then the shadows took him.
Dragged him backward. Tore him from Kaelren's grasp. Ripped him into the dark.
"Kaelren—!"
The scream echoed through the vision.
Kaelren screamed back.
He reached again. He failed again.
The King vanished.
And Kaelren's heart broke for the first time.
The vision shattered.

Kaelren collapsed to his knees, sobbing — a raw, broken sound torn from somewhere deep, somewhere he had locked away for years.
The squad froze.
The Voyager stepped toward him, hand trembling, runes flickering faintly beneath his skin.
"Kaelren—"
But the Gate cracked open.
A sound like stone splitting under the weight of a god tore through the courtyard.
The air collapsed.
Everyone gasped, clutching their chests as the pressure crushed their lungs.
The dawn dimmed. The pyres guttered. The shadows lengthened.
And then the world went silent.
Not quiet.
Silent.
No wind. No breath. No heartbeat.
Even the flames froze.
Kaelren lifted his head.
His eyes widened. His breath caught.
"No…" he whispered. "No, no, no—"
A figure stepped through the Gate.
Slowly. Inevitably.
Like a memory returning to finish what it started.
His armour was the same. His cloak was the same. His stance was the same.
But his face—
By the Realms.
His face.
It was the King of Flameborn. The man Kaelren had loved.
The man he had failed to save.
But twisted. Rotting. Hollowed out by the Void.
One eye burned with sickly blue fire. The other was a black pit. His skin was cracked like old stone. His jaw hung slightly open, as if the muscles had forgotten how to hold it closed.
He looked at Kaelren.

And Kaelren broke completely.

He screamed — a raw, agonized sound that tore through the courtyard.

He crawled forward, reaching for the King like he had in the vision.

"Please—" His voice cracked. "Please, no—"

The Harrowed King tilted his head.

And then—

A second voice slipped through the first.

Not the hollow rasp of the monster. Not the void-rotted whisper.

A voice Kaelren knew. A voice he had bled for. A voice he had loved.

"Kaelren…"

His King's voice.

Soft. Warm. Human.

Kaelren's breath shattered.

"Why did you let me fall?" the human voice whispered.

Kaelren sobbed. "I tried— I tried— please—"

The void voice cut through him like a blade.

"You failed."

The Harrowed King reached out — not physically, but with something deeper.

Something cold. Something ancient.

Kaelren felt fingers close around his soul.

He gasped, back arching, vision fracturing into shards of memory and pain.

Flameborn. The breach. The King's scream. Thalen's death. Jorren's last breath.

Every failure. Every loss. Every wound he had buried.

The King dragged them all to the surface.

"You let me die," the human voice whispered.

"You let them ALL die," the void voice snarled.

Kaelren screamed.

The squad tried to rise — Rynn crawling, Talla dragging herself forward, Lysa reaching for a broken arrow — but the King flicked his hand.

They were thrown back like leaves in a storm.

And then—

The King turned.
Toward the Voyager.
The Voyager froze — runes flaring, breath catching, eyes widening with terror.
"No—" Elyndra gasped. "No, please—"
The King lifted his hand.
Voidlight shot upward.
The Voyager was ripped into the air — dragged upward by invisible claws of ghostlight and shadow.
He choked, hands clawing at his throat, feet kicking helplessly.
Elyndra screamed. "STOP! STOP!"
The King didn't even look at her.
He laughed.
A horrible, broken sound — half human, half void.
Then he looked at Kaelren.
"Do you really think," the human voice whispered— "you could protect him?" the void voice finished.
The King leaned closer, smile widening.
"From me?"
The Voyager's body jerked — once, twice — as if the King were tearing something out of him.
Ghostlight bled from his skin. His runes flickered violently.
His breath came in strangled gasps.
Kaelren tried to stand.
He collapsed.
The King's grip on his soul tightened.
"You cannot save him," the void voice hissed.
"You never could."
The Voyager screamed.
Kaelren's vision blurred with tears.
"Please—" he begged. "Please, let him go—"
The King leaned close, his ruined face inches from Kaelren's.
The human voice whispered:
"Kneel, Kaelren."
The void voice followed:
"Or watch him die."
The Voyager's scream tore through the courtyard.

Kaelren's heart broke open.

He looked at the squad — broken, bleeding, helpless. He looked at Elyndra — reaching for the Voyager with shaking hands. He looked at the King — the man he had loved, the monster he had become.

And he knew—

Whatever choice he made next would break him forever.

Kaelren lowered his head.

His hands shook.

His knees buckled.

The Harrowed King smiled.

ACKNOWLEDGMENTS

Stories are forged in solitude, but they are never carried alone.

To everyone who walked beside me through the long nights, the rewrites, the doubts, and the sparks of inspiration — thank you. Your belief kept the lantern lit when the path grew dark.

To the readers who stepped into this world and chose to stay — you are the heartbeat of this saga. Every page exists because someone out there wanted to turn it.

To my family, whose love and patience gave me the space to build a universe from shadows and fire — this book is part of our legacy now.

And to those who have lost something, or someone, along the way — may you find strength in the stories that remind us we are never truly alone.

This is only the beginning. The Gate has opened. The world is changing. And the Voidhammer has yet to fall.

ABOUT THE AUTHOR

John is a storyteller from Wollongong, Australia, crafting mythic fantasy worlds filled with heartbreak, hope, and cinematic intensity. He builds universes where light and shadow collide, where ordinary people face impossible choices, and where every victory comes with a cost.

When he isn't writing, he's building communities, designing lore artifacts, and shaping the Voidhammer Saga into a multi-book epic.

This is his debut novel — the first strike of a much larger storm.

OFFICIAL

AUTHOR'S NOTE

When I began writing this story, I didn't know where it would lead. I didn't know these characters would become family, or that their grief would echo my own, or that their courage would teach me something about my own life.

Kaelren's burden. The Voyager's fear. Elyndra's resolve. The squad's loyalty. The King's fall.

These moments shaped me as much as I shaped them.

If this book reached you — if it made you feel something, or remember something, or breathe a little deeper — then it has done its job.

Thank you for walking this path with me. Book Two awaits.

PREVIEW OF BOOK TWO — VOIDHAMMER: SHATTERFALL

The Harrowed King has returned. Kaelren has fallen to his knees. The Voyager is awakening. The Gate is open. And Emberhold is no longer safe.

In the aftermath of the King's arrival, the squad must face a world unravelling at the seams. Old loyalties will fracture. New powers will rise. And the truth behind the Void will finally begin to surface.

But the greatest threat is not the King.

It is the choice Kaelren made in the courtyard — and the price he will pay for it.

The storm has only begun.

VOIDHAMMER LORE GLOSSARY

The Veil The boundary between the mortal world and the Void. Thin in some places. Broken in others.

Ghostlight A luminous energy drawn from the Veil. Used by lantern bearers, healers, and those touched by the Void.

The Gate of Emberhold A sealed breach beneath the fortress. Now open.

The Herald A creature of the Void. A hunter. A messenger. A warning.

The Harrowed King Once the King of Flameborn. Now something else entirely.

The Voyager A man from another world — or perhaps many worlds. His mind is a door the Void wants open.

The Squad Kaelren, Rynn, Talla, Lysa, Bren, Mareth, Mira, Elyndra. Bound by loyalty, grief, and the battles they survived together.

THANK YOU

Thank you for reading *Voidhammer: Volume One*. Your support brings this world to life.

If you enjoyed the journey, consider leaving a review — it helps more than you know.

To join the community, explore lore, or follow the creation of Book Two, visit: **patreon.com/c/Voidhammerofficial**

Socials:

Instagram: @voidhammerofficial
TikTok: @voidhammerofficial
YouTube: @voidhammerofficial